On the Edge

T.S. Krupa

On the Edge is a work of fiction. Names, characters, places and incidents are the products of the author's imagination or are used fictitiously. Any resemblance to actual events, locales, or persons, living or dead, is entirely coincidental.

To My Family and Friends who have supported me along this journey.
Without you there would be no adventure.

Chapter 1

I continued to pace in the hallway by the front door, glancing out the window every so often, waiting for headlights to sweep across the driveway. It was well after seven in the evening and Hayden Grace was late, which wasn't completely unusual. Molly, our golden retriever, was on the upstairs landing looking down at me, following my back and forth movements while Casey sat on the stairs fiddling with her phone. I exhaled more sharply than I intended, startling them both when I heard the gravel crunch outside.

"It's about time…you're late," I said with exasperation, when she finally made her way into the house with strands of her long blonde hair sticking out under her knit cap, her book bag and snowboard bag in tow.

"Sorry," she mumbled with no real remorse, as only a fifteen-year-old can do.

"I'm headed out, but Casey is here to babysit you," I said, raising my voice at her retreating figure as she darted straight up the stairs brushing past Casey and Molly, headed to her room, dragging her bags on the floor.

"I don't need a babysitter, Andy," she shouted back as she slammed the door to her room.

"It's 'Mom'…" I shouted back as the deafening sounds of Fall Out Boy could be heard from her room. Just then, a faint sound of a horn beeped in the driveway.

"That's me," I said, taking a deep breath and looking at Casey who was still sitting on the stairs.

"No sweat, Mrs. Parker," Casey said, giving me a half-hearted smile.

"I'll be back around eleven," I began to say as I glanced at my watch. My mind drifted to the hectic schedule I had the following day, "umm…maybe more like ten-thirty," I clarified to the top of Casey's head as she continued to play on her phone.

"Molly, how do I look?" I asked playfully, twirling around as I grabbed my long gray winter trench coat off the staircase banister. Molly raised her head and gave me a wag of her tail.

"That will do," I said quietly and slipped out the front door to the waiting silver Nissan Altima in the driveway.

***

Noble's Grill was far more crowded than I expected for a Tuesday night. I could see couples huddling over their dinner plates engrossed in conversations, the twenty-something professionals swarming the bar and not very far away from them the older business men were drinking while trying to keep a subtle eye on those twenty-something professionals. One couple in particular in the far corner caught my eye. They were done eating, now holding hands and whispering to each other over the table, but I couldn't stop staring at the man. The gentleman was about thirty years my senior, but from his broad shoulders he looked to still be physically fit. He reached back raking his fingers through his short gray hair and laughed over something the women said. Something caught in my throat as I continued to stare shamelessly—he looked like I imagined Stefan would have, had he lived that long. A sudden sadness crept through me.

"Andy?" Gregg said across the table, breaking through my thoughts.

2

"Sorry, daydreaming," I said shaking my head and trying to bring myself back from the past into the present.

"I was asking if you were free Friday night?" he repeated as he handed the waiter back the check. I tilted my head slightly to the side, mentally flipping through my calendar.

"Hayden Grace doesn't have practice because of the competition on Saturday," I mumbled to no one in particular.

"I'm sorry, did you say something?" he asked confused.

"It was nothing."

"Does that mean you are free?" he asked again, waiting patiently for a reply with a tight smile.

"I could see if Casey is available," I said, looking at him only to find his dark chocolate eyes staring back at me. "What?" I asked, suddenly self-conscious that I had food on my face.

"You're beautiful," he said simply, and I smiled.

"Yes, I'm free Friday."

"That's great because I was thinking…" he started saying, but I couldn't help and glance back to the couple in the corner…they were no longer there. Clearly distracted, I tried to focus back on Gregg and what he was asking me. He wore black rimmed glasses that I imagined matched his once jet black hair now peppered with gray. Gregg was only a little taller than I was when we were standing side by side, but seated across from me he carried himself with confidence and a sophistication that I found alluring. Breaking away from his norm of wearing dress slacks and a suit jacket, tonight he wore a blue button up shirt with a maroon tie and khakis. I heard him cough, and I could tell he had

3

asked me another question and was waiting for a proper response.

"That sounds nice," I said taking a gamble with a generic answer and hoping it was adequate.

"Ok, good. Not everyone loves seafood so I wanted to ask," he followed up. I sighed, knowing that I had answered correctly.

***

The drive home was quiet as I stared out the window, watching the snow flutter down among the small beacons of light from the surrounding houses. It was only the second week of January and already the meteorologist on the local news station was promising record breaking snowfall by the end of the winter season.

"Andy, are you okay? I feel like you have been somewhere else this entire evening," Gregg said when he pulled into my driveway.

"I'm sorry. I've just had a lot going on," I said, making up a reasonable excuse. I could see the clock on the dash; it was just past ten-thirty. This only increased my distraction as my mind raced about all the things I had to do to get Hayden Grace and myself ready for tomorrow.

"I understand," he said, leaning over and brushing stray strands of blonde hair from my face, capturing my attention. Slowly he moved his fingers ever so softly down my cheek to my lips, sending small pulses of electricity racing through my body. Leaning in even closer he kissed my lips gently. "Have a good night," he whispered, pulling back. I closed my eyes, letting the moment sink in before exhaling.

"Goodnight, Gregg. See you Friday," I said at long last opening my eyes and staring out into the night.

phone stays unlocked. I look through it every night, and it charges in the kitchen, not in your room," I said in a neutral tone, trying very hard not to start a fight so early in the morning and with so little caffeine in my system.

"Dad and his stupid rules," she mumbled while rolling her eyes. I winced at her comment, hoping she didn't see my reaction but continued to sit quietly. Several more moments passed before she spoke again. "Yeah, coach said my tricks are getting tighter, and he thinks this weekend is going to go well for me." I gave her a slight nod of encouragement but secretly cringed inside. Her coach had been saying things were 'going to go well' for several years now. Don't get me wrong—Hayden Grace was an excellent rider and at six years old showed amazing promise. But something changed when Stefan died. Not suddenly, but gradually. She was still a great rider, but her concentration wavered. She used to ride with such passion, but it seemed to have fizzled out and now she was just going through the motions. I had asked her repeatedly over the last couple of years if she still wanted to ride, and she was vehement that this is what she wanted to be doing.

"Remember, I have to work on the mountain this weekend and your grandparents are coming up from Long Island to watch your competition." While I worked a normal job as a senior marketing associate at Unique Aspects during the week, on the weekends I worked at Mount Sunapee. I had been teaching ski lessons and working other odd jobs there since I was eighteen. It was convenient that Hayden Grace was on the snowboarding club there; this allowed me to sneak away from lessons every now and then to watch. Like it or not we were both pretty well known on the mountain; it was one of those places that truly felt like home. But this particular weekend was a big deal. The top three female and male winners qualified for a larger competition, Regional 6, which was like junior nationals, and that competition exposed the riders on a national level. The only hitch was that the Regional 6 was in Aspen, Colorado. All of the other competitions Hayden Grace had competed in thus far were in the New Hampshire and Vermont areas. She had had moderate success at these more local competitions over the years but still had not managed to qualify for any national competitions. So naturally, Regional 6 was all Hayden Grace talked about. In actuality, this was all she ever talked about, and every year at this time she had always been so close to qualifying, placing fourth or fifth the last four years—she was always just out of contention. Feeling bad I had to work during such an important competition, I had persuaded my parents to come up and cheer her on while I worked just to make sure she felt supported. With the competition going on, the mountain was seriously short-staffed, and we could really use the extra money. Even though Hayden Grace and I had already talked about me having to work, I found that constant reminders worked best.

"Do you think Uncle Drew will come?" she asked between bites.

"I don't know. He hasn't called me back. I will try him again today," I said, and she just nodded. Drew was my younger brother and a financial consultant in New York, but he was Hayden Grace's favorite person after her father.

"So, how was the date last night? ... That's date number three," Hayden Grace asked, trying to be casual.

"It was just okay," I answered honestly. "We are going out again on Friday. Casey will be here to watch you," I mentioned as she rolled her eyes at me, *again*.

"One more after Friday and I get to meet him," she reminded me.

"You are correct," I replied, responding to Hayden Grace's eye roll with one of my own. I had made a deal with Hayden Grace several years ago when I finally started dating that I wouldn't bring anyone home until we had been on at least five dates. I didn't want to make her life any crazier than it already was. Since then she has teased and gossiped and speculated about my dates because in the entire time I had been dating, no one had ever made it past the fifth date.

"Time to go," I said, looking at my watch, "you got everything together?" She nodded and pointed at her cup. "I'll pour it over to a travel mug; go grab your stuff," I said, taking our mugs to the counter. She got up and headed down the hallway.

***

"Have a good day at school," I said as we pulled up in front of the high school. We were uncharacteristically early for once which didn't seem to brighten Hayden Grace's day at all. She mumbled something under breath about the ability to enjoy high school being an impossible task.

"I'll be back from Boston in time for dinner. Is Madison's mom going to bring you home from practice?" She nodded. Madison was newer to the snowboarding club but had made fast friends with Hayden Grace and was a pretty good technical rider. She and her family had just moved to the area. Her mom Lisa was a bit over involved in Madison's life (if you asked me) but was super organized and always willing to drive Hayden Grace home. Madison had a younger sister, but she was very introverted from my understanding, and her dad traveled a lot for business. The friendship had been good for Hayden Grace, and Lisa was a whiz with a car-pooling schedule.

"Today's your big presentation isn't it?" she exclaimed after several moments, bouncing in her seat, and I nodded. "Mom, you're going to do just fine…remember what we talked about. Try not to be old and boring—be excited and fresh. You will nail those bas…" I raised my eyebrows at her before she said the word, and she paused, "you will nail those guys to the wall."

"Thank you," I said simply trying not to get emotional over her interest and support. With that she leaned over and gave me a quick squeeze and a kiss and then grabbed her bags and headed off towards the large brick building that read, Newbury High School. I idled momentarily watching her before heading off to the city.

***

The commute into Boston from our home in Newbury, New Hampshire, took about two hours on a good day. I hated the drive into the city and was grateful that I only needed to venture in to Boston a couple of times a month, working from home or from the offices in Manchester the rest of the time. It had stopped snowing sometime in the middle of the night, and the light accumulation danced along the roadway as the cars passed by. Glad that traffic was light today, I made it to the office in record time, allowing me to set up the presentation and enjoy my second cup of coffee in silence. My mind raced over my presentation as people filtered into the room while my palms started to get sweaty and my heart raced just a little in anticipation. I nodded in acknowledgment as Tony and Mark sat down next to me with stacks of paperwork. Today each of us, being the three senior associates, had been tasked to give a presentation on marketing ideas and strategies for a women's activewear campaign. It was decided late last week that I would go first. Our boss, Gary Thomas, had assigned each of us this project two weeks ago, placing great emphasis on its importance for our jobs within the company. I had worked on the presentation every spare minute I had and still wasn't sure if it would pass his approval. Last week I had been working on it at home when Hayden Grace came into my makeshift office and watched over my shoulder. She stood quietly for a long time before declaring that the presentation was old fashioned and boring. She then pointed out several flaws in my campaign; I stood back and looked at the presentation through her perspective and decided she was right. I scraped the whole been-working-on-it-for-sixty-five-hours thing that night. The following night I sat at the kitchen table and started over; Hayden Grace joined me at the table doing her homework, looking over and chiming in suggestions or comments every fifteen or twenty minutes. We worked that way for several nights as my campaign shaped itself into a much fresher and stronger campaign. I remember thinking that if snowboarding didn't work out, Hayden

Grace had a future in marketing.

***

The three presentations took all morning, but after lunch the day dragged on with a conference call and strategy meeting. By four-thirty I was ready to hit the road to try and get ahead of the rush hour traffic. Just as I was packing up my stuff, Gary called me into his office.

"Now Andy, you have been with this company how long?" he asked from behind his large vintage oak desk. Had it been thirty years earlier, I would have expected him to be smoking a cigar, drinking whiskey and maybe even have his feet kicked up on the desk. But instead he leaned back in his chair and ran his hand through his hair, smirking in my direction.

"Ten years." *Ten years* I thought to myself. I had started with the company in the smaller Manchester office when Hayden Grace started kindergarten—I was twenty-five and she was five.

"Ten years, that's what I thought. You are the most senior of the senior associates here Andy, and I need you to start taking a more active leadership role. I had you all do these presentations this morning because in reality we just landed a huge account with an up-and-coming sports and activewear company. I am making you the lead on this—your presentation this morning was fresh, innovative and young. It's just what this company needs." He looked right at me and raised his eyebrows indicating that this was not up for debate. In the past I had been overlooked for these opportunities because of my commute and my commitment to Hayden Grace. I know that if I had been more willing to miss more competitions, more practices, more dinners, I might have been further in my career, but the little things matter, and with Stefan not being around I had too much guilt already for the things I did have to miss that were beyond my control.

"Thank you for this opportunity. When do we start?" I asked, hoping I sounded excited, but I felt more terrified than anything. It wasn't that I wasn't up to the challenge, because I was, but the timing was horrible. Hayden Grace still had four competitions this year, and if she won any of them she might have more; I could feel the stress and anxiety starting to build as I fidgeted with my watch. Maybe the account was still thirty to sixty days before becoming active, I thought to myself. It wasn't unheard of for the company to make these big announcements yet the project to be delayed by paperwork or the legal department.

"The clients will be here Monday, and I'll need you in the city all next week. This project is going to require some serious time and dedication, and I know you have the ability to put the work in... Now Andy, if the work isn't up to par, it might be time to seriously evaluate your position with the company," he warned. "Take the rest of the week off and relax—be ready to have your head in the game Monday," he said, dismissing me with a wave of his hand. My heart was racing, and I had a pit in my stomach during my drive home. It was fantastic news. This was an opportunity of a lifetime, but how was I going to balance work and Hayden Grace? It had long been an unspoken understanding that from November to April I was often working remotely to balance the crazy practice and competition schedule Hayden Grace had. It's not that I didn't work hard, but I never took the lead on projects because I didn't have the time to do it all. I still had nothing figured out by the time I pulled into the driveway back home. Looking at the clock, Hayden Grace was due home in about thirty minutes; it was time to start dinner and get cleaned up, but instead I sat down on the sofa to process the day. When Hayden Grace walked in the door I was still sitting on the sofa in my work clothes.

It was almost eight-thirty by the time we sat down to dinner. Hayden Grace had gotten home from practice and had run straight to her room to shower and get cleaned up which wasn't uncommon for her. While Hayden Grace was cleaning up, I tried to clear my head so I could pull together a fabulous gourmet meal of salad, rice, carrots and re-heated chicken. I knew I was never going to win any 'cook of the year' awards with my culinary talents as I looked at the sad options on the table. While I was waiting on Hayden Grace to emerge from her room, my phone rang.

"Andy?" I heard a male voice from the other side.

"Yes?"

"It's Ron."

"Oh, Coach Davis, how are you?" I asked in confusion. It was rare that Ron actually called. I usually got debriefed about Hayden Grace on the weekends when I was on the mountain.

"Hayden Grace had a rough practice today. She fell on almost every run—one of those falls scrapped her up pretty badly," he paused to let the information sink in. I thought of Hayden Grace and how quickly she had rushed in straight to her room.

"I haven't seen her yet; she went straight to her room," I confessed after a moment.

"Andy, she has more God-given talent than most of the boys and girls we have here, but there is something keeping her back," he exclaimed, raising his voice in frustration.

"I know."

"Despite the performance today, I'm going to put her in the line-up this weekend because I'm not ready to give up on her. Maybe you can talk to her and see what's going on. She had a great practice the other day, but today was the polar opposite."

"I understand. I will talk to her. I really appreciate you calling with your concerns."

"You're welcome," he paused, "…how are you doing, Andy?" he asked after a moment. Ron and I had known each other a very long time. He was making waves on the mountain as a snowboarding talent when I was eighteen. We even dated a short while, but then he got injured, and I met Stefan. We have remained friends, and he always looked out for Hayden Grace.

"Things are good," I lied. Ron didn't need to know about the stress and anxiety. He was just being polite, and I didn't need to burden him with my life problems.

"That's good," he replied, leaving an awkward pause. I could hear Hayden Grace coming down the hallway.

"Ron, she's coming. I'll talk to you later," I said and disconnected quickly without giving him a chance to say anything further. When she rounded the corner I could immediately see the scratches on her check and a black eye starting to form on her left eye.

"Oh honey," I said, rushing to her to examine her further.

"Mom, it's no big deal," she said, trying to push me away.

"You know better," I said, taking a closer look. Satisfied with my examination, I went to the freezer and made up a small bag of ice.

"Who was on the phone?" she asked, taking a seat at the table.

"Coach Davis."

"He thought practice was that bad that he called you?" she sounded surprised and hurt.

"He was worried about your injuries and just wanted to update me," I said as a half-truth. "What was going on up there today?" I asked, handing her a bag of ice and a dishtowel for her eye.

16

"What's this for?" she asking, holding up the dishtowel with two fingers.

"To wrap around the bag of ice," I said with exasperation.

"Oh."

"The mountain?" I asked, bringing her back to the issue at hand.

"I don't know…" she said, struggling with her words. I knew better than to push her and instead sat dinner down in front of her and waited. "I was just over thinking it," she finally said.

"Was that all?" I asked. Her saying she was 'over thinking it' was a generic response. She stopped what she was doing and looked up at me. We had a stare down; the fact that she only had one good eye did nothing to deter me. Neither of us wanted to be the first to talk about the elephant in the room. Finally, unable to keep up the staring contest, she looked down at her food.

"I miss Dad…I want him to be there with me so badly," she finally whispered.

"Oh honey, we both miss him very much," I whispered back putting down my fork and coming around the table to squat down in front of her. I rested my hands on her knees. "You need to know he is always with you," I said, and a small tear slid down her cheek.

"Do you think he's proud of me?" she asked as more tears welled up in her eyes.

"Hayden Grace, of course he's proud of you. You were the love of his life, and you continue to grow into a beautiful young woman," I said, wrapping her into a hug. She dropped the ice and leaned down and hugged me back, crying into my shoulder. Molly who had been lying under the table came over and whined at the sight of us, licking both our faces causing us to laugh. The moment was so touching, yet it was breaking my heart.

"Come on," I said after a long moment, grabbing her hand. Hayden Grace hesitated but got up as I led her out onto the back porch. The cold night air was crisp causing us both to shiver. The moonlight bounced off of the snow which was covered in a thin layer of ice, making it look like glass and illuminating the backyard. Molly bounded down off the porch and frolicked in the crunchy snow.

"Look up," I told her, and she obediently gazed up into the sky. "What do you see?"

"The moon, the stars, the dark sky," she responded.

"Okay, focus on the stars," I said, and I could tell she was looking at them intently.

"Remember what I told you right after we found out that Dad had passed away? Whenever you miss him, look up and know he's there among the stars looking down on us," I quietly commented as a small hitch developed in my throat.

"What about during the day?" she whispered while not breaking her stare with the stars.

"The stars are always there day and night. Just because you can't see them during the day doesn't mean they aren't there. Just like Dad, you can't see him or touch him, but he's always there…he's always cheering you on," I whispered as the tears fell down my cheeks, causing me to quickly wipe them away so Hayden Grace wouldn't see.

"Can I talk to him?"

"I do all the time," I said, and she looked up at me with questions in her eyes.

"I know he can hear me, and when I look at the stars, I feel like he's talking back," I said, looking up at the twinkling starbursts.

"Okay," she said and looked up.

"Okay."

"Mom," she said after a moment.

"Yes?"

"Can I have a moment… alone… with Dad," she asked shyly.

"Of course," I said in surprise. "Molly, come," I called out to the retriever that was now rolling in the snow. Molly and I stepped inside, and I watched Hayden Grace as she walked to the edge of the porch looking up. I could see her talking, but I wasn't sure what she was saying. The tears flowed freely down my cheeks over the heartbreak I was feeling for Hayden Grace. I could live with my own heartbreak I thought, but her pain felt as if it was going to suffocate me. After several minutes Hayden Grace turned to come back inside, and I quickly made myself busy at the kitchen counter.

"Mom?" she asked, and I turned around.

"Yes."

"I love you," she said and embraced me in a big hug.

"I love you too."

Chapter 3

That evening, after Hayden Grace finally went to bed, I lay in bed constantly repeating the evening's conversation and events in my head. Unable to sleep, an idea started to form, and I crept up into the attic. Being an old house, the attic had a full set of stairs that were hidden behind a closet door in the hallway. They creaked loudly as I ascended; at the top stair I fumbled for the light switch. Once the lights flickered on it took my eyes a moment to adjust to the dim and crowded attic space. It had only been a short while since I had been up here, but everything remained the same—dust and cobwebs collected on the boxes and old furniture that was arranged in the far corner. Various holiday decorations were stacked closest to the door as those were the most frequently used items stored up here. Some of Hayden Grace's toys from her childhood poked out of boxes which were piled next to a wide array of dated snowboard and ski equipment. I scanned the attic for a hunter green footlocker and eventually located it towards the back of the attic next to a clothing rack that was covered in plastic to protect the garments that hung on it. I could hear the pitter patter of paws and the jingle of Molly's collar behind me as she made her way up the stairs. She sniffed around at all the boxes as I dragged the footlocker out into the open space.

It was a large, vintage metal footlocker and in black paint on the lid was scrawled, CPT STEFAN PARKER. I sighed and sank down next to the solid case. I ran my hand across the dusty lid which caused me to cough slightly. Molly made her way over and smelled the trunk before whining slightly and lying down next to me—she remembered too. It had been six years, but it still felt like yesterday. It was a day that will always be etched into my memory. It was a warm Saturday in April, and thankfully, Hayden Grace was at her friend's house for a sleepover; she was nine. I was home alone with a then two-year-old Molly, attempting to make carrot cake cupcakes for Easter the next day. Molly started barking and pacing at the front door before the doorbell even rang. I remember rushing to wash my hands, not wanting whoever was there to wait. The second I opened the door and saw their faces, I knew. The notifying officer and chaplain introduced themselves and escorted me to the sofa. They spoke a lot about honor, service and country—I don't remember the details, but I do remember when the officer reached over and put his hand on my arm and said 'he died saving a life'.

'Of course, he did,' I remember mumbling; it was so Stefan.

I thought it was painful learning that my husband had died while serving his country, but nothing compared to telling Hayden Grace the next day. By the time she had arrived back at the house from the sleepover my parents and younger sister, Jennifer, who was still in high school, had already driven up from Maryland where they were living at the time. My brother Drew was getting ready to graduate from law school and was in the middle of preparing for exams so he wouldn't be able to make it for another day or two. My dad was close to retiring after spending thirty-five years in the army. Out of everyone there that day he understood more than any of us did; he never said a word to me. Instead he just gave me a big hug and held me while I cried. He later told me that a day like that was a day he dreaded the most for my mom, sister, brother and me—he thought about it every single day of his time in the service. I had called and asked Stefan's parents to come over, but they preferred to stay at home and grieve.

When Hayden Grace entered the house she was a normal nine-year-old girl worried about braces and obsessed with Hannah Montana—it broke my heart that I was about to change that. I asked her to take her things to her room and then to come sit with me on the back porch. She fussed a little that she wanted to see Grams and Grandpa but finally agreed. We sat in silence for ten minutes before I worked up the courage to speak. When I finally told her that her daddy had been hurt while he was away and wouldn't be coming back, she cried. At first she wouldn't let me hug her and instead ran to the corner of the porch with such anger in her eyes. When she finally sunk to her knees shaking, I went over and engulfed her into a hug, and she wouldn't let go for hours. It wasn't until she finally fell asleep, still hugging my neck, that I was able to put her down.

With a reluctant sigh I opened the footlocker. It now carried mostly sentimental items and memorabilia of Stefan, most of which I was saving for Hayden Grace. I had long ago given away his clothes and many personal effects to his parents and brothers and sisters. He was just as much a part of their lives as he was ours. I rifled through the items when I came across several letters. They were labeled '16', '18', '21', 'Wedding Day' and 'The Big Win'. I had hidden them in the footlocker knowing Hayden Grace never ventured into the attic. She had a very practical fear of everything that involved the dark, cobwebs, spiders and 'creepy' things as she once told me. I set the envelope labeled 'The Big Win' to the side and put the rest of the envelopes back as they each awaited a specific time in Hayden Grace's life. Stefan had written letters to Hayden Grace before his first deployment in case something ever happened. He gave them to me to keep safe and made me promise to wait for each occasion. After his second tour I thought I would be able to throw them all away as he would be around to tell her in person, but then he got called for a third tour and he never came home.

Next, I came across a letter I knew all too familiarly. It was all creased from being unfolded and refolded a million times. I recalled finally having to put the letter up in storage because I was reading it every night, and instead of trying to live in the present, I was reliving the past. Slowly unfolding the letter I hesitated a moment but then realized it didn't matter because I had long memorized each line; thankfully it no longer evoked the same torrent of emotion that it once had on me.

Dear Andrea,

If you are reading this letter, I'm so sorry. It was never supposed to end this way but we both understood the sacrifices it might take.

Words cannot express how much my life with you has meant to me. You brought me meaning, hope and love. Then you gave me the greatest gift of all, the gift of being a dad. My time with you and Hayden Grace has been the greatest joy in life.

I can only imagine how hard this will be on both of you. I know you are strong and can live through the pain – I always told you that you were the tougher Parker. But Hayden Grace is so young; I fear this might break her tender spirit. Please let her know that she was and always will be my little girl, and I am and always will be so very proud of her.

There is nothing more I have to say that we haven't already said or vowed to each other. Know that I loved you more than my own life, and you now deserve the love and happiness of someone that truly understands you for you.

Look for me in the stars as always. I will be there looking down on both of you.

Love,

Stefan

    Tears streamed down my cheeks as I carefully folder the letter back up. Flashes of memories from our wedding flooded my thoughts. The sadness that crept through me was different than the sadness that I felt six years ago; this sadness was bearable. I now knew life would go on and that he was true to his word because I had already felt him among the stars. Next in the trunk was a piece of college ruled paper labeled 'Rules'. This one brought a smile to my face although it often made Hayden Grace very grumpy. It was a list of rules for both of us, but mostly for Hayden Grace in his absence. It hung on the refrigerator during his last tour and stayed there for nearly two years after his death. It wasn't until Hayden Grace finally asked me to take it down that we moved it.

Again, even though I had this list memorized, I couldn't help but read through it.

Hayden Grace:

Rule 1 – No dating until you're 18.

Rule 2 – No cell phones in your room at night, no passwords we don't know.

Rule 3 – No boys in your room.

Rule 4 – No staying home alone until you're 16.

Rule 5 – When you drive, both hands on the wheel at all times.

Rule 6 – School is important – As and Bs are expected.

Rule 7 – Chores are a must – mow the lawn, clean the house, do the laundry – you get the idea.

Rule 8 – ~~Don't fight with your mother~~. (She said that is not realistic) Talk to your mother. There is no room for secrets and don't bottle things up inside.

Rule 9 – Remember to say please, thank you and you're welcome. Show respect to those around you.

Rule 10 – Love unconditionally no matter who comes into your life (this one is REALLY important).

Andy:

Rule 1 – Take a deep breath, have patience.

Rule 2 – Don't forget to ask for help, you don't have to do this alone.

Rule 3 – Find happiness every day.

Rule 3 was much harder than Stefan could believe, but I was slowly working on it, I thought to myself as I put the 'Rules' back in the trunk. Scanning the trunk, I finally spotted the corner of the small plastic bag of patches I was looking for and gave it a big tug, causing a small avalanche of items. When the slight cloud of dust settled, I examined the baggie. They were patches that had either been on Stefan's uniforms or extras waiting to be added. I grabbed two patches and set them to the side with the letter. I took a couple of extra minutes to sort through the rest of the items before finally closing the lid and pushing it back into place. After gathering the few items off of the ground, Molly and I finally made our way back downstairs.

Once downstairs I quietly crept into Hayden Grace's room in search of her snowboarding jacket. Stopping only momentarily to check on her eye and other minor injuries and assessing that she was fine, I continued my search. Finding the white and black jacket on the ground by her closet door covered by another winter jacket and at least three pairs of various colored jeans, I crept back out of the room, trying not to wake her. Sitting on the sofa while a late night talk show buzzed in the background, I slowly stitched the two patches into the inside lining of her jacket. Finished, I held it up to view my handiwork. The first patch was one that was in the traditional digital camouflage fabric—a rectangle with black stitching that read 'PARKER' and the second was the United States flag. Of everything that was on his uniforms, these were the ones I thought Hayden Grace would remember the most. Proud of both my idea and my handiwork, I finally headed to bed only to find Molly had already beaten me there.

Chapter 4

I woke up to a wide array of noises coming down the hallway. I looked over at the nightstand and saw that it was just past seven in the morning. I must have forgotten to set my alarm the night before.

"Mom, I'm going to be late," Hayden Grace said, bursting in through the door.

"Calm down," I mumbled as I sat up and rubbed my eyes. Molly hopped down from the bed and walked over to Hayden Grace who rubbed her head. "Do you have any tests this morning?" I questioned her.

"No, but I have a geometry test this afternoon," she replied with suspicion.

"I was thinking you might be late to school today. Would you like to have breakfast with me?" I asked, finally getting out of bed and heading into the bathroom.

"Seriously?" she exclaimed with a whoop.

"Also, I think we should get your head checked out after your crash yesterday," I added calmly.

"I knew it! Mom, I'm fine...no headaches, no bright flashes or dizziness," she said in exasperation as she flopped down on the bed.

"Are you sure?" I questioned from the bathroom.

"Yes! Now where are we going to breakfast…Wait, don't you have work?"

"I will go in later; now quit asking so many questions," I joked, tossing a pillow at her. She laughed and rolled over now clutching the pillow underneath her.

"How about the Diner," we both said at the same time and burst into giggles. Officially it was called The Hometown Experience, but everyone in town referred to it as the Diner. From its outward appearance it looked like it had been transported to modern day straight from the 1950s. It was an added bonus that the food was good and very affordable.

"Okay, go grab your jacket. I think I saw it in your room," I said coyly, pulling on some jeans and searching for my red plaid button up shirt. I made some final adjustments to my appearance and grabbed the letter that was hidden under a book on my nightstand.

"Mom. … Mom! … Mom?" Thinking she already discovered my handiwork, I headed down the hall. Instead I saw she was dressed in her jacket holding my car keys in one hand with a sheepish grin.

"Can I drive?" she practically begged. She had gotten her driver's permit several months earlier but with everything going on we had little time to practice.

"Sure," I said very slowly. With that she bounded out of the house to the car while I locked up and prepared myself mentally for the short drive. We arrived at the Diner in one piece with only one incident and all my nerves still intact. Hayden Grace failed to understand the meaning of a 'yield' sign at a busy intersection, but as luck would have it, nobody was in the lane she careened into. We were quickly seated, and the waitress came over and took our order, giving us a strange look when we both ordered the same thing. After a couple of silent moments I decided to broach the subject I had been thinking about since last night.

"Hayden Grace, I can't stop thinking about our conversation from last night," I said, looking at my teenage daughter across the table very closely. She had grown so much and yet had so much more to learn. She stopped stirring her coffee and looked up at me.

"Don't worry about it Mom," she said causally.

"That's funny. In case you forgot... Hi, I'm your Mom," I said with a joke and reached across the table to take her hand which she playfully batted away. "Seriously, Hayden Grace, you are all I worry about. But you say you miss your Dad, right?" I asked, and she nodded.

"I can't bring him back honey, but I thought of a way that maybe you can keep him close to you. Look inside your jacket," I said, holding my breath. There was a slight chance this was going to go over badly. Confused, Hayden Grace lifted up her jacket and saw the two patches sewn in.

"How did I miss that," she mused to herself, carefully tracing the patches with her fingers. She looked up from the jacket with tears in her eyes. "Where did you find these?"

"Apparently I had them lying around," I commented.

"This is so cool. Thank you, Mom," she exclaimed, reaching over the table to hug me. I sighed with relief.

"There is one more thing," I added before the moment passed. "Here," reaching into my purse I brought out the letter. She knew what it was before I even had it all the way out.

"It's not my birthday," she said in confusion. She had already gotten two letters from her dad: a week after he passed away and then again on her 13th birthday. They were all in simple white envelopes with his thin handwriting on the front.

"No, it's not your birthday, but this letter is different. I was supposed to give you this letter when you won ..."

"I have won several competitions," she interrupted me with accusation.

"Let me finish. When you won your first national event, but I think that you need this more now than you will then," I explained. She looked startled.

"Mom, there is a chance that won't ever happen," she said, looking appalled at the chance of there being a letter from her Dad she wouldn't receive.

"No sweetie, your Dad and I knew that it would happen—it was just a matter of when." She nodded and opened the letter. She read silently to herself and kept reading even after our food arrived. I watched her emotions swing back and forth as she read. She finally set the letter down and started to eat her food without saying a word. I knew better than to ask her about the letter or to try and read it. We ate in silence for most of the meal before she spoke.

"Mom?"

"Yes?"

"You were right…I needed this now," she said and then slid the letter across the table for me to read before going back to her food. I picked up the letter up as my hands shook slightly.

Hayden Grace,

Congratulations! I knew from very early on that you had the talent to become the best. You later surprised me with the passion and competitiveness that left me with no doubt you would achieve your goals. You ride with the grace of your mother but with my reckless abandon. You are and always will be the true balance between us.

Don't think the work stops today...take a moment and remember the day, remember how you felt and what it took to get to this moment and then tomorrow get back to work. I know it may not be fair but being the best is hard work. If it were easy, everyone would be doing it.

I'm so proud of you and know that your only limitation is you.

Love Always and Forever,

Dad

I couldn't stop the tear that fell down my check as I put the letter back in the envelope for Hayden Grace. Even though the letter was addressed to her and Stefan was connecting with her the only way he could, I felt a sense of connection to the letter. It was like getting a moment with him again, and I was grateful Hayden Grace shared it with me.

"Thank you," I said across the table.

"You're welcome."

***

After breakfast I made sure that her emotions were in check and that she showed no signs of a concussion, and then I dropped her off at school, wishing her luck on her geometry test. After the last few days I felt mentally drained and decided to take my boss up on his offer to take the day off, so instead of heading to work I headed to the mountain.

The parking lot was unexpectedly full for a Thursday. There were several large media trucks set up in the far lot as the mountain prepared for the weekend competition and activities. I made my way through the lodge to the employee locker room where I kept most of my ski clothes and equipment. After changing into warmer clothes and putting on my ski pants and jacket, all I wanted to do was escape up the mountain. Several employees were shocked to see me there on a Thursday mid-morning and stopped to chat but quickly sent me on my way after sensing my impatience. I had just about made it all the way to the high speed quad ski lift when I heard my name.

"Andy! Andy!" I heard, shouted from behind, causing me to turn around. Joel Warner lumbered toward me, waving his hands in the air.

"Joel," I said when he got closer, lifting up my goggles so I could see him better.

"What a pleasant surprise seeing you here," he said, making small talk.

"Joel how did you know I was here?"

"News travels fast," he said, offering no further explanation.

"What do you need?" I asked with a touch of annoyance.

"Where are you headed?" he answered my question with a question of his own.

"It's my day off, Joel. I'm headed to the top of the mountain and then the backcountry," I said. The backcountry was mountain terrain outside of the resort trails that had wide open spaces, no set paths and lots of natural obstacles—it was mostly off limits to our guests. Having grown up skiing and then skiing Mount Sunapee since I was 18, I probably knew the mountain better than anyone else and enjoyed skiing predominately in the backcountry.

"That's what I was hoping," he said, confusing me. Joel usually hated it when any of the employees ventured off into the backcountry. He was always talking about what a huge liability it was. "I need a favor. I have several VIP guests here that want a tour of the backcountry. I was going to send Teresa with them, but you're a better skier, and you know the area much better," he said. I shuddered at the thought of sending anyone with Teresa and reluctantly agreed. He motioned to a group of four snowboarders down by the lodge, and they walked over talking amongst themselves.

"You didn't say they were snowboarders," I mumbled to Joel as the riders approached.

"Gentleman, this is Andrea Parker. She is the best skier and backcountry guide we have," he said with flare and enthusiasm.

"Andy," I said pulling my goggles back down, wondering what I had gotten myself into. We made introductions, and I found out that the group consisted of Paul, Trip, Davie and Scott. They were in town from California for the weekend competition.

"Have you guys been riding long?" I asked when we reached the summit.

"You can say that," Scott said, and the others chuckled at some inside joke.

"Fine, let's go," I snapped, narrowing my eyes at them under my googles already annoyed with my group. I was not up to showing the backcountry to a group of arrogant jerks from California who probably didn't know the first thing about riding. Gathering them together and making sure everyone understood the hazards and dangers, I steered them over to a roped off section, lifting it up to let the riders underneath. I waved at Joel who had made the ride up to the top of the mountain with us, and he waved back, giving me a small nod. He was going to owe me I thought to myself.

Standing at the top of the summit was an amazing feeling. From this side of the mountain you were engulfed completely by nature's beauty. I warned the riders that the trees were sparser at the top and gradually got denser as you got to the bottom of the mountain and to watch out for large objects like rocks and downed trees obstructing the terrain. They nodded in understanding, and we set off down the mountain at a good pace; the guys actually surprised me and turned out to be pretty good snowboarders.

I loved sailing through the backcountry. It felt so freeing and peaceful racing down the mountain with no one else around. Each trip in the backcountry was a different adventure; the mountain landscape was always different unlike the ski trails. Often the only noise on the trail was the wind whipping off your jacket and your own breathing; it was my favorite place in the whole world. I almost forgot that the Californians were with me—almost. We paused about fifteen minutes into the trip at one of the larger drop offs, and I pointed out some larger rocks and waited for them to descend first. The first three went down without a problem. The fourth guy, I think his name was Trip, went down and then caught his board on something and went tumbling down about fifty feet.

"Oh no!" I exclaimed and took off after him. I reached him much faster than his buddies. He was rolling in pain, and I could see his legs were caught up beneath him and twisted with his board in an awkward position. I quickly clicked out of my skis and made my way over to him.

"Trip, I'm going to detach your board," I said, and he nodded. I slowly made my way around him and detached his board, standing it up in the snow.

"Does anything else hurt?" I asked, and he shook his head no as he shifted slightly, bringing his legs around in a less awkward angle.

"That's good, but I need you to lay still just in case," I said. By this time his friends had reached us; they were talking over each other about what to do

33

next.

"Guys, calm down," I finally said. They each looked at me in surprise. I knew from our location that we couldn't climb back up for help, and our best bet was getting to the bottom and alerting ski patrol.

"Okay, I'm going to head down and get help. I need you all to stay with him. Do not move him but keep him talking," I gave firm instructions, and they just nodded. I was about to head down when one of the guys, I think his name was Paul, spoke up.

"Andy, I'm going to go with you," he said, standing up and adjusting his bindings. I rolled my eyes under my goggles. I really didn't need anyone slowing me down.

"Trust me, I can keep up," he said as if he could read my mind.

"Okay." With that we took off racing down the mountain. True to his word Paul kept pace with me, and side by side we descended down the mountain in record pace. When we emerged from under the roped off area at the bottom, Joel was there waiting for us.

"Andy, what's wrong?" he asked, seeing only two of use emerge.

"Trip twisted his knee pretty badly just after the cascading point," I said, trying to give him a reference; he nodded with concern and radioed for ski patrol. With ski patrol Paul and I headed back up the mountain. This time we descended at a slower pace until we could see Trip's snowboard sticking out of the snow, and then the three snowboarders came into view. Davie and Scott were sitting around Trip, and they were all laughing and joking when we got closer.

"Andy, you found help," Trip called out to me with a bit of a laugh. He must be delirious I thought to myself. No one gets that excited over ski patrol. The three member ski patrol team got Trip secured into the toboggan quickly and assured us all that it was most likely just a dislocated knee and nothing seemed broken. Scott and Davie looked a little cold and tired and started to head back down the mountain slowly with ski patrol.

"Do you mind if I finish out the tour?" Paul asked, coming up from behind, startling me.

"Are you sure? Your friend is hurt," I said, hoping he would change his mind.

"He'll be fine… he can sometimes be a bit dramatic," Paul said with a grin. "Plus that run down the mountain was crazy fast—you're pretty good… for a skier," he said, mirroring my earlier thought about his snowboard abilities.

"Sure, why not" I said slowly. I had already seen him snowboard and knew he was capable of keeping up. I motioned to him that we would be going right instead of following behind ski patrol, and we took off in that direction. We rode side by side for about another 30 minutes until we came to a small clearing. I stopped and pushed up my goggles. Paul slid up next to me, also pushing up his goggles.

"Amazing," he breathed.

"Agreed," I said looking at him, startled by his eyes which were electric blue and piercing. "Down ahead," I motioned down and to the left, "are some natural table top jumps, so be careful."

"Really?" His eyes lit up like a child at Christmas.

"Don't do anything stupid," I said, sliding my goggles back on and waiting for him to go ahead. He just grinned at me and took off ahead. I kept up with him until we reached the jumps, and I swerved left; he headed straight for it and did what looked like a cab 720 or two full rotations and then landed on the other side.

"Show off," I muttered to myself as we headed for the second of three jumps. Again, I swerved left and he nailed the jump, throwing his arms up in the air when he landed. The final jump was probably the largest of the three, and this time I wasn't going to let him be the only one with all the fun. He hit the jump first and again in spectacular fashion flipped with ease, completing two and half full rotations. By the time I hit the jump he was clearly over; I tried to focus my breathing and rely on my training some nearly twenty years ago, clearing my mind and letting my body follow. By some miracle I landed the jump and came to a halt where he stood at the bottom. I could clearly see shock on his face.

"We are almost at the end," I said calmly as he gaped at me speechless. Inside I was freaking out; I couldn't believe it. We finished the final portion of the mountain in good time and without any more tricks. Joel was pacing at the bottom of the roped off area when we finally cleared the tree line.

"It's about time. I have been worried sick about you," he yelled as we approached. I looked over my shoulder at Paul because I knew he wasn't talking to me.

"That was one of the best guided tours ever. You didn't tell me the guide was so talented," Paul said to Joel, slapping him on the back as we continued to the lodge. "Really, Andy, that was awesome. Your flip at the end was sick!" he exclaimed, and I blushed, thankful that the exertion from the mountain hid the color in my face.

"Thanks," I said and made a move to head to the locker room.

"Hey won't you join us for a drink? It's the least I could do…" Paul said, calling after me.

"Give me ten minutes?" I said after a moment's hesitation. What I really wanted to do was to put my equipment away and change back into normal clothes.

"Yeah, sure thing. I should probably check on Trip," he said and headed off toward ski patrol.

***

I changed quickly and noticed that it was almost three. I had spent all day skiing the backcountry. I couldn't recall the last time that had happened. Hayden Grace should be arriving at the mountain any moment for practice. Excitement grew at the realization of the rare opportunity to see her practice. Walking through the lodge, it was pretty empty at this time of day as people were just now starting to get off of work and school. Soon the entire area would be swamped with all types of people. Momentarily, I had a flash of nerves not really knowing who the guys were but also what they even looked like. People look so different dressed in all their ski stuff than they do dressed in street clothes. I soon realized that I had nothing to fear.

"Andy," Paul called, waving me over. As I approached I got a better look at my California riders. Paul was sitting in front of the fireplace, and Scott and Davie were lounging on the large sofa, laughing over something someone said. Trip was seated in the far recliner with his leg in a soft brace and propped up on the coffee table. Davie had shaggy blonde hair and seemed to be of average build; he wore jeans and a ripped t-shirt of a band I had never heard of. Trip was surprisingly thin but also had shaggy blonde hair and what I imagined a pretty permanent five o'clock shadow. Scott was the tallest of the group and had brown curly hair that hung down by his ears which he covered up with a black flat-billed baseball cap; he wore gray sweatpants and a large black sweatshirt with the Burton logo. Paul, who sat closest to me, was dressed in jeans and a black, thick thermal long sleeve shirt. He had broad shoulders and a pretty muscular build with short jet black hair. When I looked up from my observation, I was met with those sharp blue eyes and a smirk.

"Hi," I breathed as he stood and walked toward me, never taking his eyes

37

off of me.

"Hi," he commented back after a moment. Finally pulling my gaze from his, I addressed the rest of the motley crew that they were.

"Hey guys," I said, stepping around Paul and shaking all of their hands.

"That was a great ride, today," Paul said after I had settled down in another recliner near the fireplace.

"It's not as big or vast as some of the mountains out West, but I think it's pretty darn good," I said, feeling the need to defend our great mountain.

"Andy, thank you for saving my life," Trip said from his chair.

"Your life?" I said, chuckling. "I don't think you were ever in any real danger, but you're welcome," I grinned over at him.

"How long have you been skiing the backcountry here?" Davie asked from the sofa.

"The backcountry here at Mount Sunapee? Since I was eighteen. I have been skiing since I was five," I said, thinking back to my very first ski lesson. They each muttered in understanding as they had all been riding for an equally long amount of time.

"Do you ski other mountains?" Scott asked.

"I did when I was younger. My parents moved around a lot… but not recently," I explained. The truth was I hadn't been on any type of vacation in almost five years. Shortly after Stefan died I took Hayden Grace on a small trip to New York City to visit my brother Drew and to get her out of the house and take her mind off of everything, but since then there just hadn't been time. From there we fell into casual conversation and for a moment I forgot where I was. I felt like I was in my early twenties again—carefree, skiing, meeting new people and giving tours; their enthusiasm seemed contagious. We talked for a couple of minutes before I heard my name.

"Mom?" Hayden Grace called from behind me. I could hear a collective whisper of surprise from the group.

"Sorry guys, I have to go. It was nice meeting you all," I said and turned to join Hayden Grace.

"Maybe we will meet again," I heard Paul say from behind me.

'Unlikely,' I thought to myself, but I politely turned back toward the group, smiled and waved goodbye.

"Who are those guys?" Hayden Grace asked when I reached her by the back door.

"Just some group Joel asked me to take on a backcountry tour," I replied.

"You were working here today?... Backcountry tour?... You promised to take me on the next one," Hayden Grace stated in a whiny voice before asking a hundred more questions.

"Hey, slow down...how about I just watch you practice, and we talk about the rest at dinner?" I asked as we walked out of the lodge.

"Cool."

"Oh... Hey Mom, look," Hayden Grace pulled open her jacket to show me the patches once more. I smiled widely, and she took off up the mountain to catch up with her friends.

Chapter 5

I raked my hands through my hair and let out a big sigh as the strands fell down around my face. It was a little after two in the afternoon on Friday, and I was fading fast. Today, unable to sit at home, I found myself at the Manchester office as I prepared for the new account on Monday. My eyelids drooped from the lack of sleep the night before, and my thoughts drifted to the huge fight Hayden Grace and I had during dinner. The day had gone so well that, of course, there would be a fight, I mused to myself. I had been in mid-chew when she brought up the subject of attending the Killington Mountain School in Vermont instead of going to public school, *again*. It was a tired argument that she brought back up every couple of months. Last night the argument started after Hayden Grace went on and on about how Madison was going to be homeschooled next year so that she can focus more on snowboarding. Hayden Grace thought that the Killington Mountain School was her solution to stay competitive. The Killington Mountain School was a boarding school for gifted skiing and snowboarding students. I understood her passion and desire to focus on her sport and that she wanted to 'take it to the next level,' but there was no way I could afford to send her there—a single year alone cost around $45,000. As it stood we barely have enough money to cover our bills and her coach, gymnastics lessons, equipment upkeep, competition travel and entry fees. Club membership at Mount Sunapee was $800 a month and that was *with* my employee discount. Then there was the fact that selfishly I could not stand the thought of her moving away and staying in a boarding school. Hayden Grace raged on and on about if her Dad was here he would let her go and he would be there to support her. I did my best to keep cool, but somewhere in all the shouting I slowly started to unravel and started shouting back. The truth was her dad wasn't there, and it was just me and her, and I couldn't afford it.

"I HATE YOU," she yelled, before finally storming off to her room and blasting her music. I can still hear the accusation and hatred in her voice echoing through my mind this afternoon. After she slammed the door, I took about a minute to practice my deep breathing before I went and fished Molly out from under the bed. Molly didn't like loud noises which were usually relegated to thunder and lighting and sometimes the vacuum, but it now extended to loud yelling. After cleaning up from dinner that was never finished, I crawled into bed with a bowl of chocolate ice cream and Molly by my side and cried. Not just small tears, but big ugly tears and sobs into my pillow. Frustration, anger, anxiety, confusion and guilt racked my body with each sob. 'I loved Hayden Grace so much, but I can't give her everything she wants,' I mumbled incoherently to Molly and at times made my own wild accusations at Stefan. It was moments like these that I questioned whether I was cut out to be a single mom.

"Earth to Andy," Marla said over the cubical wall. Her crazy auburn hair was tied back in a high ponytail with two different colored scrunchies which clashed with the wild leopard print sweater she wore. Marla was part of the graphic design department and had joined the company the same year I had. Together we had struggled through many ups and downs in each other's lives. She carried me through Stefan's death, and I helped her through her fertility struggles and ultimately her divorce.

"Hmmm?"

"I have been talking to you for about five minutes about this awful date I had last night, and I look over the wall and you're not even paying attention…it's like my date all over again," she said, throwing her hands in the air wildly in mock frustration. "What is going on with you?"

"Teenagers," I responded and flashed an awkward smile.

"Oh honey…you need a break," she said in her fake southern accent. She came around the desk and pulled me up out of my desk chair despite my loud protesting. After several minutes, I caved to Marla's insistent urging, it was just easier that way. We rode the elevator down to the ground floor and made a bee-line for the Dunkin' Donuts. On the way I told her all about my fight with Hayden Grace while she listened intently. After several minutes she looked at me with wide eyes and in a very sarcastic tone asked, "Whatever are you going to do?"

"I have no idea," I mumbled. Once at the counter, I ordered a regular coffee, and Marla ordered a large iced coffee with milk. "Iced coffee in the middle of January? What…you don't get enough ice?"

"The key is to always stand out, my dear," she replied, taking a slight bow. I shook my head at her again and listened as she started in about her awful date.

"Andy, you're too stressed… you need a girl's night out or you're going to lose your mind," Marla finally said after circling the conversation back to Hayden Grace and our argument as we returned back to our cubicles. "How about tonight?" she suggested.

"I can't—I have a date," I said, and then the realization hit. "Oh my, I have a date… tonight! I completely forgot." I panicked, thinking of all the crazy things that had gone on since Tuesday night.

"Oh another date with the infamous Gregg," she mocked.

"I should cancel; there's too much going on," I said, reaching for the phone.

"Relax, this is good for you. You go home, put on some sexy little number, throw back several cosmos, martinis or whatever it is that you drink, and you get your freak on…it's a great stress relief," she said, winking at me.

"Ugh…that seems like so much work," I said, throwing my pen in her direction but ultimately deciding she was right; the date was a good idea.

"How about drinks on Saturday?" she asked, after skillfully ducking from my projectile.

"That works. My parents are going to be in town so they will be able to watch Hayden Grace."

"Wonderful! Let's meet at the Lucky Penny at eight?"

"Sounds great."

***

I stood in front of the mirror studying myself closely. I had picked a dark blue bandage dress and black sheer tights. I had managed to pull my hair up into a low loose knot at the base of my neck as several wayward strands had already come lose. The longer I looked in the mirror the more I could see new wrinkles that had developed around my eyes and the small purple circles that seemed to be a permanent fixture these days. I did my best with the make-up and headed down the hall to Hayden Grace's room.

"Hayden Grace?" I said, knocking on her door.

"I'm not talking to you," she practically spat through the door.

"Still mad?" There was no response this time. "Listen, I was just letting you know that Casey is here, and I'm going out. Is Madison's mom still taking you girls to the mountain in the morning for the competition or should Grams and Grandpa plan to?" I asked and waited for a response.

"You know if you are nodding your head in there, I can't see you through this thing called a door," I quipped back after what seemed like five minutes of silence.

"Yes, Madison's mom is coming at nine, the competition starts at twelve," she finally responded. "Did you call Uncle Drew?"

SHIT! I had totally forgotten to call Drew. This was not going to go over well or increase my chances of her anger with me subsiding anytime soon. "No, I forgot. I'm sorry," I said bracing for the worst.

"I figured. I called him, and he can't come. He is going to Vail with some chick Stella," she said as we continued to speak through the door.

"Really? Stella?" I mused aloud and with that the loud sounds of Linkin Park drowned out any further conversation. I was kicking myself for forgetting to call Drew but slightly intrigued by his re-interest in Stella; it was a disaster the first time around, and she crushed his heart into a million pieces.

"Looking good, Mrs. Parker," Casey practically whistled when I entered the living room.

"Thank you, Casey," I said slightly taken aback by the compliment.

"I don't know when we will be back," I told Casey when I heard the car honk from the driveway. I had a slight feeling of déjà vu from several nights ago.

"No worries, Mrs. Parker. Hayden Grace seems pretty mad. I don't think I'll see much of her tonight," she commented, settling in on the sofa. If it hadn't been for the fact that Casey had known Hayden Grace almost her whole life I would have tried to defend her, but who was I kidding? Casey was right. There was little chance that Hayden Grace was leaving her room tonight.

"No, I don't think you will," I agreed and headed out the door.

***

"Andy you look like heaven," Gregg said once we got into the restaurant and I took my coat off. I cringed a little bit at the cheesy nature of his comment but thanked him as he pushed my seat in.

"How did you get this reservation?" I whispered across the table. The restaurant was, in fact, one of the fanciest restaurants in Manchester and had just been in the paper with rave reviews. I had heard that reservations were at least six weeks out.

"I know a guy," he said as he winked in my direction, and I smiled. We chatted for a bit about work and the weather. The date was moving at a slow pace, and after the last couple of days I needed something to happen or I was going to fall asleep at the table regardless if it was a high class occasion. In atypical-Andy fashion, I ordered a Long Island Iced Tea half way through dinner. Gregg's eyebrows shot up in pleasant surprise when I placed the order. When the waitress asked him if he wanted something he didn't skip a beat and ordered a rum and coke. After the drinks arrived, the conversation at the table seemed to become livelier as we found new things to discuss.

"Would you like dessert?" Gregg asked, reaching out and placing his hand on my knee, sending tingles throughout my body. I nodded and schoolgirl giggles escaped my lips. Gregg ordered dessert and our third round of drinks. I mentally made a note to slow down or things were going to get sloppy very quickly. Dessert arrived, and Gregg moved his chair closer to mine at the table.

"Andy, you're truly amazing," he whispered into my ear, leaning slightly forward, skimming his hand along the inside of my thigh. Normally, I would have been appalled by his bold and very public display of affection, but tonight his touch felt electric and made me stir in my seat, and I giggled again.

"I have to use the restroom," I finally said, interrupting the moment when my head started to spin slightly. I wobbled my way to the restroom as the alcohol worked its way through my system. Taking an extra minute or two, I splashed some cold water on my face.

"Get it together, Andy," I said to myself, looking at the women with the flushed checks and slightly droopy eyes staring back. 'You are a grown-ass woman with a kid...act right,' I thought to myself. Taking a deep breath, I steadied myself and headed back into the restaurant. Leaving the bathroom, I ran into Gregg.

"Sorry," I mumbled, surprised by his sudden appearance.

"You were gone a while... I got worried," he said, reaching for my hand.

"I was?" I asked in confusion. I swore it was only a minute or two. He started to lead me down a short hallway. "Aren't we that way?" I tried to ask, twisting to look back towards our table. Suddenly, he pulled me down a shorter hallway and turned to face me, cupping my face in both his hands.

"You're so sexy, Andy," he breathed as he leaned in for a kiss, making my pulse race. The kiss started out slowly as I moved my hands up his back and then quickly changed into a wildly passionate kiss. My fingers weaved through his hair as he pushed me up against the wall, moving his kisses down my jaw line to my neck. I laced one leg around his thigh as he let out a slow groan.

"Andy, let's go back to your place," he mumbled between kisses.

"Can't... babysitter there," I gasped back, trying to catch my breath. "What about yours?"

"No, that won't work," he mumbled.

"That's a shame...do you like the color red?" I whispered back, suddenly feeling very daring.

"Yes," he paused, pulling back slightly to look at me with a puzzled look.

"Then you'll want to see what's under the dress," I said with a grin, knowing it was the alcohol that was making me so brave. Gregg started to say something when suddenly there were footsteps coming down the short hallway. Gregg smoothly moved to lean on the wall next to me so he was blocking me from sight as I straightened my dress a little and regained my composure. I felt like I was in high school again, about to get caught by the principal. Whomever it was stopped and turned around, going down a different hallway and leaving us to our small nook. A moment passed, and I let out a giggle for the ridiculous nature of the entire situation.

"Time for the check?" Gregg asked when the coast was clear.

"Yes, time for the check," I commented as he steered me back to the table. Once back at the table Gregg asked if I wanted another drink, and I politely declined. The crazy and wild moment from minutes earlier seemed to pass as fatigue and reality started to set in. I think Gregg also realized that the opportunity had passed as we walked to the car in silence except for the alcohol buzzing between my ears.

Chapter 6

My alarm clock was sounding, and it was entirely too early I thought to myself as I swung wildly at my nightstand, hitting the alarm. Down the hallway I could faintly hear my phone ringing as well, causing Molly to crawl up the bed and start licking my face.

"What the hell," I mumbled to myself as I sat up. Ugh, the blood rushed to my head, causing an instant throbbing sensation. This is not the morning for a hangover, I thought to myself, stumbling down the hallway.

"Good morning sweetie," I heard my mother say on the other line; it was six in the morning.

"Mom?"

"We are here in the driveway," she commented.

"The driveway?" I asked in confusion.

"You know that long path covered in tiny rocks that leads from your house…"

"I know what a driveway is. I am confused about what you are doing in it," I snapped.

"It's Saturday; you asked us to come up for Hayden Grace's competition."

"What are you doing here so early?" I questioned as I headed to the door. It was a five hour drive to the house from their house in Long Island. I had a hard time thinking they left at one in the morning.

"Last night we stayed the night at the house of one of your father's army buddies who lives near Manchester. Plus, you said you had to work early this morning and that Hayden Grace couldn't be alone for a single minute," she gently mocked on the phone. My mom had always thought that the rules were a little restrictive and that I needed to give Hayden Grace more space. What I could never fully articulate to her was that the rules were more than a set of guidelines that I followed; they were Stefan's last thoughts about how to raise Hayden Grace, and I wasn't ready to take that away from him...or her. Following the rules helped to shape Hayden Grace to be the young woman we both hoped she could be.

"Oh...I have to work!" I exclaimed, opening the door.

"Yes, you do," she said, coming through the door and giving me a gigantic hug. Molly raced down the hallway, barking with excitement.

"Shhh, Molly...you will wake the teenager," my dad commented as he came through the door. Once in the kitchen, I made coffee and poured everyone a large mug.

"Honey, you look like crap," mom said as we sat at the table.

"Thanks Mom, I love you too," I mumbled back.

"Are you taking care of yourself? I worry about you and Hayden Grace up here in New Hampshire all by yourselves. You should move in with us." It was an age-old conversation Mom had been having with me since Stefan died.

"You know I can't do that to Hayden Grace with her snowboarding career," I gave her the fiercest look I could muster under the horrible conditions I was currently experiencing, and she nodded in understanding. When I was done with my coffee I raced into the bedroom to get ready for work. This morning I was set to teach ski lessons to the intermediate club team and any guests on the mountain. Racing out the door, I shouted last minute instructions to my parents.

"Madison's mom is coming to get them at nine and the competition starts at twelve. I will be teaching lessons all morning, but if you need something just text me," I paused, "you do know how to text?"

"Yes. Now get out of here, we can take care of the rest," my dad said, shooing me out of the house.

***

The drive to the mountain was quick as there weren't many people on the road this early. The mountain, however, was already a buzz with last minute preparations for the day's competition. I had heard rumors that several high profile professional snowboarders would be in attendance as well. It didn't matter much to me who was in attendance; I had my ski lessons to teach and then Hayden Grace's competition to focus on. I headed straight to the locker room and changed for the day. My head was still spinning as I pulled a granola bar from the vending machine in the employee locker room. Outside the bright sun reflecting off of the snow hurt my eyes causing me to wince.

"Andy!!" Rachel shrilled, coming up from behind me. Rachel was a little older than Hayden Grace, and we often taught lessons together on Saturdays. Usually working with Rachel wasn't a problem; in fact, I had instructed her first ski lesson when she was six. Once in high school she started working at the mountains regularly after school and on the weekends. She didn't have enough drive to want to compete and try and make it onto any club or national team. She was perfectly content teaching lessons and skiing the trails in her free time. But today...her energy needed to be reined in or my head was going to split open.

"Rachel, I need you to bring your voice down so many levels," I whispered, taking the coffee out of her hand and slowly sipping on it waiting for the wave of nausea to pass.

"Did you hear?" she asked in a whisper, observing my hung-over state.

"Hear what?"

"PW and his crew are here!"—she was so excited that she was shaking.

"Okay and they are…?" I questioned.

"Only the greatest snowboarder ever and his famous snowboarder friends," she said waving her hand in exasperation at my lack of knowledge. Vaguely in my mind I recalled Stefan and Hayden Grace talking about a PW and watching his tricks on TV. From what I could remember, he was a phenomenal snowboarder in his prime.

"Revolutionizing the sport," Stefan would always say after watching a competition. I think that Hayden Grace even now occasionally mentions his name, but it never really clicked.

"That's great; I hope you get to meet them," I said, trying to end our conversation to work on my hangover. Thinking she was done, I headed out to the Discover Center where all the ski lessons were taught.

"Oh you better believe I'm going to meet them," she called after me.

"Andy!" A different name called after me when I was only about ten feet away from the Discover Center.

"Almost made it," I thought to myself as I sighed and hung my head. "What?" I said, turning around to find a flush faced Joel running up behind me.

"I need a favor," he said, trying to catch his breath.

"Another day, another favor... that's two in two days," I said, holding up two fingers.

"I know, I know, but you're the only one that can do it," he said.

"You say that a lot. Maybe you should give me a raise," I said, feeling strangely bold...or sick—I couldn't decide which.

"I'll think about it," he said, finally able to breathe.

"Okay, what do you need?" I asked. Joel always had interesting odd tasks for me to do, and I usually didn't mind doing them. But this morning my head was still spinning, and I could have used about three more hours of sleep and some ibuprofen.

"Mitch called in sick on ski patrol, and I need someone to check all the trails at the top of the mountain before we can open up," he said, getting all excited again. Joel hated when things didn't run smoothly. He hated it even more on competition or event days.

"What about my lessons?"

"Rachel can cover them until you get back," he said, thrusting a radio and key into my hands.

"You can get the ski patrol bag from the patrol shack at the top of the mountain," he continued with instructions as if I had never opened the trails for him before.

"Sure, not a problem," I said, secretly relieved. At least it would be quieter on the mountain, and people would stop shouting at me. Rachel, on the other hand, was not going to be happy, I thought to myself as I grabbed my skis and headed to the lift.

In no time I was up on the mountain looking around the ski patrol shack for the emergency bag and other essentials needed to check the trails. Opening duties on ski patrol included checking all the trails starts and making sure that the closed trails were clearly marked. It wasn't a job everyone loved, but I enjoyed being alone on the mountain... and on a day like today it was a blessing. As I checked each trail I radioed down to the ski patrol station at the bottom of the mountain, and they crossed each trail off the list. Once all the trails were checked, they would open the lifts to the guests. The last area I checked was the backcountry entry point I had used yesterday with Paul, Davie, Scott and Trip. As I got closer to the trail I noticed that it had been disturbed, and I could see a small trail of footprints and edge marks from a snowboard from the second chair lift. I radioed down to ski patrol that all the trails were set, and I was going to check something out in the backcountry. I followed the tracks of what looked like a snowboard down the through the slopes and valleys. I got to a familiar clearing and saw the two riders: one rider standing by the tabletop jumps from yesterday and the other one had just cleared the first jump. I knew exactly who it was by his riding style.

"Paul," I said, waving my hands in the air, trying to get his attention as I glided up next to Scott. Paul saw me and waved back, changing his direction to come join us.

"What the hell are you doing on this side of the mountain," I fumed in anger, as best as I could since my head still pounded, when he finally joined us.

"Joel said to make ourselves at home," he commented, ignoring my irritation.

"Who let you up the ski lift?" I questioned, trying to figure out who would be losing their job as soon as I got back down the mountain.

"Joel," Scott said with a grin.

"He failed to mention it," I huffed.

"Joel owed me a favor," Paul said with a wicked grin.

"Those seem to be going around," I mumbled to myself.

"You guys could get hurt or injured like your friend Trip, and no one would know you were here," I said, changing my tactics to try and get them to understand but not hiding my serious annoyance over the situation.

"Joel let us up the ski lift so that's not entirely accurate," Paul clarified, only making me seethe even more.

"But you're here now so we are all good," Scott said, giving me a thumbs up. I could see a small camera in Scott's hand and figured they were filming stunts or tricks.

"We really should get down to the bottom of the mountain because you really shouldn't be here," I said again with less force.

"Come on… is there any way we can stay a little longer?" Paul pleaded, slightly flashing a huge grin. Against my better judgment I sighed and called down to ski patrol and asked for Joel. Joel all too quickly confirmed the story and told me to stay with our guests until they were ready to come down.

"Looks like I'm all yours," I commented when I joined the group after making my radio call.

"Fantastic, we won't be too much longer," Paul said. He then motioned to Scott again who got the camera ready, and he took off down the jumps. I sat down and eventually leaned back on my elbows and watched the theatrics. I was ticked I was stuck on the mountain babysitting with a thunderous headache; there were a thousand places I would rather be, starting with my bed back home. After a couple of runs, Paul glided up to me and asked if I wanted a turn.

"No thanks, I'll pass," I said, squinting up at him.

"What's wrong? Yesterday you were killing it," he commented, looking down at me in concern as he put his hands on his hips.

"Bad date last night left me with a headache," I motioned to my head, hoping he would stop with the questions.

"Nothing serious I hope," he said.

"The date or the headache?"

"Both," he said, flashing yet another grin and nudging me with his foot to get up.

"Really, I don't think this is a good idea," I said, struggling to stand up.

"Fresh air is really good for you," he said, extending his hand. I normally would have agreed with him, but he didn't have someone with a hammer banging around in his head. I reached up and grabbed his hand. He pulled me up with more force than was needed, causing me to become off balance and stumble forward, knocking him down. Still off balance, I continued to fall forward until I landed on top of him. Anyone watching would have seen a tornado of arms and legs flying in different directions before landing with a quiet thud in the snow. Opening my eyes I found myself staring into those electric eyes as excitement danced through them.

"You are right—it is dangerous up here," he said after several seconds.

"I'm so sorry," I mumbled, struggling to untangle myself from him. Finally free, I stood myself upright as Paul stood next to me. I couldn't help but start giggling, and he soon joined in the laughter.

"Hey, are you done up here?" Scott called to us from where he was standing. "I'm freezing and ready to eat, man."

"Just a couple more," Paul gestured to him.

"Fine," Scott said and repositioned himself with a clear view of jumps.

"Join me?" Paul asked, holding out his hand.

"It's not a good idea," I said, trying to hold my ground. Instead he fixated his blue eyes on me and raised his eyebrows. It was a subtle expression, but it was as if he was questioning my ability. Not able to back down from a challenge, I agreed. I let him go first unsure if all this movement was about to cause me to be sick all over the mountain. Taking a moment to make sure I was in control of myself, I set off behind Paul as he landed the first jump with some crazy spin. I followed behind still trying to get my wits about me and did a simple back flip. Landing squarely on my skis, I followed to the next jump where Paul was already executing his jump. I waited a moment and followed behind doing a simple spin as I worked up to the last jump. Yesterday I had done a rodeo which was a back flip with a spin. I was pretty confident that I could do it again with enough speed as Paul finished his last trick. I took a deep breath and again stopped thinking when I hit the jump. Yet again I was able to land safely on my feet. 'I need to stop pushing my luck,' I thought to myself as I skied over to where Paul and Scott were now standing.

"That was awesome!" Scott exclaimed, giving me a thumbs up.

"It's been a long time since I did those kinds of tricks," I commented mostly to myself.

"Okay, I'm going to do one last run, and we can head down. Want to join me again?" Paul asked. I shook my head no as my head continued to pound. The only bright side of the situation was that I didn't get sick after all the twisting and flipping; given the way I was feeling it had been a real possibility. Paul looked at me for another moment and then headed back around to do the jumps one last time.

"This is tiring…does he ever run out of energy?" I asked Scott.

"Never," Scott said before yelling some final instructions to Paul. When he was done I radioed down to Joel and let them know we were coming down. The three of us then whipped down the mountain in no time without incident. At the bottom of the tree line, I could see a small crowd at the roped off barrier.

"What the heck is going on?" I said as we slowed down. I just heard a loud sigh next to me, and Paul and Scott whipped ahead where a larger man that looked like security was waiting for them. They ducked under the ropes, gave a small wave to the crowd and were whisked away. I made a much slower approach and by the time I made it to the ropes the crowd had dispersed. They must be some important Californian snowboarders I thought to myself as I pulled out my phone.

***

I looked down, and I had four missed calls from Hayden Grace and then another two from my mom. Panicking that something had happened, I called Hayden Grace first and got her voice-mail. Looking at my watch, it was already eleven-thirty. 'Where did the time go?' I thought to myself. I placed a call to my mom who answered on the first ring.

"Andy?"

"Yes Mom, it's me, is everything okay?" I asked in a panic.

"Yes, everything is fine. Hayden Grace said she left a bandana in your car, and she desperately needed it for the competition. We have looked everywhere here and can't find it." I sighed with relief that something horrible hadn't happened.

"Okay, I will look in my car and get it to her," I said, hanging up the phone. I put my skis up the by lodge and jogged out to my car. Stefan had worn your typical red bandana under his helmet whenever he rode. I never really understood it because his being in the military always guaranteed a clean well-kept buzz, but he told me when he was younger he had long hair and it kept the hair out of his face. After he joined the military it was a habit he couldn't shake; it became his crutch. It was no exaggeration—in almost every picture we have of him on the mountain he is wearing it. After he died I found it packed away with his snowboarding gear. I wasn't sure what I was going to do with it, and I was carrying it through the house when Hayden Grace spotted it in my hands. She ran over and grabbed it from me and ever since she has always worn it while riding. At this point it is as important to her riding as her boots and board—now becoming her crutch. She once told me that it was so important to her because when she saw the bandana she could picture Stefan and it was like he was there with her. After she said that I couldn't say anything about the bandana, and I just went along with its importance.

Looking through the car I found it on the floor under the passenger seat. Sighing with relief that a meltdown would be avoided, I headed to the lodge for a quick stop before going out to the pipe. My stomach had started to growl, and I needed to raid the vending machine in the break room for lunch and ibuprofen if I had any chance of making it through the day. Once I had secured the bare necessities, I turned to leave the break room and bumped into Joel, literally bumped into him.

"Joel, we need to stop meeting like this," I exclaimed, straightening myself up.

"I have been looking for you, and you didn't answer your phone," he said exasperated as always.

"Need another favor?"

"No, I just needed to give this to you," he said, handing me a note.

"Passing love notes?" I questioned him.

"You tell me, it's from PW."

"PW? I don't know him," I said with confusion.

"Andy, come on…you have been showing him around the backcountry for the last two days," he said, puzzled over my lack of comprehension. "I thought you knew."

"I had no idea," I said, eyeing the note with suspicion. I waited for Joel to leave before I opened the note. Slightly nervous I tore open the small white envelope. Inside was a half sheet with the Mount Sunapee logo on it.

Andy

Sorry to leave so abruptly. Thank you for the tour, again.

I hope you can join us all for dinner tonight at the lodge around 7.

Paul Westcott

At the bottom of the note he had scribbled his phone number. I stared in disbelief at what was happening. My mind drifted back to his blue eyes and his grin, and I let out a slight sigh, shaking my head to clear my mind. This was ridiculous; I didn't have time to get caught up with someone like Paul Westcott. I scribbled a response, declining his invitation. I had a sensible job, a daughter with a slew of responsibilities and I was dating a practical guy. That is how it was supposed to be. I made a mental note to give the note back to Joel so he could deliver it, like a telegram messenger, to Paul Westcott. Remembering the bandana, I looked at my watch. Hayden Grace had only a couple minutes before her first run, causing me to rush out the door.

Chapter 7

I found Hayden Grace at the top of the pipe in line waiting for her turn. She was so happy I had found the bandana that she forgot how mad she was at me and embraced me in a big hug. I wished her good luck and made my way back down the pipe. I ran into Joel at the bottom and passed him the note. He gave me a questionable look but didn't press any further. I then took over the rest of the ski lesson that Rachel was instructing. She was so grateful that she squealed with delight and ran off in search of 'PW' and 'his gang'—'I should have saved his number and given it to her,' I thought to myself; it probably would have made her life.

The competition was announced over the intercom on the mountain so I was able to keep tabs on Hayden Grace's early runs. She did well in each round, and her final qualifying run earned her a spot in the final. At the last minute one of the other ski instructors offered to cover my lesson for me so I could watch the final run. Now I sat with my parents in the grandstands at the bottom, cheering on the riders as they prepared their final two runs. Hayden Grace's friends, Madison and Lucie, were also having a pretty good day and had easily qualified for the final. The men were up first; my eyebrows even rose slightly when I heard the announcer call Preston in the men's division. 'Must be the guy Madison has a crush on,' I thought to myself, feeling like I was a little in the know. Preston finished third in the men's competition and qualified for Regional 6 in Aspen. For the women, Madison was in first place so she would go last, and Hayden Grace would ride fifth—not a great position but she could fight back. During her first run, Hayden Grace was solid on every trick until the end; she fell backwards after her landing and washed out. I was a ball of nerves, and I fidgeted in my seat during her entire run. I was not made to watch these events live, I thought to myself. Looking up as they announced her name for her second run, I could make out her silhouette on the top of the mountain and my palms started to get sweaty. She paused for a moment and patted her jacket before she set out for the pipe; the moment she dropped-in I felt like I was holding my breath, unwilling to exhale. I knew her routine by heart, and this is what it should have looked like:

Trick 1	*Air-to-Fakie — She goes airborne without rotation and grabs her board and then lands*
Trick 2	*Backside 540 with Mute Grab — She rotates one and one half turns and then grabs the board between her bindings on the front side*
Trick 3	*Cab 360 — She completes one frontside rotation*
Trick 4	*Japan Air — Another trick with no rotation she goes up and grabs the board between the bindings and pulls the board back behind her*
Trick 5	*Switch Backside 720 — She goes up and completes two full rotations spinning backwards.*

With each trick, I could hear my parents whistling and calling her name, but I remained seated where I was. She cleared her last trick, and I finally exhaled as we all erupted in cheers. She pumped her fists in the air. It was one of the best runs I had seen her put together in a long time. She was able to complete all the tricks with no mistakes; her height was good, and she looked confident. There was still a lot of competition left, but it was a solid run for Hayden Grace. She waited impatiently at the bottom while the judges scored the run. After what seemed like forever her scores were announced: she was in second place. She jumped up and down and pointed to us in the bleachers. We waved wildly while she took her seat at the bottom under the sponsor banner and waited. There were four more riders to go. Lucie was up next and nailed her run as well. Her middle tricks were a little harder than Hayden Grace's, and she had a little bit more height. Lucie's scores earned her second place, and pushed Hayden Grace to third. Next up was a girl named Kelly Franks who, according to the announcers, rode with a club in Vermont. She made it half way through her run and then she washed out. My mom grabbed my arm and squealed in delight.

"You know you're getting excited over a teenage girl falling down," I reminded her, and she ignored my comment.

Up next was Abbie; she was a little older than the rest of the group at eighteen. She was a senior in high school in the same school that Madison attended. She was a little more experienced, but her attitude really sucked as Hayden Grace and Madison often told me. Now she was the only thing that stood between Hayden Grace and her qualifying for the next competition and going to Aspen. She started her run smoothly and hit her first trick and the next trick and the one after that—she hit them all. I held my breath while the judges scored her run, and when a loud cheer erupted at the bottom I knew she had taken first place. Abbie taking first forced Madison who was previously first to do her final run in hopes of finishing first. It also meant that Hayden Grace was in fourth place no matter what. I scanned the bottom of the pipe and saw her still sitting by the sponsor banner hugging Lucie as Madison finished up her final run. I knew this was going to crush her; she had wanted this so badly for so long. "There is always next year," I heard my dad say next to me. Madison finished her run with the same score as her first run and ended up second, Lucie third and Hayden Grace the alternate. Less than one point separated all four girls.

I sighed and told my parents we would meet them at home, and they understood. I slowly tried to fight the crowd of spectators to where Hayden Grace stood. Many of the spectators were frequent skiers themselves or parents of the children I taught ski lessons to. Several of them stopped me and complimented Hayden Grace's performance, passing on words of advice or wisdom. I just smiled and nodded, appreciating the support but needing to reach my daughter. As soon as she could see me Hayden Grace took off on a dead sprint towards me.

"Mom, you made it," she cried, grabbing me around the waist.

"I wouldn't have missed this for anything," I said into her hair.

"I almost had it this time," she mumbled into my jacket.

"I know sweetie… it was such a good run. I'm really proud of you." It was all I knew to say at the end of such heartbreak.

"I think everything… helped," she said calmly, pulling away. I was expecting more tears and emotion. "I was able to just do the tricks without thinking about it just like Dad said in his letter," she said with the sophistication of an adult. I nodded as a tear threatened to escape. Just then loud voices and shouting could be heard from the judges' area.

"What's going on?" I asked.

"Oh, the judges are coming down to meet the riders," she commented, standing next to me.

"Is that normal?" I wondered out loud, thinking back to past competitions.

"Not always, but in this case the judges asked; they told us before the competition began," she said, taking off her helmet and slipping off the bandana. Her blonde hair fell down around her face as she fussed with it.

"Hayden Grace?" Coach Davis called from several feet away.

"Here?" she answered back in confusion.

"The judges wanted to meet the alternate riders as well; they need you to line up on the left side of where Lucie is standing." He rushed over and pointed to the exact location.

"Hi Andy… whatever you said to her made the biggest difference. She was like a different rider today," Ron said quickly before disappearing to find a couple of the male riders. I smiled with pride and stepped back as the judges came forward. I gaped when I saw who Joel was ushering in from the judges table: Paul or 'PW', Scott, Davie and lastly Trip hobbled in on crutches. This day was just full of surprises I thought to myself as I stepped back a little bit into the crowd of parents. I found myself next to Madison's mom in the crowd.

"Lisa, how are things going?" I tried to ask casually, keeping an eye on the judges.

"Can you believe they are meeting PW?" she said with a rushed excitement as if this event was the second coming of the Beatles.

"I mean, yeah, I guess that's cool," I said half-heartedly. "Did you come alone today?" I asked, trying to change the subject. It would not have been unusual for Lisa to come alone. From what Hayden Grace told me Madison's dad spent most of his time traveling, and Madison's older sister Laura was some sort of piano prodigy.

"They were here earlier but had to leave…Laura had piano practice," she said, dismissing the subject as she looked on. "Oh look, they are talking to Madison," she gushed, rushing forward and asking for several photos with Madison and the judges to which all the judges quickly obliged. Hayden Grace was making eyes at me that I had better not attempt such theatrics. I put my hands up, indicating I had no such intentions, and she giggled where she stood. As the judges finally made it to the alternates there were not many parents left in the crowd, and I had less and less people to hide behind. When Paul reached Hayden Grace he shook her hand and asked her a couple questions. I could tell one of them caught her off guard as surprise washed across her face and she pointed in my direction. He stood and searched until his eyes met mine, and I smiled shyly and waved, knowing my attempt to hide was in vain.

"Mom! Come over here," Hayden Grace yelled to me frantically, waving me over. Cursing the stars I slowly made my way over to where Hayden Grace stood. Paul had a large Cheshire cat grin sprawled across his face as I approached. Scott, Trip and Davie turned around to see what he was looking at, and recognizing me, they all shouted my name in a collective greeting, causing my cheeks to turn red in embarrassment.

"Fellas, we meet again," I said, extending my hand to them.

"Oh no. Hugs all around Andy," Scott declared and crushed me in a hug.

"Your mother saved my life," I could hear Trip telling Hayden Grace as she hung on every word they all said.

"Mom, you didn't tell me," she hissed.

"Remember the story about the backcountry riders from yesterday," I hissed back and recognition flashed across her face.

"But you said they were…"

"From California," I said, interrupting her for fear of what she might say to finish that statement based on the conversation I remember having with her.

"Hayden Grace, it was a pleasure to meet you. You have a very awesome mom here," Davie said, and Trip quickly agreed. Hayden Grace was on cloud nine and just nodded in agreement.

"I heard you declined my invitation this evening," Paul said, coming up close behind me, startling me. I could feel his breath on my neck, and a warm sensation developed in the pit of my stomach.

"I had plans already," I commented, trying to sound casual. He seemed to mull this over before replying.

"Hayden Grace, how would you and your friends like to have breakfast with us before we leave tomorrow?" he asked, and my mouth gaped open, *again*. Her mouth drew into a big 'oh' and she tried to play it cool but quickly lost her façade and jumped up and down in excitement.

"Mom, can we?" she asked, looking very hopeful. I threw an evil look at Paul who just shrugged his shoulders.

"Why don't you ask Madison and Lucie first," I barely finished saying as she sprinted over to her friends to ask them. I could tell from the shrieks and high pitched squealing it had gone over well.

"You fight dirty," I whispered at Paul when she was out of earshot.

"I'm not above fighting dirty to get what I want," he said smugly.

"Do you always get what you want?" I questioned with annoyance.

"Usually," he said, flashing a grin. We were interrupted in our stare down when Joel called the four of them over for press photos with the winners.

"Tomorrow at ten a.m. in the lodge," he said before he turned and walked away. The ride home was nothing but a thousand questions from Hayden Grace. How did you meet them? What kind of riders are they? What is PW like?

"His name is Paul," I corrected, uncomfortable with calling him by his rock star name. How did Trip hurt himself? Did you really save him? Where did you find them today? When are you going to take me to the backcountry? She continued the entire drive home without pausing for a breath.

"I can't believe my mom skied with PW," she finally exclaimed, flopping herself down on my bed. By this time we were home, and Molly and my parents were watching us like a tennis match continually moving their heads back and forth from Hayden Grace to me and back. I sighed in exasperation.

"Hayden Grace, it's not a big deal. They are just normal people," I finally said.

"Normal people? They have collectively changed the world of snowboarding! They have tricks named after them..." she rambled on as I brushed my teeth and changed in the bathroom.

"Aren't they retired?" I commented at one point.

"Kind of... they still ride at the big competitions like X Games—well sometimes...I think. Mostly they judge and coach riders on the Olympic and National teams," she said with a touch of jealously.

"Are you going to be alright home tonight with Grams and Grandpa?" I asked, coming out of the bathroom. I had changed into a pair of dark jeans and a purple silk shirt. I had put a little volume in my pin straight hair but otherwise left it down.

"Yes," they all said collectively, causing me to put my hands up in defeat. I got a movie started for my parents as Hayden Grace lay on the floor watching

YouTube videos of the snowboarding legends of Paul, Scott, Davie and Trip on her laptop; I couldn't help but roll my eyes.

"Normal people," I whispered to Hayden Grace as I leaned down and kissed the top of her head.

"Not in this world," she commented back.

"Goodnight Hayden Grace…I'm proud of you."

"Love you Mom. You're so cool…you skied with Paul Westcott," she exclaimed in a fit of giggles. I stuck my tongue out at her and waved goodnight to my parents.

Chapter 8

The Lucky Penny was fine dining and social debauchery at its finest. On one side it was a great restaurant that served creative and date friendly dishes. On the other side the bar area was often packed tight with lots of energetic, fun but sometimes desperately single people. Marla once told me it was like extreme dating trying to get from the bar side to the restaurant side with a person you just met.

On this particular night it, it felt more crowded than usual. I wormed my way through the masses of people until I saw Marla. I was not surprised that she was already talking up some tattooed, muscle bound gentleman dressed in all black. I thought I would give her a chance to get his number and tried to make my way little further down on the bar until they were done talking, but she saw me right away.

"Andy, over here," she called, waving her purse in the air.

"I'm here, I'm here," I said changing my direction, trying to find a small space to stand.

"Andy, this is Jett. Jett, this is Andy," she said as a way of introductions. Jett leaned over and mumbled something to Marla and then got up and left.

"Is he coming back?" I asked. She shook her head no, and I instantly grabbed his seat at the bar.

"Jett is an old friend. We are just two ships passing in the night," she said somewhat cryptically. "How are you?" she asked, giving me the once over.

"I've been better," I said, giving my trademark sigh.

"You need a drink," she stated. I groaned internally, thinking back to this morning. It was rare for me to be in a social setting with the ability to drink; it was even rarer for it happen twice in the same weekend. 'Was that only this morning?' I thought to myself in alarm as my stomach turned a little; it seemed like ages ago. Marla leaned over to the bartender and ordered two shots of Patrón tequila.

"I'm gonna' die," I thought to myself when the bartender returned with the two amber filled glasses, salt and limes.

"What is all that?" I asked, pointing to the accessories that had accompanied our shots.

"Haven't you ever done shots before?" she asked in alarm.

"Not really," I admitted. In high school I was so focused on skiing that I never had any interest in drinking. I mean, don't get me wrong, I would sneak out of the house, and I got in my fair share of trouble, but alcohol was never an interest. Then, while my peers were going off to college and partying, I was married at nineteen and was pregnant with Hayden Grace at twenty. I had different priorities in my life.

"Lick it, drink it, suck it," she said, demonstrating the proper tequila drinking technique.

"Is this really necessary?" I asked, eyeing the lime and salt skeptically.

"It is tonight," she said, pushing the shot towards me. Sighing, I followed her direction.

"So who were these guys?" Marla asked again after I finished telling her my backcountry adventures.

"Possibly retired professional snowboarders," I said, placing extra emphasis on the word retired.

"And you, Andrea Parker, were doing flips in the woods with them?" she questioned.

"It's the backcountry and just some basic tricks," I said, suddenly feeling defensive.

"Andy, this Paul guy is totally hitting on you," she said after several moments.

"That's not possible," I said, groaning as the second round of shots arrived.

"It is possible. Look at you! You're still young, in your mid-thirties, you've got gorgeous, long blonde hair, that I'm slightly jealous of by the way, those crazy hazel eyes, you're a terrific skier, an awesome mom and a kickass senior marketing executive," she exclaimed, raising her shot.

"That is *not* my world," I said after the burn of the tequila subsided.

"What's not your world? Handsome men?" she said, eyeing the bartender again and gesturing for another round.

"No. Jet setting across the country, having no cares in the world, skiing all day…" I exclaimed.

"Now you just sound jealous," she commented. I hesitated for a moment, mulling over her comment.

"Maybe I am a little jealous. Who wouldn't want that life? But it's not my life. I live in Newbury, New Hampshire, I have a fifteen-year-old daughter and I work two jobs – I pay bills. That is my life," I said, slamming the shot back, thinking the burn wasn't too bad anymore. "Anyway, you forgot I'm seeing

71

someone, and it's going pretty well," I added for extra measure.

"Oh yes, Gregg," Marla said, leaning closer to me. "Tell me about this guy."

"What do you want to know?"

"Well, besides everything? Let's start with where you met him. You only go to work, the mountain and possibly the grocery store so it has to be one of those," she mocked.

"Hey!" I pretended to be offended before I mumbled, "the grocery store."

"I knew it! Andy Parker, you need some spice in your life," she said with a sad smile.

"Gregg is great. He works as an insurance salesman. He makes me laugh, he's a good kisser and he's a normal guy," I said, shrugging my shoulders.

"Andy, do you hear yourself? He's a normal guy—you're shrugging your shoulders. No! You want passion, fire, someone oozing sex appeal. You want someone who actually makes you feel something, and you can't settle for anything less. You want this Paul guy," she said, getting all fired up and waving to the bartender again.

"I don't want Paul, and the person you are describing isn't real. That's not a real relationship—it's a fantasy. Plus, I have to think of Hayden Grace. She needs a stable figure in her life, not a rock star or someone she thinks is *cool*," I said, making air quotes. I knew I had to slow down on the shots, or I was going to be face down on the bar soon. Marla shook her head to disagree with me and was about to say something when I interrupted her.

"Want to get some air?" I asked, thinking that moving around was going to help. I could feel my head starting to get fuzzy, and everyone started to appear more interesting around me. She pouted slightly, but agreed. Marla paid the tab after refusing my money, and we moved our way from the bar towards the dining area as we headed for the door.

"Fine, you like boring. What does this Gregg look like?" she asked, sliding a glance at me.

"He's handsome," I said enthusiastically, ignoring the sarcasm in her voice. "He has these wonderful deep chocolate eyes, he wears black rimmed glasses and his hair is slightly peppered with gray," I said, distracted by a couple sitting by the front window.

"Is that all?" she said, clearly unimpressed.

"He's average build," I mumbled, staring harder at the couple by the front window until I bumped into a waiter, causing dishes and food to crash all around us. The restaurant and bar suddenly went silent; everyone was staring in our direction. Thinking quickly, I ducked down, trying to hide until the noise in the restaurant picked up again.

"What are you doing?" Marla asked, kneeling down next to me.

"He's wearing a green sweater and black slacks," I whispered.

"Who?"

"Gregg."

"Wait, he's here? Where?" she asked, standing up and looking around.

"He's sitting by the window, with… his WIFE," I hissed, pulling her back down.

"How do you know that's his wife? Maybe it's his sister," she asked, peeking back up.

"Because her name is Lisa and she has a daughter named Madison who is Hayden Grace's best friend," I whispered as panic and dread spread in the pit of my stomach, causing my pulse to race. I had originally thought Gregg looked vaguely familiar, but when I couldn't place him I shrugged it off. Thinking about it now as we were crouching down on the floor behind a table in the restaurant, looking absolutely ridiculous, I realized that the last and only time I saw him he was at least seventy-five pounds heavier. I think at the time he was also sporting a full beard and mustache that were jet black. There is no way the man sitting by the window would have reminded me of the Gregg I knew to be married to Lisa, I justified to myself.

"What are you going to do?" Marla asked with a surprised but very amused expression.

"I don't know, but we are leaving," I said, still crawling on the ground towards the door.

"For goodness sake, get up," Marla said, dragging me to my feet as I bolted to the door.

***

Marla convinced me it was a bad idea to go home, and instead we ended up walking two blocks to a smaller, more local bar called the Tap Room.

"Not so normal now, is he?" Marla teased as we sat down at the bar. I rolled my eyes at her and ordered two beers.

"Too soon?" she asked with an innocent expression.

"Too soon," I said, putting my head down on the bar.

"Andy, you really had no idea?" Marla asked after several silent minutes.

"No," I wailed. "I had no idea. We met at the grocery store; he wasn't wearing a ring. I've never really been formally introduced to the man before, and he looked so different... I mean, I think we were once introduced when they first moved to town, but we didn't say more than two words to each other and since then I only ever see Lisa. OMG, I'm a home wrecker," I said, flopping down on the bar again.

"Andy, you're not a home wrecker. He is a lot of things, but this is not on you," she paused. "Are you going to see him again?"

"NO."

"Then this is totally not on you," she said, taking a sip of her beer and making a face. "As a general rule, shots are better in these kinds of situations."

"Probably, but I still have to get home and face my parents and daughter," I said with a horrible sinking feeling my stomach. "I have to tell Lisa," I practically whispered, thinking how awkward that conversation was going to be.

"No... No, No, No, No. Andy, you do not say anything. This will come back and hurt you more than them. They might even turn this into you trying to get Hayden Grace some competitive edge by messing with Madison's mental state," she said with a serious expression.

"You're insane—no one will think that," but as I said the words, I knew her statement was preposterous enough to be true. Marla sat with me at the bar for another hour or so before the mysterious Jett from the Lucky Penny wandered into the Tap Room and gave Marla a look.

"Are you going to be okay?

"Yes, I'm going home and going to bed and hoping to wake up from this nightmare," I mumbled. She gave me a smile and a quick hug as she made her way over to Jett. He leaned over and whispered something in her ear, and then they slipped out the front door.

***

I pulled into the driveway around one in the morning. The small front porch light shone bright as the house was dark. I was re-playing the last twenty-four hours in my head and thinking just how improbable it was. Just as I reached the front door, the phone in my pocket buzzed. I sighed loudly to myself, thinking that Marla needed something. I was shocked to see Hayden Grace's picture light up my screen.

"Hayden Grace?" I asked in confusion.

"Mom," she cried into the other end.

"Are you okay? Where are you?" I asked in a panic, guessing that she was not asleep in her room.

"Mom, I need your help."

Chapter 9

Hayden Grace had texted me the address of the party giving me vague details. Something about everyone from the snowboarding club going and that Madison had driven them. I could only assume that 'them' meant Lucie and herself. Panic and anger washed through me as I raced down the dark winding roads, thankful it was so late that not many people were in the way as I ignored many rules of the road. 'I was wrong,' I thought to myself—this night was so much worse than I ever thought possible.

As I pulled onto Jackson Street, I looked for the house number that Hayden Grace had given me but soon realized that was not necessary. Four houses down on the left was a large white colonial house with at least thirty cars parked in the driveway, on the front lawn and in the road. I had to drive past the house and turn around to find a spot to park my car. As I approached the house I could see that every room in the house had lights shining brightly; the music only got progressively louder as I got closer. Reaching the front door, I was unsure about whether or not I should knock. However, when I got to the stairs the door flung open and several kids ran out laughing and giggling. A girl in pigtails stood at the door and looked at me.

"Are you friends with Abbie? Come on in...the beer is in the fridge, and I think there might still be pot floating around here somewhere," she said, giggling and disappearing down the hallway. My stomach felt sick, but it wasn't from the alcohol. I cautiously stepped into the house, and what I saw caused my hand to quickly rise to my mouth in surprise. The house was packed with people in every room; it was like a pre-pubescent version of the movie *Animal House*. The music was so loud I could barely hear myself think as I carefully stepped through the house, looking for Hayden Grace. The call with Hayden Grace had been disconnected before I could find out exactly where she was. When I called back it kept going to voice-mail only increasing my anxiety level.

When I exited the kitchen I ran across a couple in the hallway that was making out for everyone to see. At one point I thought the guy was going to swallow the girl in one piece, and they sure didn't care about who was or was not watching. Shaking my head and trying to focus on finding my daughter first, I stopped a guy who was coming out of the bathroom.

"Excuse me...have you seen my daugh...Hayden Grace?" I corrected myself, trying not to identify myself as a parent and cause an immediate mass exodus.

"Who?" he said, slurring the word. It appeared that he was highly intoxicated as he could barely walk straight, that or the floor was crooked, and seeing as though I was having no problem with the floor, I knew it must be him.

"Long blonde hair, hazel eyes, snowboards..."

"Cute ass?"

"Sure," I said, seething inside.

"Last I saw her she was upstairs," he slurred and staggered off down the hallway. He needed help, and I vowed to myself that after I found Hayden Grace I would come back and check on him. Making my way upstairs, I came across another couple that was in the throes of a passionate kiss. Interrupting this couple, I tapped the girl on her shoulder.

"Mrs. Parker?" Madison said, looking up at me, her eyes getting really big in what I hope was fear, but knew was probably shock.

"I think you need to go home now, Madison," I said quietly. I could see a hickey already forming on her neck.

"Yes, Mrs. Parker."

"Preston, I presume?" I asked, looking at the boy, and he just nodded. "I think it's time for you to go home as well." Both continued to stare at me in horror.

"Where is Hayden Grace?" I asked, slightly shouting over the music. Madison pointed to the door in the hallway. I took several steps toward the bathroom, and when I turned around to say something to them, they had both already disappeared. Sighing to myself, I turned back to the door and tried the door handle only to find it was locked.

"Hayden Grace?" I called through the door.

"Andy?" I heard her call back.

"Yes," I acquiesced to her request only to hear the door unlock. Hayden Grace pulled the door open and grabbed my arm, pulling me into the bathroom.

"What the hell is going on Hayden Grace?" I erupted when we were both in the bathroom.

"Andy…I mean, Mom. I will tell you everything, and you can ground me forever, although I think that would be a little extreme…" she paused when she noticed the look I was giving her. "Abbie is really sick, and I didn't know what to do," she said, pointing to the corner of the bathroom. I hadn't noticed in my anger, but Abbie was slumped against the toilet, and she looked unresponsive. From there my anger subsided as I focused on the situation.

"Has she thrown up?" I asked Hayden Grace as I crouched down next to Abby to check her vitals. She was still breathing, but it was really labored and weak.

"Yes, she has thrown up three or four times," Hayden Grace recounted.

"Do you know what and how much she drank tonight?"

"No, she was already pretty drunk when we got here. Before I knew it she was getting sick in the kitchen so I brought her up to the bathroom, and she seemed fine. We were talking and joking, and then she stopped talking and her eyes rolled back," Hayden Grace said as she twisted her fingers in her hands.

"Did she do any drugs tonight?" I asked.

"I'm not sure."

"Did you?"

"Mom, don't be ridiculous," she responded quickly, and I raised my eyebrows. "No, I did not. That would jeopardize everything," she stated simply. I nodded and motioned for her to help me pick up Abbie.

"She needs to go to the hospital. Let's get her downstairs, and we can either call for help or take her to Newbury Hospital," I said as we got on each side of her, hoisting her up.

"Mom, we can't call the cops. I can't be that girl. That's why I called you" she exclaimed in exasperation. I could see her logic, no matter how flawed I thought it was. I figured we could get Abbie downstairs first, and then I would go ahead and make the call whether or not Hayden Grace approved. We were able to pull the door open only to find two policemen coming down the hall with flashlights. Quickly seeing we were in distress they rushed over to help us bring Abbie downstairs while we waited for an ambulance to arrive.

The ambulance arrived about fifteen minutes later and by then most of the kids at the party had scattered. I looked for Madison, Lucie or Preston in the crowd of people that were running in every direction, but never saw them. I did tell the officer about the young man from earlier. He said they had found him asleep on the front lawn and that his parents were on their way. There was a humorous moment that gave me a good laugh when the young couple I had observed earlier outside the kitchen continued to be oblivious to everything until a policewomen tapped them on the shoulder. Their shocked expressions were priceless.

When the ambulance arrived, they strapped Abbie to the gurney and immediately started fluids before they closed the doors. Abbie was then taken to the hospital with suspected alcohol poisoning; her mom had been contacted and would meet the ambulance at the hospital. After the ambulance left I turned to leave when an officer stopped me.

"Ma'am, we are going to have to ask you some questions down at the station," he said as he approached me.

"Wait, what are you doing?" I asked, taking a step back. He started talking about endangering minors, underage drinking and felony charges.

"I don't live here," I said, raising my voice, causing another officer to come over.

"Mom, what's going on?" Hayden Grace said with a look of confusion on her face.

"Miss, we are just going to have to take your mom with us," the same officer said, coming toward me again. Panic flashed across Hayden Grace this time as she jumped in between me and the officer.

"She didn't do anything wrong. I called her for help when Abbie started getting sick," she paused, taking a deep breath. "I'm the one who snuck out of the house; if you have to arrest anyone, arrest me," she said holding out both her hands to the officer. I placed my hands on her arms, lowering them down.

"No one is getting arrested," I said to Hayden Grace, touched by her act of selflessness.

"They're not?" she said, turning to face me.

"No. This isn't our house, and we did nothing wrong," I said firmly, looking at the police officers. The officer who had walked over finally nodded in agreement. He did ask us both some follow up questions; through this line of questioning I learned that the house belonged to Abbie's dad, who was in Paris with his new girlfriend.

"Abbie said her dad wouldn't mind if she had a couple people over while he was gone," Hayden Grace had told the police officer, causing me to roll my eyes.

'I bet he minds now,' I thought to myself. I also learned that Hayden Grace had snuck out of the house after Grams and Grandpa had gone to bed around eleven. She even bribed Molly with a treat not to bark when Madison, who had just turned sixteen before Christmas, came to get her. Thinking it was just going to be a handful of people, Madison, Lucie and Hayden Grace were all surprised to see more and more people arriving. Apparently, Lucie got scared and asked to leave, and Madison didn't want to leave because she was waiting on Preston to arrive, so they had a big fight. Hayden Grace was going to leave with Lucie, who had found someone to drive them home, when she noticed Abbie. Making a quick decision, she told Lucie to go, and she would stay with Abbie. From there I could fill in most of the blanks with what Hayden Grace had already told me.

When we were finally allowed to leave the house, I took in the scene one last time. I could feel my shoes sticking to the floors, and a dark film covered most surfaces. Every table, counter or piece of furniture had empty cups, beer cans and trash scattered on them. I observed a broken lamp on the floor in the living room and expensive looking vases being used as trash cans. I felt pity for the person who would have to clean this all up and suspected it was going to be Abbie.

As we drove home in silence my emotions floated between anger and pride. I was so angry with Hayden Grace for sneaking out of the house, being at a crazy, out-of-control party with alcohol and drugs and for almost getting both of us arrested. But I was proud that she was looking out for her friend and knew enough to try and take care of her instead of leaving her alone. I was also proud that she called for help when no one else did. I was even a little proud over her theatrical stunt with the officer where she was taking responsibility for her actions. By the time I pulled into the drive it was after three in the morning. The house was still dark, and the porch light still shone brightly. As I opened the door Molly came down the stairs and let out a little bark.

"Now you bark? … You are fired," I said to the dog as we climbed up the stairs. Hayden Grace stopped in the hallway and looked at me.

"How much trouble am I in?" she asked quietly.

"I haven't decided yet. It's been a very long night—go to bed, and we'll talk about it in the morning," I said rubbing my temples. She nodded and headed to bed.

Unable to sleep as my mind raced with thoughts of Gregg, Madison, Lucie, Preston, Abbie, Abbie's poor mom and dad, and Hayden Grace. I finally gave up and crawled out of bed and padded to the kitchen. Rummaging through the freezer, I found the chocolate ice cream I had been eating earlier in the week. Taking the ice cream to the living room, I grabbed a blanket and curled up on the sofa. After a couple of minutes I heard the soft pitter patter of Molly coming down the hallway as she curled up on the floor by the sofa. I sighed and turned on the TV and flipped through the channels until I found some sitcom that would take my mind off of the crazy events that had just transpired. First Gregg and then Hayden Grace – I wasn't able to process everything.

"Mom?" I heard Hayden Grace whisper. I turned to see her standing there in her pajamas, holding her pillow to her chest.

"Timeout?" she asked sheepishly. When she was little we used to put her in timeout whenever she was acting out. As she grew older it became our thing; if we were fighting or bickering and she needed a hug or needed us for something, she could say 'timeout' and we would put our differences aside to offer our support. But we would always go back and deal with whatever was going on before the 'timeout'. I studied her carefully as she stood in the doorway; I could tell she was unsure of what my reaction was going to be.

"Timeout," I finally said, lifting the blanket up. She smiled and ran over, climbing in, snuggling up next to me. I continued to eat the chocolate ice cream as she lay in my lap.

"I was so scared," she said after several minutes.

"You did the right thing," I said softly. "Sweetie, why did you call me?" I asked the question that had been on the tip of my tongue all night.

"Who else would I call? I knew you would know what to do. Should I not have called?"

"What you did showed a lot of maturity tonight, minus the whole sneaking out thing," I said, looking down at her, and she crinkled her forehead in worry. "But in all seriousness, Hayden Grace, you probably saved Abbie's life," I said, and she smiled broadly, causing me to give her an odd look.

"We both saved lives this weekend," she mumbled as she drifted off to sleep.

"Yes, we did," I mumbled to myself after several minutes.

Chapter 10

I could hear whispering as I stirred. Trying to stretch, I realized I was unable to move. My eyes popped open as I tried to orient myself. The room was much brighter than I expected, causing me to squint. I could feel someone moving next to me. Looking over, I saw Hayden Grace still curled on my lap. Realization washed over me of what had happened last night, causing me to groan.

"Andy, are you okay?" I heard my mom ask me from somewhere behind me.

"I've been better," I commented again, trying to stretch my limbs which felt numb and heavy.

"What time did you get in?" my dad asked.

"What time is it now?"

"A little after eight," he said after a moment.

"I've been asleep for about three hours," I clarified. Twisting to watch my parents' faces, I could see concern etched in their expressions.

"Don't you think that's a bit late?" my mom asked, clearly disapproving. I slowly eased myself off of the couch, moving Hayden Grace slightly until she was curled up, still hugging her pillow.

"Oh, you must mean what time did I get in from my girls' night out. Well that was around one, but here's the funny thing mom: when I got home, my daughter wasn't home," I paused to let this information sink in as I made a beeline for the coffee and continued. "So, after going back out to get my daughter, putting one of her friends in an ambulance, then almost getting arrested, we returned home at three in the morning. Then I felt the need to finish the last of the chocolate ice cream and watch bad late night TV," I said, my voice oozing with sarcasm as I leaned across the kitchen counter on my elbows, coffee in hand.

"What are you talking about?" my mom said, clearly in denial.

"It's all true…" Hayden Grace said, suddenly kneeling on the sofa looking at us. "I snuck out with my friends, went to a party and things went bad. I'm a terrible person," she lamented, flopping down.

"Stop it. You're not horrible, terribly grounded perhaps, but not horrible," I said as my parents looked stunned from where they sat at the counter. I could tell my mom was still unsure if we were trying to pull a prank on her or if it really happened.

"Mom, it all really happened, but everyone is okay," I said, reaching a little further and grabbing her hand. "It just turns out Hayden Grace took only fifteen years to learn what took me sixteen," I smiled wickedly at her.

"What does that mean, Andrea?" my mom said in frustration.

"I used to sneak out all the time," I said, letting out a sigh, confessing to an almost twenty-year-old secret. I slid a sideways glance at Hayden Grace, who had by now gotten up, also fixed herself a cup of coffee, and was leaning on the counter next to me. I watched slowly as my mother's cheeks turned red, and she got flustered.

"Hayden Grace, why would you sneak out on your Grams and myself?" my dad asked as my mom digested all the information I had just sprung on her.

He was always one to ask a direct question and expected direct answers.

"I just wanted to be with my friends...I didn't know it was going to be as bad as it was," she said, shrugging. Her action caused my mother to sigh and look at both of us with her head tilted slightly to the side.

"Hayden Grace, you are just a younger version of your mother. Look at the two of you now," she said, crossing her arms and leaning back in her chair as if she had proved a point. I again glanced over at Hayden Grace and could see that we currently mirrored each other's stance. If my mother was trying to prove a point, I had missed it. My daughter was a product of me regardless of my flaws, just as I was a product of my mother, and she of hers. There was no greater compliment, I thought to myself.

We eventually moved into a healthy discussion about the previous evening's event. I talked some about my time with Marla, leaving out the part about Gregg, as we mostly focused on Hayden Grace and her misadventure. Hayden Grace recounted the entire story again for her grandparents and patiently answered questions as they thoroughly dissected every action and reaction.

"Mom, are you going to tell Madison and Lucie's parents?" she asked, looking at me. I took a moment to think it over.

"Well, I never saw Lucie, so I don't have anything to tell them." Madison's family on the other hand, I could fill Lisa in on some serious issues going on with her family. 'For starters, a cheating and deceiving husband and then a daughter who sneaks out at night to make out with her boyfriend,' I thought to myself.

"What about Madison's parents?" she asked, almost reading my thoughts when I didn't fully answer her question.

"I honestly don't know what I'm going to tell them, if I tell them anything." It was more truthful than Hayden Grace could ever understand.

"Mom?"

"Yes?"

"I know I am in a lot of trouble but can we PLEASE still go to breakfast with Paul, Trip, Davie and Scott?" she asked, now facing me with both her hands clasped together. Looking at her, I groaned, then turned to get another cup of coffee.

"Is that really this morning?" *Would this weekend never end*, I thought to myself.

"Please Mom? I'll do anything," she again pleaded as she followed me around the kitchen. I sighed and looked over at my parents.

"Don't look at us. You did this to us all the time. It's satisfying to watch you get some of your own medicine," my mom smirked, and I stuck my tongue out.

"Mature," my mom added. I took a moment to think about the pros and cons of taking Hayden Grace to breakfast with the snowboarders. On the one hand, she showed great maturity by calling for help and staying with her friend, but she would never have been in the position if she'd stayed home. I thought about my own youth and if I would have made those decisions at that age. I surely would have snuck out of the house, but I was also sure I would not have called for help like Hayden Grace did. This realization led me easily to my decision.

"Yes to breakfast," I barely had the words out of my mouth when she started loudly shrieking and shouting with joy. "Hayden Grace, look at me," I said, waiting for her to finish her ridiculous dancing. "We are going to breakfast, but when we get back we will discuss the proper punishment for your behavior," she nodded in understanding and sprinted off toward her bedroom, mumbling something about calling Madison and Lucie. My parents and I talked for a bit longer before they decided to pack up and head out as they had made plans to visit friends in Boston for the night before heading home on Monday.

It was almost time to leave when Hayden Grace raced into my room with two shirts in each hand.

"Mom, which one?" she asked in an almost panic.

"Hayden Grace, it's not like you to get this way—remember, they are normal people," I commented.

"Why do you keep saying that?" she asked, frustrated.

"Normal people can't disappoint in the way that people we look up to can. Normal people all have flaws that we can accept. Idols, celebrities, athletes—we take away their ability to have flaws and then they inevitably disappoint us—it's unrealistic. All people have flaws; if you accept that, it makes your expectations more realistic." She looked at me, tilting her head to the side as my mom did earlier, mulling over my statement.

"Perhaps," she said not entirely agreeing. She held up both tops for me again, and I shrugged. I knew no matter what top I picked, she would pick the opposite one.

"I like the green one," she said, making her own decision on what to wear. "Is that what you are wearing?" she asked before leaving the room.

"Yes. Why?" I asked, glancing in the mirror at my jeans and my oversized pinkish cream sweater, which I had layered over a white v-neck, long sleeve shirt and my hair in a casual braid down my back.

"You look nice. I'll be ready in ten," she said, dashing out of the room and back down to her room. Molly whined from the bed where she had been laying.

"I know…teenagers," I mumbled.

***

We arrived at Lucie's house, and she was ready without incident. She bounded into the backseat of the car with Hayden Grace, and her mom waved from the door. Madison's house was an entirely different story. When we pulled in the driveway, I honked and we waited. After five minutes Hayden Grace said she was going in to see what was going on. I knew I wasn't about to go inside, knowing Gregg was home after I spotted the Nissan Altima in the driveway. Seriously, how had I missed that the Gregg I was seeing was the same Gregg as Madison's father; I just shook my head as I continued to stare at the front door, waiting for Hayden Grace and Madison to emerge. Lucie had opted to stay in the car because, apparently, she was still mad at Madison. After about another five minutes, Hayden Grace and Madison emerged; Madison was flush in the face, and you could tell she had been crying. I gave Hayden Grace a curious look, and she shook her head at me as they got into the car. Just as I was about to back out of the driveway, Lisa came flying out the front door and ran down the front walk.

"Andy!" she called, and I rolled down my window. "Why didn't you tell me," she said with accusation. Not sure how to answer or what she was referring to, I kept quiet.

"My husband…" she started, and my pulse quickened, and I could feel my palms go sweaty.

"…caught Madison trying to sneak back in the house last night. She spilled the details about the party and how she had driven Hayden Grace there. She also said that you were there." She raised her eyebrows at me, as if she were my mother. I looked in the review mirror and saw Madison sink down further in her seat; the hickey from last night was now very prominent on her neck as she tugged on her sweater trying to cover it up. Unsure of how to answer in a manner that would appease her but not completely 'out' Hayden Grace in front of her friends, I improvised.

"Hayden Grace told me about some friends hanging out, but when she wasn't home by one I went out looking for her," I said, looking in the rearview mirror again, this time at Hayden Grace who was silently exhaling with relief. "I'm sorry I didn't call, I thought you knew. Of course, I didn't know it was meant to be a rager—I just thought it was a small group of friends hanging out," I followed up, using Hayden Grace's words. My excuse seemed to mollify Lisa who eventually stepped back and waved us on our way.

***

We arrived at the lodge about fifteen minutes later than planned. All three girls sat in the backseat of the car huddled together in conversation during the ride while I shamelessly eavesdropped. The topic of conversation was the party last night and what had gone on as would be expected. This was probably the most exciting thing that the three of them had been involved in outside of the mountain. No one had mentioned Abbie, so I guessed that information about her trip to the hospital had not yet become common knowledge. Lucie had forgiven Madison in the process of the discussion soon after she realized Madison hadn't told anyone that she was at the party. Hayden Grace had told me that Lucie was there, but I wasn't going to tell anyone. The fine web of secrets and gossip of teenage girls had me exhausted by the time we finally reached the lodge.

The parking lot at the mountain was filled with patrons, but the media circus of trucks and vans had already left. I had barely parked the car when the three girls jumped out of the backseat and raced ahead to the lodge. I took my time getting out of the car and slowly made my way up behind them. The weekend had taken its toll on me, and I could feel the fatigue in my body as I finally entered the lodge. I scanned the crowded area looking for Hayden Grace, Madison and

Lucie, thinking they weren't that far ahead of me, but I didn't see anything. I looked for Paul, Trip, Davie or Scott in the crowd and again came up with nothing.

"Looking for someone?" I heard behind me, causing me to immediately spin around. I came face to face with Paul. He was wearing jeans and a plaid button up shirt with his characteristic smirk, and I couldn't help but smile. My smile caused him to pause, and an unnamed emotion flickered across his face before he regained his composure.

"You need to stop sneaking up behind people," I commented in slight annoyance. "Have the girls already found you?" I asked after my annoyance passed.

"Yes, can't you hear the shrieks?" he replied in jest, pointing to the upper balcony of the lodge. I could make out the three girls as they stood together engaged in a lively conversation of some sort with Scott and Davie.

"That must get tiring," I said, referring to the yelling and screaming.

"You have no idea," he replied back in a lower tone as he led the way up to the balcony. By the time I had joined the group, everyone had already filled their plates and now sat in different areas of the balcony. Hayden Grace sat with Scott, and I could hear them discussing something about the mechanics of specific spins and tricks. Madison and Lucie sat next to Davie as he fiddled with the guitar, swooning. Trip was not at breakfast, I was informed, as he had gone to get x-rays of his leg before the trip home. Apparently the swelling had not subsided in the manner that the doctors had hoped. Not hungry, I sat down on the loveseat with my third cup of coffee for the morning and took the scene in. Minutes later Paul came over and sat down beside me.

"I didn't think you were coming," he teased, referring to our very tardy arrival.

"Sorry about that…we almost didn't come," I added after a moment.

"Oh really?" he asked.

"Let's just say it was a very long night, and some rules were broken."

"Rules were meant to be broken."

"That's a matter of opinion if you're the one setting the rules," I quipped back.

"Andy, how's it going?" Davie said, wandering over to join Paul and me.

"Where are your groupies?" I asked, looking for Madison and Lucie.

"They took your daughter and went downstairs for something, I didn't ask," he said looking relieved, and I nodded in understanding.

"How do you handle teenagers all the time?" Scott asked with a perplexed look, also joining the conversation.

"You get used to it," I commented back, and he gave me a rather skeptical expression.

"Did you ever ski professionally?" Paul asked after a couple silent moments, changing the subject. I gave him a questionable look at the lack of transition and the directness of his question.

"If you answer the question, I will explain myself," he said, replying to my look.

"I started skiing at a young age. I told you that the other day," I said a bit defensively. When no one made any attempt to add anything further to the conversation, I continued hesitantly.

"My dad would take us to the mountain on the weekends to give my mom some alone time," I chuckled to myself; to this day my mom has only been on skis once or twice in her life. She was much happier with her feet firmly planted on the ground. "When I was fourteen I got on the junior national team and then won the junior world championships, but to ski professionally it would have made more sense to move out West and my family didn't want to make that move," I said with a shrug.

"I knew it!" Paul exclaimed, looking at Scott who shook his head.

"Knew what?" I asked with suspicion.

"I recognized you from somewhere but couldn't place it. It was at the '94 junior championships." he confidentially stated.

"Are you sure? I can't even remember what Friday was like, let alone who I competed against twenty years ago."

"I'm sure. Plus your friend Ron kind of filled me in on your skiing career yesterday," he admitted sheepishly.

"And from all that you remember me?" I asked again, suspicious.

"It's not so much you, but your riding style. It's so laid back and graceful that it's hard to forget, and it hasn't changed one bit," he added as Scott and Davie exchanged a look.

"I doubt it," was all I could say. In fact, I felt a little breathless thinking that Paul would remember my performance. It made sense he would have probably been on that national team as we were about the same age. At that age I was singularly focused on skiing and competing. I never knew who was on the team with me, and at the time I didn't have room for friends in my life.

"Mom!" Hayden Grace yelled as she raced up the stairs looking for me, and I waved from my spot on the sofa, grateful for the interruption. Paul, Davie and Scott looked around in alarm, but the theatrics didn't faze me at this point.

"I haven't moved since you left," I quipped as she raced over, dressed in her snowboarding gear. She leaned over and started whispering rapidly in my ear.

"Slow down…I can't understand you," I said, and she repeated herself.

"I don't know. Why don't you ask them?" I asked, looking around the room. She paused, suddenly looking very shy, but finally asked her audience if they were up for a little competition to which they all but too quickly agreed.

Chapter 11

While everyone went to gather their gear, I went to find Joel. I knew he was on the property somewhere…he was always here. I found him in the ski patrol station speaking with the parents of a teenage boy who had just broken his arm when he lost control and swerved off the trail into a tree. I waited patiently while he finished up. I then asked him for two favors—he owed me. The first favor was easy. I needed him to find someone to cover my afternoon ski lessons; I knew I didn't have the energy for them today. He nodded and agreed that was an easy fix, then he eyed me carefully as I asked for my second favor. It wasn't really my favor, I explained, but one last favor for his favorite California snowboarders. Normally on the mountain the practice pipe was open for all patrons to use; the competition pipe stayed closed and was only used for competition or for the ski/snowboard club for practice. I asked him to make an exception, to which he very reluctantly agreed.

I found the group dressed and ready for competition at the bottom of the competition pipe. I walked over and let them know that Joel had agreed, and they all cheered in excitement.

"Okay Mom, we decided it will be boys versus girls, and you're going to be the judge," Hayden Grace said after everyone settled down.

"Alright, I'm up for the challenge," I said, trying not to chuckle. The girls quickly headed to the top to practice while I headed for the bleacher section at the bottom ready to 'judge' the competition.

"What are you doing?" I heard Paul call after me.

"Watching?" I said in confusion.

"From there?"

"Where else?"

"Come with me," he said, extending his hand. I hesitated for a moment and then grabbed his hand. He walked me up to the deck of the pipe towards the bottom and instructed me to sit about four feet from the edge, or coping, as it is more commonly referred to by snowboarders. Complying, I made myself comfortable as they finished warming up. Finally, I saw them huddle together at the top for a little talk before lining up in order. First up was Davie; watching him board over the last several days I noticed he had a more relaxed approach to the way he rode. He entered the pipe and flipped and twisted. In his final trick he set himself up several feet away from where I sat. It was amazing to watch from this perspective as he whipped by me. Next up was Madison—her tricks were not nearly the height of Davie which was expected, but there was a sluggish nature to her riding today. Given her lack of sleep and new found interest in Preston, it didn't surprise me. She made it cleanly to the bottom, and Scott was up next. He was definitely a more technical rider and landed each trick with precision. Lucie seemed nervous at the top, and she let the moment get away from her, washing out after her second trick. I thought Paul would go up next as that seemed the order, but instead Hayden Grace sat at the top waiting for Lucie to clear the pipe. I saw Paul lean over and whisper something to her, and she nodded seriously. She patted her jacket and started her run. It didn't matter that it wasn't a competition; I felt anxious as she entered the pipe. But there was something new to her riding— she hit the first trick and transitioned seamlessly to the next one. The jumps were cleaner and higher, and she rode with an excitement I hadn't seen in a while. When she got to the bottom she threw her arms up in excitement, and I clapped with excitement for her. Finally, Paul was up last, he entered the pipe, and his first trick soared higher than the rest of the group. 'It might have been higher than all three of the girls put together,' I thought to myself. Paul rode with a flare and a competitive edge—he had the best of Davie and Scott rolled into one run. As he set himself up for his final trick, he came up the wall directly in front of me, and it seemed as if he was suspended in slow motion for a moment.

"Wow," I whispered in wonder before he flipped and landed soundly on the inside wall. He glided over towards the girls and at the last minute turned, sending a wave of snow at them as they cheered and laughed. I slowly made my way down the pipe and joined them.

"Who won?" Hayden Grace asked excitedly as I approached.

"That was some really great riding. Guys you were awesome, but I have to give it to the girls—they were on fire," I finished to cheering from the girls.

"Tough competition," Davie said with a smirk, and I nodded

"Hayden Grace, that was awesome," I whispered, leaning down to hug her.

"Thanks, Mom. Paul gave me some last minute pointers. I think they really worked," she said into my shoulder. I nodded in agreement. We stood there in our odd little group for a while and chatted about the riding before Scott realized the time. The guys had a flight to catch and needed to get going. The girls pouted but managed to talk everyone into a group photo. They all grouped together as I snapped the photo on several different phones. There were hugs all around, and finally the girls glided off to the locker rooms to change.

"Andy, thank you for such a great weekend," Scott and Davie said before heading off to the private lodges where I assumed they were staying, leaving Paul and me standing at the bottom of the pipe.

"That was a pretty decent run you put together," I commented, and his eyes shone with excitement.

"I'm glad it meets your approval," he smirked.

"Thank you for whatever you said to Hayden Grace; it really seemed to make a difference." The words caught slightly in my throat.

"Andy, she's a great rider. She just needs a little confidence and minor pointers. But if she keeps it up, she will be on the circuit shortly," he commented, turning to look at me. "Thank you," he said simply and leaned down to kiss me on the cheek before riding off after Scott and Davie, which was probably a good thing so he didn't see how flushed my cheeks became or my goofy grin. It didn't feel like a good-bye, but what more could it be? When would I ever see them again? I wondered to myself as I headed to find the girls.

***

I dropped off Lucie and Madison successfully without any more drama. Hayden Grace talked non-stop about the riding and the pointers that Paul gave her. When we got home I could tell she was exhausted, and I suggested a nap for everyone. She scrunched up her nose and made a comment that she wasn't a little kid anymore. I changed my tactics and asked if she wanted to watch a movie. She agreed and went to change into something comfortable. We both settled in on the sofa as *Harry Potter*, her favorite movie, started to play. Within fifteen minutes she was sound asleep; I smiled as I closed my eyes and soon drifted off as well.

I awoke to the sound of pots and pans in the kitchen. I looked around and the TV screen was blue indicating the movie had ended. Stretching, I noticed I was now alone on the sofa. Turning around and looking into the kitchen, I saw Hayden Grace at the stove with Molly at her feet; I cleared my throat.

"Oh good, you're up. Dinner is almost ready; do you need to get cleaned up?" she asked, looking over her shoulder.

"What's for dinner?" I asked, trying to hide my surprise.

"Hot dogs and mac n' cheese," she said. I smiled at her response. It was probably the only meal she knew how to cook, but it was a classic in our household.

"Sounds wonderful... Let me go freshen up." When I returned she had a small picnic on the living room floor set up, and the movie had been reset back to the beginning.

"I thought we could start over," she said, motioning to the TV. Taking a seat on the floor, I nodded in agreement, thinking we could start over in more ways than one.

"This looks great," I said, looking at the spread and suddenly feeling very hungry. I hadn't taken two bites before Hayden Grace cleared her throat.

"Mom, I've been thinking," she said, looking at me. I slowly lowered my bowl to the floor and looked at her in anticipation. She then slid her phone over to me, "as my punishment you should take my phone away." I could tell it hurt her to part with her phone. I had already been thinking about this conversation since breakfast. It was hard to truly punish Hayden Grace. I couldn't really take away snowboarding. We had invested too much time and money; it was more like a budding career than a hobby that I could take away like a Playstation or Xbox. I couldn't really ban her from her friends; she didn't have much of a social life as it was between school and snowboarding. I thought about her phone, but it truly was the only way I had to reach her in case of an emergency. I thought about what my dad had done with me and figured it was worth a try with Hayden Grace.

"Sweetie, I'm not going to take your phone, but I appreciate the gesture. Instead, I am going to break one of the house rules and give you more responsibility. I'm going to let you stay home alone and not call for Casey anymore," she looked at me with big wide eyes as I continued. "You showed great maturity calling for help. I listened to you with Madison and Lucie, and you never once talked bad about Abbie or brought it up. You also did not pick sides between Madison and Lucie. You have great loyalty to them and I understand, but you have to be your own person and I believe you are trying. So you can keep your phone, and we will continue to operate as normal with the understanding that if something like this were to happen again, no matter what the reasoning, you will be banned from snowboarding for the remainder of that season regardless of what time of year it is. Do you understand?" I looked her straight in the eyes, and she nodded. "Also, you will be spending two weeks this summer with your grandparents in Long Island helping them around the house," I threw in for good measure as she groaned and nodded again.

"Okay then," I said, now that we were in agreement.

"Okay then," she repeated, and then flung herself at me. "Thank you, Mom."

"You're welcome." Eventually we settled in and started the movie again. Hayden Grace made it about half way into the movie this time before she fell back to sleep. I sat there for a long time after the movie ended thinking about the weekend and the week ahead of me. Sitting there with Hayden Grace wrapped up around me made everything worth it.

CHAPTER 12

The alarm clock sounded early, and I rolled over slowly to turn it off. Molly stirred next to me, causing Hayden Grace to shift. Last night when I woke her up to move her to bed, she grumbled something and headed down the hallway while I cleaned up. When I made it to her room to check on her she wasn't there; instead I found her curled up in my bed sound asleep. Crawling out of bed, I took a long hot shower. When I got out, I woke Hayden Grace so she could start getting ready for school. After getting dressed in my best navy blue suit, I went into the kitchen and made two cups of coffee, bagels with cream cheese and lunch for the both of us. Molly was still crunching on her food when Hayden Grace rounded the corner. She was dressed in a maroon dress and brown knee high boots with cream socks sticking out the top. Her long hair hung loosely down her back. I raised my eyebrow in a question mark.

"Picture day," she said simply sitting at the table, her coffee and bagel in hand.

"Today is gymnastics?" I asked to reaffirm the schedule I had in my head, and she nodded.

"Lucie's mom is bringing me home," she added.

"Okay…I'm in the city all week so I hope to be home by the time you get home but if not, go ahead and have her drop you off at home," I said, sliding a spare key across the table to her. In the past if I wasn't going to be home she would go next door to Casey's house or stay with her friends until I was able to pick her up.

"Really?" she said, taking the key from me, looking at it curiously.

"You'll be fine."

"So your presentation went well," she asked, thinking back to last week.

"Too well...I got the lead on the account, so it's going to be a lot of late nights this week working on it," I said, hoping she would understand the implication. She just nodded without asking any further questions. I was able to drop her off on time for school before heading to the city. I was not as lucky as I had been last week and got caught in traffic entering the city, causing me to be fifteen minutes late. I got several grumbles and waves as I walked into the office suite. I wasn't the only one who had a long weekend, it seemed. Being late, however, provided me no time to check my e-mails before Gary called me into his office.

"Have you read your e-mails?" he questioned.

"Good Morning, to you too," I mumbled but shook my head no, that I had not yet read them.

"Andrea, I need you on top of these things. Our clients are from out of town, and we have a limited amount of time with them. Today we have lunch with the marketing director, Alan, and then dinner tonight with the CEO, Malinda, of what used to be ValueTech Apparel and is now Guardian Angel Apparel. Dinner reservations have been made for seven, so dress appropriately," he said, and then dismissed me.

Seven. My head was spinning about Hayden Grace and getting her dinner and being home really late. I also had to deal with the fact that I didn't bring an additional outfit with me to work. My suit would work for lunch, but it would be frowned upon for dinner. I spent the rest of the morning cleaning up my presentation to give at lunch causing the time to pass quickly.

I had given presentations before, but for whatever reason, I felt additional pressure giving it this time. The hour went by slowly as the marketing director asked a lot questions, some of which I had the immediate answers for and some I did not. I did learn that the company, formerly known as ValueTech, was in the middle of splitting into two divisions: Guardian Apparel for the men's division and Angel Apparel for the women's division which would be collectively known as Guardian Angel Apparel. I would be exclusively in charge of the marketing for the women's division. They wanted to target younger females that were on the move—teenagers who were into being outdoors, sporty and athletic—'a precise description of my daughter,' I thought to myself. Alan seemed satisfied with my presentation and before he left, gave me a box of women's apparel to use and get better acquainted with as we worked on the campaign. Scanning through the box, I could see sweatpants, sweatshirts, yoga pants, long sleeved active shirts, sports bras, socks, knit hats, gloves, scarves and two winter jackets. It was a massive amount of apparel, I thought to myself as I lugged it back to my desk. After the meeting, I quickly texted Hayden Grace to let her know I would be much later than expected, and if she needed anything, Casey and her parents would be home. It was an awful week to leave her home alone for the first time, I realized.

As with most Mondays, the afternoon dragged on slowly; it was filled mostly with a long and boring strategy meeting. After the meeting Gary and I had another meeting to put together my marketing team for this project. I petitioned to pull Marla in from the Manchester office and he agreed—at least I would see a familiar face, I thought to myself. At five o'clock the office cleared out as I packed up my stuff. Gary walked by my desk on his way out to remind me about dinner and to congratulate me on my first day's work on the campaign. I smiled, trying to hide the panic, as I stuffed as many items as I could from the box Alan gave me into a bag and headed to my car. I unloaded my briefcase and the apparel, grabbing an extra pair of black pumps I had in the back seat. I changed my shoes, knowing I would need the pumps instead of the kitten heels I had on after I was done shopping.

I then set off for the closest T station and headed further into the heart of Boston. I knew there was a Nordstrom on Boylston Street where I could find something quickly to wear for dinner tonight. The sales lady looked at me in excitement when I described my dilemma and that I would be wearing a new outfit out of the store as she showed me to the dress department. I settled on a jersey off-the-shoulder dress in dark gray. The dress had a wrap-over front and a cowl back. While I changed, she ran off and got me a pair of nude tights. I looked at my hair in the mirror and sighed; having no resources, I pulled my hair back into a slight poof and then fished bobby pins out of my purse, pinning my hair into a twisted loose bun. I added some tinted lip balm that I had in my bag as well as mascara. By the time the sales associate returned with tights that she slipped under the dressing room stall, I thought I looked presentable.

"I found these as well, and you need them," she said, handing me a pair of gray drop earrings. I had to agree with her, as I pulled out my studs and replaced them. Stepping out of the stall, she stood back and looked at me.

"Exquisite," she said, clapping her hands together.

"I'll take it," I said, agreeing. I was able to cram the suit I had been wearing into my oversized bag as the sales associate rang me up. I gasped at the final price tag, but knew there was nothing I could do at the moment. Finishing up at Nordstrom, I grabbed a taxi and raced over to the restaurant. I arrived a couple minutes early, which allowed me to check my light gray knee length jacket with my very large bag. I headed to the bar and ordered a drink, hoping to settle my nerves before dinner.

"Andrea?" I heard behind me. As I turned I saw my boss, Alan and a woman who I presumed to be Malinda, standing in the doorway. Malinda was a slight woman—her hair was slicked back in a short, expensive-looking bob. She wore a little black dress with black tights and tall heels. She had on bright red lipstick and oversized eye glasses which, as she got closer, I saw had a tortoiseshell print on them. I must have had a slight look of confusion on my face as they approached, because Gary gave me a worried look.

"Andy," I said, introducing myself to Malinda.

"You look wonderful," Gary whispered and gave me an approving smile. I nodded slightly, and we headed to the table. Dinner conversation was dull as we went over the formalities of introducing ourselves and going over the nuances of the presentation that I gave that morning. As we neared the end of the dinner, Malinda looked at me and asked about my family.

"I have a fifteen-year-old daughter, Hayden Grace," I said in response.

"Is she home with her father?" Malinda asked.

"No, he died six years ago," I stated, matter-of-factly.

"Oh, I'm so sorry to hear that," she said, clearly not shocked by that information. I could tell by the huge rock on her finger that she was married.

"Do you have any children?" I asked, trying to change the subject.

"Yes, twin daughters—they are eight," she said proudly, and I smiled, actually shocked by that information.

"What are they into?" I asked. Looking around I could see that the gentlemen were bored with our talk of families and children and excused themselves to the bar.

"Finally," Malinda said, surprising me. "Those two are as old as dirt and fairly antiquated," she said, turning her chair towards me.

"Andy, where do you see yourself in five years?" she asked bluntly, catching me off guard. I started to stumble through a generic response of growing with the company and taking on leadership opportunities…blah…blah….blah… before she cut me off.

"No, where do you really see yourself. I've done my research on you Andrea Parker. I know you were a skier on the national team until you were 18. You got married and had Hayden Grace at twenty. Your husband died serving his country, as you said, six years ago. You have been with this company for ten years but have never really taken a leadership role," she paused, talking to herself. "I had to ask myself when Gary called about the account—telling me that he put you in charge—why that was. This new company is my baby, and I needed to know it was in good hands. But then I looked a little further, specifically into Hayden Grace…she is pretty special," she said with a smile, and I nodded, not knowing where this conversation was going.

"I know it must be hard managing this job and being a single mom to a driven kid like that." Again, I had nothing and sat there speechless, looking at her as she continued. "It helps that you're friends with Marla. She is a friend of my husband's, going pretty far back, and has been pitching your name for this account for at least six months. It's why I offered your company the opportunity to pitch for the account. She was right—the presentation is amazing, and it's just want I want."

"Andy, I want to offer you a position at Angel Apparel. You would run our entire women's marketing division. Alan is moving over to the men's division, and I need young blood in my women's division. I'm not usually in the business of stealing my co-worker's employees, but this is an extreme case and I always get what I want," she stated, matter-of-fact. "Oh, you would need to move out to the West Coast. I like to have my key people close to headquarters in Sacramento," she said, as if I had agreed to her original question.

"One problem, I don't know if I can move Hayden Grace," I whispered, completely overwhelmed with information. She raised her eyebrows at me as Alan and Gary returned.

"You'll think about it?" she asked vaguely.

"Of course," I stammered.

"Think about what?" Gary asked.

"Switching the location of the marketing prints from woodsy New Hampshire to the majestic mountains of Vail or Tahoe," she said, without skipping a beat. The gentlemen just nodded in agreement, and we continued on, as if nothing had just happened.

***

It was well after ten by the time my taxi dropped me off at the parking garage at work. I could tell Malinda would have preferred if I stayed after dinner to talk about her offer, but I couldn't. Instead, I cleared out of there as fast as possible. The drive home was quick with no traffic on the road, and I soon pulled in the driveway around midnight. I couldn't help but smile to myself when I saw all the lights on throughout the house. I let myself in and after turning all the lights off, headed to my bedroom to change. I was startled to see Hayden Grace curled up in my bed again. Molly let out a half-hearted bark when I entered the room, waking Hayden Grace.

"Mom?" she mumbled, rubbing her eyes.

"It's just me, go back to bed," I said.

"What are you wearing?" she asked, staring at my dress.

"I had dinner with the CEO of the company we are representing, and I had to buy something last minute," I explained.

"I really like that...you look good," she said and then rolled back over. I changed and joined her in bed, falling into a dead sleep.

***

The alarm sounded all too early, and I hit snooze. I was not cut out for the commute to Boston, I determined, finally getting up when the alarm sounded the second time. I took a quick shower and headed straight for the coffee.

"Late night?" Hayden Grace asked, as she came around the corner. I grumbled a response, and she didn't ask any more questions. It was several moments before I had enough clarity to speak.

"How was gymnastics last night?" I asked, thinking about her schedule.

"It was good. Abbie wasn't there, and everyone was asking a lot of questions."

"What did you say?"

"I didn't say much of anything. It wasn't my business, and I really don't know what happened after she went to the hospital. I texted her, but she never replied," she commented, shrugging her shoulders.

"What's on your agenda today?" I asked, trying to think of her calendar, but drawing a blank.

"Pipe practice today with the whole club. The winners of the competition are going to be traveling all next week, so Coach Davis wanted us all on the mountain today." I nodded in understanding.

"Who is bringing you home?"

"I think Madison's dad, which is weird because he never drives us anywhere. But Madison said her mom is out of town for several days or

110

something." I nearly spit my coffee across the table. "Are you okay?" she asked in confusion.

"I'm fine. That's nice. I will be in the city again today. I have no idea of my agenda. Yesterday that last minute meeting caught me off guard—sorry for not being home."

"Mom, I get it. Molly and I survived the night," she smiled, easing my anxiety.

"Are you ready for school?"

"Give me ten minutes," she said, darting down the hallway. I put my head down on the table and closed my eyes.

"Mom… wake up…," Hayden Grace was saying, standing over me in the kitchen.

"What? Sorry… let's go," I said, standing suddenly – which made me dizzy.

"Are you going to be okay?" she asked with the concern of a parent.

"Yes, I'm going to be fine," and we headed out of the door.

***

Just like my commute the day before, traffic was again at a standstill for over thirty minutes. I was fighting very hard to stay alert. Before heading to the office, I went straight to the Dunkin' Donuts on the corner and ordered the largest coffee I could get. I just needed to survive the day, I thought to myself. I got to the office and oddly enough, not many people were in. I was able to sit at my desk, answer e-mails, and return several phone calls, before I heard Gary call my name.

"Andy, good showing last night at dinner. I think we impressed Malinda," he said, puffing his chest out in pride.

"Yes, sir," I said, still unsure if last night happened, or if I had dreamed the whole conversation.

"Let's move forward with those story boards with the minor changes from last night. I really liked the idea of setting the campaign at Vail, as she suggested." I rolled my eyes slightly, but nodded in agreement. "Also, have you got your team together?" he asked.

"Not yet. I've made several inquiries amongst the staff, but I'm still waiting on confirmation," I said. He thought over my statement and finally dismissed me from his office. About an hour later I had a break in my day, so I snuck out of the building and called Marla.

"You could have told me!" I said, without any need for pleasantries.

"Whatever do you mean?" she said, innocently.

"One word, MALINDA," I said, with sarcasm.

"Oh, you met the good witch," she replied. "Andy, she is an amazing leader and CEO. You can go far under her watch, but don't play games with her offer or she will make your life a living hell," she added, dropping all pretenses in her warning.

"I figured that out from our conversation. She wants me to move out West," I said, pacing up and down the city block outside our building.

"Again, not surprising…she likes to keep everyone close."

"You recommended me to her because…?" It didn't sound like something a friend would do.

"Because you're better than all of this. You need a new opportunity for both you and Hayden Grace. There are tons of snowboarding opportunities for her out there; more chances there than in Newbury, New Hampshire. You should take the job," she said.

"I don't know," I said after a pause. "Oh, by the way, I'm putting you on my campaign team for this project," I threw in for good measure.

"Really... I hate driving into the city," she moaned. We talked logistics for several more minutes before I got too cold and had to head back inside. My conversation with Marla did nothing to calm me down about the offer. Back at my desk I saw I had a missed call from Guardian Angel. My fingers were shaking as I punched the number into the phone.

"Malinda Mitchell's office," a voice answered on the other line.

"This is Andrea Parker. I'm returning a missed call."

"Andy, she is expecting your call," the young voice said, putting me through.

"Andy, good to hear from you," Malinda's voice rang through the phone moments later. Like I had another choice, I thought to myself.

"Are you calling to accept my offer?" she inquired.

"I'm at work, and you called me," I replied, confused.

"You are correct. I was looking at the presentation again this morning, and I really think this is the best direction to take Angel Apparel. I want someone young and energetic to be the face of the apparel brand. Let's do some research into budding athletes ages 16-18 and see what we can come up with. It can be in various sports; the more the better," she rattled on.

"That sounds great. I'll have that list to you by the end of day tomorrow,"

I said, looking at the clock and figuring out the time it would take me to do it.

"Friday is fine. I'll be out of town the rest of this week and won't have a need for it until then." I thought the conversation was over, before she continued.

"Andy, I don't expect you to answer me since you're at work, but listen to me very closely. I can double your current salary. You can work from home most of the time, and we will work with you and Hayden Grace's schedule. I know those things are really important to you as a single mother, and I want to accommodate them, but I can't wait forever. I will need your answer by Friday as well," she said.

"If I accept this 'change', when would I start?" I whispered carefully, looking to make sure no one was around.

"It would take us a week or two to work through the legalities of backing out of our contract…probably three weeks to a month. Of course, you wouldn't have to be settled in here permanently by that time, but we would need the ball to be rolling." I could hear her drumming her fingers on the desk.

"Of course."

"Any further questions?"

"None at this time," I lied, thinking of a million questions I actually had.

"Talk to you Friday," she said and disconnected. Looking at the clock, I still had a couple hours before the workday ended; it could not come fast enough, I thought to myself. Sighing, I focused on the project Malinda had given me until it was time to go home.

***

The traffic on the way home wasn't as bad as it had been in the morning, but it was still bad. Half way home my phone rang, and I picked it up before looking at the screen.

"Andy?" Gregg said on the other line.

"Gregg," I said in a monotone.

"I haven't heard from you in several days. I thought we could arrange for another date, maybe pick up where we last left off?" his voice oozed with sexual suggestion, while my stomach turned. Hayden Grace just told me this morning that Lisa was out of town for several days, and the first thing he does is call me?

"I don't know if now is a good time, Gregg. I just landed a major account at work and expectations are really high," I offered as an excuse.

"That big account you were working on the presentation for? Congratulations. I know you worked really hard. What about next week? I have several days open."

'I bet you do,' I thought to myself, knowing that Lisa and Madison would be in Aspen.

"Gregg, I just don't think this is going to work." 'Oh, and you have a wife and daughter who I know, you sleezeball,' I was mentally shouting. Undeterred, Gregg said he would give me a call in a couple days to see if things had changed.

After that call and more traffic, I got home a little after eight. I found Hayden Grace in the living room working on school work; she looked startled when I came through the door, as she had on headphones and couldn't hear me.

"How was pipe practice?" I said, setting my briefcase and the bag of apparel from the other day down in the hallway.

"It was awesome! I had a great day…a little too late since the competition was last week, but my run is getting better. Coach Davis talked to me about adding some new tricks," she said, with excitement.

"That's great to hear. What do you want for dinner?" I asked, wandering into the kitchen.

"I ate with Lucie, Madison and both of their dads at Subway, then Lucie's dad actually brought me home since it was on his way," she said, looking back to her books, sending waves of anger down my spine. I knew Gregg didn't know Hayden Grace was my daughter, but the nerve of him calling me to ask me out while with her and his own daughter made my blood boil with fury. I looked in the fridge and found leftovers, slamming the door with frustration. Putting them in the microwave, I went and changed into my comfort sweatpants, trying to put Gregg out of my mind. My mind drifted to work, and I started thinking about Angel Apparel, which made me go back and change into some of the samples that Alan had sent me home with.

"Where did you get those?" Hayden Grace asked, when I came back into the living room.

"New client gave them to me to try out...help yourself...the bag of stuff is in the bedroom," Hayden Grace was sprinting down the hallway before I finished the entire statement. Smiling to myself, I took the food out of the microwave and settled in on the sofa.

"This stuff is so cool," she said, coming back down the hallway, modeling a range of items.

"Hayden Grace, I need to talk to you about something," I said, pausing and wondering how to start. Just then her phone rang.

"It's Coach Davis," she said as she grabbed it. I nodded, shoveling in a mouthful of broccoli and potatoes.

"NO WAY...," she screamed, jumping up and down, causing me to choke on my dinner. "This is so awesome!" She was now pacing and playing with her hair. "Yes, I understand…I will….THANK YOU!" she said, hanging up the phone and jumping on me.

"Mom, I got in," she yelled again.

"Got into what?" I asked in confusion, as I tried to understand what was going on.

"Abbie-got-disqualified-for-testing-positive-for-marijuana-from-the-party-but-also-rumor-was-that-her-parents-pulled-her-so-as-the-alternate-I-get-to-go-to-ASPEN," she rambled.

"Slow down and breathe…you're talking too fast," I said, trying to comprehend everything.

"We are going to ASPEN," she said again, jumping up off the sofa and looking at me.

"You are going to go, right?" she asked, and I just stared at her in disbelief.

"I have to call Madison and Lucie," she said, continuing on. She ran down the hallway, where I heard more shrieking and yelling moments later. I just sat on the sofa glued to the same spot, wondering what the heck had just happened.

CHAPTER 13

As I sat at my desk in Boston, with another large cup of coffee in front of me, I was processing the fact that Hayden Grace had suddenly qualified for the national competition in Aspen and what that meant for our family. After Hayden Grace had calmed down and finished her homework, I had tried calling Coach Davis to talk about the competition, the price, the travel, etc., but he never answered. It was typical of Ron. It would take him three days to return my call, but today I didn't have to wait long—my phone rang just after lunchtime.

"Ron?" I asked, when his number popped up.

"Actually, this is Anna," the voice on the line commented.

"Hi, Anna." Anna was Coach Davis's administrative secretary at the mountain.

"I'm calling to make travel arranges for the competition," she said, in a very business-like manner.

"I thought the parents were responsible for that?" I asked in confusion.

"Typically they are, but for Regional 6 there are a lot of stipulations and team rules, so we help the parents in making arrangements," she said.

"Just not in payments," I mumbled to myself.

"What was that?"

"Nevermind. Lay it on me—what are we looking at?" I asked.

"I assume that you will be accompanying Hayden Grace to the tournament?"

"Yes," even if I wanted to stay home, it was required that participants under the age of 18 were accompanied by a guardian.

"Okay. I can get you and Hayden Grace on the same flight as Madison and Lucie. There are still seats available. It leaves Monday morning from Boston at eight a.m. with a layover in Denver arriving in Aspen at lunchtime for about $1200 total. Now Madison and Lucie's families have each booked suites at the St. Regis," she paused, and I knew the price tag was going to be large. "Those suites are about a $1,000 a night; of course, there are other properties in a much more manageable price range," she quickly added.

"Yes, more manageable would be better," I nearly choked out. By the time I got off the phone with Anna, my mind was spinning. I felt like it had been spinning for days with no end in sight. Hayden Grace and I were booked on our flight for Aspen; we had a room at the Comfort Inn that was 23 miles from Aspen City Center at $98 dollars a night and a rental car to get us to and from the hotel and the resort. Her dream was very quickly becoming our reality.

***

In my frazzled state over the last several days, I had barely been paying attention to the weather forecast. I had heard people around the office talking about it, but it wasn't a priority to me. Now I wished I paid better attention as I watched the snow race down onto the city streets and cars from the tenth floor of the office building. I finally decided to leave the office at three in the afternoon after the flurries began coming down faster. Gary wasn't pleased about me leaving early, but finally mumbled something about my safety after several other co-workers started to leave. My commute home got worse the closer to home I got, taking me nearly three and half hours total. Based on the weather, it didn't surprise me that when I got home Hayden Grace was already there.

"They cancelled practice," she grumbled, when I walked in the door. She was actually one of the few kids that hated snow days because it meant it was one day less on the mountain and in the pipe.

"Sorry, the roads are really bad. I don't blame them. Go grab some firewood from the garage" I said, stomping up the stairs to change into something warmer. After I had changed and started a fire in the living room, Hayden Grace helped me with dinner. We talked generally about school and work, but I didn't bring up Malinda's offer, not yet.

"Oh, did Anna call you today?" she asked, as we were almost done with dinner.

"Yes, she did. We are booked on the same flights as Madison and Lucie. Are their parents coming too?" I asked casually, thinking of what small piece of personal hell the flight would be if I had to spend an entire flight with Lisa and Gregg.

"Madison's mom is coming for the full length of time. Her dad and sister are coming up later in the week, maybe for the weekend depending on how Madison does. Lucie's dad is coming because her mom has to work."

"Where are we staying?" she said with excitement.

"Hayden Grace, I couldn't afford the St. Regis. We are staying a little further out of town, but I promise that we won't miss anything. We are only sleeping out there," I said, as her face fell a little bit before she recovered.

"No, I understand. I am really excited to be going...I came up with a list of things I will need before the competition," she said, rattling off several things that I had already thought of. The total price of everything kept adding up, and I started to wonder if this trip was going to bankrupt us.

"Let's watch some TV before bed," I suggested, needing a change of subject. As we settled in on the sofa, Channel 8 News alerted us to the fact that all schools were closing the following day, causing Hayden Grace to grin with glee over spending one less day droning on in high school. That news was followed quickly by Hayden Grace getting a mass text from #Coach that practice was again cancelled the following day, causing her mood to swing from elation to brooding in the span of a couple seconds.

"That sucks," she complained, before bed.

"Goodnight, sweetie," I said, kissing her and ignoring her mood.

"Goodnight mom."

**

My alarm went off at five which was becoming my new 'normal' as I slowly got out of bed. I was about to shower when I thought about the weather from the night before. Looking out the window I could see that we had gotten about three feet of snow outside. I went and looked at my phone in the kitchen and saw several e-mails from employees unable to get to work. Evaluating the conditions, I knew I wasn't going to be able to go far today, let alone the Manchester or Boston offices. I sent an e-mail to Gary and several other key members of the office that I wouldn't be able to make it into the office either. Sighing with relief, I crawled back into bed. It was several hours later that I heard Hayden Grace coming into my room.

"You didn't go to work?" she asked, yawning.

"Nope," I mumbled, not opening my eyes. She must have stood there a couple minutes before I felt the bed shift under her weight. She curled up, causing Molly to adjust and the three of us fell back to sleep. It was around eleven when I finally pulled myself out of bed. Peeking at the roads, I could see that they were in better shape. Thinking I should go back to work, I looked at my phone, more than half the office had stayed home because of the weather. Knowing I had finished my biggest project the day before, I felt no remorse about not working the rest of the day. I looked out at the powder and I thought about the mountain and a great idea started to form.

"Hayden Grace, wake up," I said, going back into the bedroom to change.

"Why, no school," she pouted.

"I thought we might go to the mountain."

"Why, no practice."

"No practice, but the backcountry…" I didn't even finish the sentence, and she instantly sat up in bed, looking at me as excitement danced in her eyes.

"Really? I'm in," she said, not waiting for a response as she got out of bed and practically danced to her room to get changed. While she seemed to be in a sudden hurry, I wasn't. I took my time getting ready and making sure we ate lunch before heading out to the mountain. The drive was slow, but again, we weren't in a big hurry. During the drive Hayden Grace regaled me with stories about how Madison and Preston had already broken it off as a couple and the extreme lengths Preston was going to try and get her back. This information, while amusing, only elicited an exaggerated eye roll from me. We arrived at the mountain, finding a handful of cars in the parking lot. Hayden Grace headed to the locker room to change into her gear, and I headed to the employee locker room to get mine. Fifteen minutes later we met at the bottom of the lift. Before we got on the lift, I helped Hayden Grace adjust her bindings slightly. Riding in the pipe and in the backcountry was different, and she would need to carry her weight more towards the back of the board. This would help ensure she was gliding on the snow and not digging into it. Before we ascended, I looked around for Joel and found he was nowhere in sight. Sighing in relief that he wouldn't stop us or ask me for some crazy favor, we headed to the top of the mountain. Once at the top, I could feel the excitement build as I held the rope up while Hayden Grace glided underneath it.

"Okay…let's go over some rules," I said, adjusting her helmet.

"Mom, really?" she asked in annoyance.

"Really…the backcountry is not like the park with cleared paths and defined ski areas. There is a lot that can go wrong, so stick close to me and don't take any unnecessary risks," I stated, and she nodded. With that I pointed out the way I usually traveled, and we set off at a slighter slower pace with all the fresh snow. It was becoming a beautiful day; the sun was finally coming out from behind the heavy gray clouds, shining bright and bouncing off of all the white snow. The trees were still heavy with snow and felt like they were being pulled closer to the ground. The biggest hazards were rocks and debris that, once easily distinguishable, were now hidden deep in the snow. But I wasn't worried—I had these areas memorized and could have skied the area with my eyes closed. I kept a close watch on Hayden Grace as we descended down the mountain. She was careful, but I could tell she was enjoying the freedom that the backcountry allowed. We got close to the tabletop jumps, and I signaled for her to stop.

"Why are we stopping?" she asked.

"I thought this was a good place to break," I said, sitting down and patting the soft ground beside me as I pulled out two granola bars from my backpack. Hayden Grace sat next to me and pulled out a bottle of Gatorade from hers, which was only slightly frozen. It was a peaceful moment, and I felt that here in the backcountry, Hayden Grace might be slightly more open to the idea of moving without the distractions or reminders of our current lives. I hoped this would allow her to envision what could be.

"Hayden Grace, we need to talk about something," I said slowly, not wanting to ruin the moment, but knowing I needed to share the news with her.

"Sure Mom, what's up?" she asked, twisting to look at me.

"I've been offered a new job with Angel Apparel."

"Is that the clothing you brought home the other night?" she asked thoughtfully, and I nodded. "That stuff is so comfortable and warm." She quickly unzipped her jacket to show me that she was wearing one of the undershirts I had brought home during the week. She gave me a big grin for good measure.

"The CEO, her name is Malinda, offered me the job overseeing the entire marketing department. It's more responsibility and more money, but they know about your snowboarding and would allow me to work around your schedule," I paused, but she sat quietly and continued to listen.

"But…"

"But the job is based on the West Coast; near Sacramento, California. We would have to move."

"To Sacramento?"

"Not necessarily. We could move anywhere as long as we are close to Sacramento, from my understanding."

"Like where?"

"We could live near Tahoe, for example," I said, trying to gauge her reaction.

"What about my friends? School?"

"I don't know about school, but your friends would stay here—this is where they live."

"What about Grams and Grandpa?" she asked, with a slight hitch of concern.

"I don't have all the answers, but I know they aren't moving with us. It would be just you and me."

"The snowboarding is better out there," she commented after a moment, and I nodded. "When do you have to decide?"

"I was supposed to decide by Friday, but I'm going to ask for an extension until after Aspen," I said, making that decision as I spoke. She nodded in agreement.

"I can think on this too, right?"

"Yes, that's why I wanted to tell you. We both have to decide that we want to go."

"Mom," she said after a moment.

"Hmm…"

"If it was just you and you didn't have to worry about being a mom, would you go?" she asked very seriously.

"Sweetie, I am a mom. I'm your mom, and I do have to worry about you. I can't even think of a scenario in which you don't exist," I said wholeheartedly, hoping she understood how much she meant to me. We sat for a couple more minutes in silence.

"What are those," she asked, pointing to the natural jumps. I knew that we had moved past the moving conversation for the time being, and I was okay with that.

"Remember when I told you about skiing the backcountry with Paul, Scott, Davie and Trip?" she nodded in response. "These are those jumps they were doing tricks on," I explained, as I pointed to the specific outline of each jump.

"Oh cool, can I try?" she asked, jumping up.

"Just the first one," I said, leaning back to watch. She took off toward the jump and hit it right down the middle; she did a simple grab and landed cleanly. I heard her shout in excitement, and I smiled. It made me happy that she continued to enjoy riding, even after she spent nearly seven days a week on the mountain and in the snow while in season. I always told myself that the second she started considering this as work, it might be time to walk away. She came up to where I was sitting and asked if she could go again. I nodded, and she raced back toward the jump. This time she approached the jump riding her non-dominant side and did a double twist in the air.

"Mom, did you see that?" she exclaimed, and I clapped. "Have you ever gone off of these jumps?" she asked, coming back up to where I was sitting and plopping down next to me.

"Yes," I said, hoping she would move on.

"When?"

"Recently," I whispered.

"What? You have to show me!" she exclaimed. Hayden Grace had no concept that when I was her age I was on the national team, and I was doing what she was doing. All Hayden Grace had ever seen me do is ski mountain trails or teach ski lessons. She had no idea of the person I used to be.

"Okay, just once," I said, standing up, and she clapped with delight. I glided to the first jump and headed down, repeating my rodeo flip from several days earlier. I landed with a little wobble, but still on my feet. I skidded to a stop at the bottom of the jump and looked up to see Hayden Grace standing and cheering.

"Stop it—it was just one trick," I shouted, feeling slightly patronized.

"Mom, you must have been such a cool skier back in the day," she said, after joining me where I was standing.

"Ouch, back in the day? How old do you think I am?" I asked.

"Old enough…you are my mom after all," she smiled at me, and I returned the smile. We decided to head back to the lodge, going a slightly different way to the left side of the backcountry which took a little longer, but had a somewhat lesser decline. Hayden Grace did a good job keeping up with me, staying by my side. Whenever I noticed she would drift behind, I slowed my pace and she was able to get back into the rhythm. We cleared the tree line at the bottom about two hours after we had first ascended. I asked Hayden Grace if she wanted to ski the backcountry again or any of the other trails, and she declined. We both went to our respective locker rooms to change before we met in the lobby for some hot chocolate.

"Mom, that was awesome. Did you ski the backcountry often with dad?" she asked.

"All the time. It was our favorite thing to do." It felt so private and intimate that we often referred to it as our own personal playground. "It wasn't here at Mount Sunapee, but we were skiing in Vermont, and it was in the backcountry where he asked me to marry him. He pretended to fall down in the snow, and when I got to him he had the ring out and was down on his knees," I explained. Hayden Grace had probably heard the story a hundred times, but she always looked so engrossed whenever I told it, so I just kept repeating it. In reality, it had been such a quick romance. Meeting Stefan was love at first glance for me, and he later told me it was the same for him—it was so fast and overwhelming. Within six months of meeting we were engaged and married by the time I was nineteen. I don't think we had planned on having kids at such an early stage, but not long after, I found out I was pregnant, and we never looked back after that.

"Can we do that again in the future?" she questioned. "It was so much fun and so much different than practice." I agreed to take her again after we got back from Aspen.

"How soon would we have to move, if we went?" she asked, out of the blue.

"Probably within four to six weeks after Aspen," I replied, unsure of an exact time.

"Okay," she said, and her phone dinged with a message. She texted back and forth for several minutes before looking back up.

"Can I go to Lucie's house to watch a movie?"

"Sure, I can drop you off on the way home," I said. "Hayden Grace?"

"Yes?"

"Please don't tell anyone about the job or the possible move until we make our decision," I said, in hopes of avoiding any drama that this might add to our lives.

"Sure." After we finished our drinks, I dropped her off at Lucie's house. Lucie's mom said she would have her home by eight, as it was a school night. When I finally got home I started to do laundry and pull things out in order to start packing.

***

"Hey Mom, how are you?" I asked, when my mom picked up the phone.

"Hey, Andy. I'm good— how is Hayden Grace doing?" she asked.

"She is doing well—actually better than ever. Remember that girl Abbie, who threw the party?" She acknowledged that she remembered the name. "Well, she withdrew from the competition or was disqualified, rumors of both have been circulating; but that means that Hayden Grace is now competing in Aspen next week." My statement was followed by a barrage of questions and excitement. My mom called my dad to the phone, and I repeated my story. We talked for the next hour about the competition, travel, expenses and Hayden Grace. I was never able to approach the subject of possibly moving and decided it would be best not to. My parents did agree to drive back up and stay at the house for the week to watch Molly.

By the time Hayden Grace returned home, I had pulled out her snowboarding travel case and both our suitcases from the attic. Hayden Grace's excitement rose when she saw the suitcases.

"This is really happening," she squealed, wrapping me in a big hug.

"It really is," I said, grinning at her enthusiasm. We made another list of all the things we needed to get from the lodge over the weekend and soon headed to bed.

***

The next three days flew by in a blur with little excitement. On Friday, I sent two e-mails to Malinda. The first was with all the information she asked for about the up-and-coming 16-18 year old female athletes in all fields. I had done most of the project earlier in the week, but spent some time on Friday putting final touches on the list. The second e-mail stated that I needed more time to think about her offer, as I had more to consider than just myself. I promised a definite answer when we returned from Aspen. I sent an e-mail to Gary to remind him that I would be working remotely several days next week and then I had several days off and would not be working. He was not happy when I told him I was leaving for a week just after we started this project. I reminded him that my team was mostly assembled and Marla would be taking the lead here in Boston while I was in Aspen. We had no current pressing deadlines and things would continue to run smoothly. Reluctantly he finally agreed, but what he didn't realize was I was going with or without his approval – though his approval made things easier. On Saturday and Sunday, for some normalcy, I still taught ski lessons, and Hayden Grace took extra runs in the pipe to prepare. By Sunday evening we were both excited and exhausted. We weren't sure what exactly we were in for, but we couldn't wait to find out.

CHAPTER 14

The flight was pretty uneventful, with the exception that once we were on the plane the girls all wanted to sit together, naturally, so we had to orchestra a multi-seat switch. We landed in Aspen right around lunchtime as planned. Lucie and Madison and their parents caught the St. Regis shuttle to the hotel while Hayden Grace and I headed down to the car rental area. We made it to our hotel in pretty good time and checked into room 238. The room was just a plain standard hotel room with two double beds and a fantastic view of the parking lot. I had to admit it was a little snug with all of Hayden Grace's equipment and stuff, but I was trying to stay positive for her. I suggested we head to downtown Aspen to walk around and grab lunch, and Hayden Grace all too eagerly agreed.

We were quickly swept into the hustle and bustle of the quaint and very picturesque town of Aspen. Hayden Grace and I giggled over the women walking around in more fur than I had ever seen in a ski town. The flipside was that everyone was dressed to be able to jump onto the slopes at any given moment. But mostly, I felt like we had walked into a European winter fashion shoot, and Hayden Grace was enthralled. She kept pointing at different people, amazed with everything around her; one would have thought she had never left Newbury before. While we had traveled extensively for her snowboarding, it was primarily throughout New England. Twenty years ago, when I traveled for Nationals, most of the competitions were based on the East Coast. Aspen was new to both of us. Walking around, many of the restaurants looked really crowded. We finally settled on a small deli called Fresh Slice, that was down a much less crowded side street. The waitress who served us was able to answer all our questions and even pointed us towards the event check-in when we were done.

It was nice for the waitress to point us in the right direction, but in reality, you could see the event set up from several blocks away. Two large colorful tents covered the block at the base of the mountain. Music was playing, and people milled around more like it was a street festival than a sports competition. Both Hayden Grace and I observed that the area was crowded with not only eager skiers and snowboarders, but also visitors from around the world based on the many accents and languages we both overheard. We waited in line patiently, but the longer we waited, the more Hayden Grace fidgeted and starting biting her fingernails. I nudged her slightly, and she looked at me in confusion, mouthing the word, 'what'.

"Next?" a young man said, calling us forward. He looked like he was sixteen or seventeen. He had sandy blonde hair spiked up, with clear green eyes and freckles that covered his cheeks. Hayden Grace stood there not moving, again—I nudged her.

"Name?" he asked, looking directly at Hayden Grace.

"Oh…Hayden Grace Parker," she said very quietly.

"Well, Hayden Grace Parker, here is your bib number and information packet," he said, smiling at her after sorting through some folders.

"Thank you," Hayden Grace mumbled, trying to turn and walk away. Instead, I grabbed her arm taking the opportunity to ask several questions about the area, and the competition in general, before thanking the young man.

"He was so cute," Hayden Grace mumbled when we were out of earshot of the tent. "The boys don't look like that back home." I smiled, rolling my eyes by how quickly she could be distracted.

"Focus Hayden Grace, this packet says you can report for practice around ten a.m. tomorrow," I said, shuffling through the information. From there it looked like the schedule was practice on Tuesday, qualifying rounds on Wednesday and the finals on Thursday and Friday. The packet indicated that the top three finishers from Regional 6 would qualify for the Big Bear Exhibition held in Vail two weeks later. Not being able to process what the implications of Hayden Grace qualifying for that would mean, I quickly stuffed that paper into the back of the packet.

"Coach Davis wants us here around 9:45 a.m. so we can be one of the first riders on the pipe," she said, after a moment.

"Ron is here?" I asked. I mean it made sense the coach would be here with so many qualifying competitors from his club, but no one had said anything about it earlier.

"Yeah, I think he got here yesterday or something," Hayden Grace said, still looking over her shoulder back at the tent.

"You can go talk to him you know," I finally said, clearly understanding that a coherent conversation was not going to happen until the boy situation had been resolved.

"Nah, I can't…you think?" she said, suddenly looking at me with a twinkle in her eye.

"Hayden Grace, do what you want, but make up your mind; I don't want to stand here all day," I firmly stated, knowing if I told her to go over there she would rebuff my suggestion. I found that showing disinterest was usually very helpful in these situations.

"You're right… I'll be right back," she said, jogging back over to the tent.

I sighed and sat down on a nearby bench and watched the interaction. She walked up, took a deep breath and tapped the young man on the shoulder. He turned around and smiled, and I think I actually saw her melt just a little, which caused me to smile. They exchanged a couple sentences with each other and he finally nodded. She waved and very calmly walked back over to where I was.

"Is he still looking?" she asked, through gritted teeth.

"Nope."

"OMG, Mom… his name is Jonathan, he is from California but volunteers with check-in; this is his second year competing in Regional 6. He's more like you, a skier. Anyway he invited me to small get together tomorrow night." She practically danced in her spot. I was more amazed at all the information she got from that two minute interaction.

"Breathe Hayden Grace….party?" I questioned, unsure if I could do another party in a two week time span.

"Oh, not like that party," she said, rolling her eyes. "This is at Poppycock's—it's a small café, in a public place," she added, reading my very skeptical expression.

"Okay," I said, jotting down the time and location on the larger schedule that Hayden Grace was given.

"What would you like to do next?" I asked.

"Can we window shop?" she asked me back.

"Of course." We spent the rest of the afternoon wandering around the streets of Aspen, slowly falling in love with the town, people and atmosphere. For the most part, we just browsed storefronts, occasionally venturing into several boutique shops. There was so much to see and do just in the city center of Aspen, before you ever ventured onto the mountain. We were about to head home when I heard someone calling Hayden Grace's name. We turned around to find Lucie and Madison running up behind us.

"We have been trying to call you!" Madison said in exasperation.

"Sorry, I must have forgotten to turn it back on," Hayden Grace said, taking her phone out of her back pocket.

"Listen, rumor has it that PW is here!!" Madison and Lucie shrieked with excitement.

"His name is Paul," Hayden Grace responded automatically, causing me to smirk. I could tell she was excited over this information, but was not as impressed as her friends were. I was slightly fascinated by her behavior as the girls leaned in toward each other in a huddle, whispering and gossiping. I stood off to the side, waiting patiently for them to join the rest of society from their inner bubble. The girls finally righted themselves and exchanged notes over their adventures from the last four hours since they had been separated. I noticed that Hayden Grace did not mention Jonathan or her invitation to Poppycock's to either girl, causing me to raise my eyebrow in curiosity.

"Where are you going now?" Hayden Grace finally asked, after a lull in the conversation.

"To check-in," they said in unison, which only caused more giggles between Lucie and Madison.

"You?" Lucie asked.

"Mom and I are headed to dinner," she said, taking my arm. The girls nodded and said they would see each other at practice as we parted ways.

"Dinner?" I asked, after several blocks.

"We don't have to, but I was ready to go. Sometimes they are just too much…ya know," she said, looking straight ahead. I knew exactly what she meant, but was surprised she knew what she meant.

"You surprise me every day, Hayden Grace," I said after a moment, and she smiled broadly. We settled on burgers and fries carryout for dinner, as we headed back to our hotel. I had to admit that the hotel was not as close as I thought when I looked at the map. It was not going to be as convenient as I imagined it would be with everything going on.

***

Tuesday we were up early. Hayden Grace grabbed a quick breakfast in the hotel lobby, while I called and checked in with my parents.

"How's Molly?" I asked.

"Fine."

"How's the house?" I asked again.

"Fine."

"How are you both doing?"

"Fine," my mother repeated for the third time. "Andy, you have been gone one day…everything is fine. Relax, enjoy the trip and try to have a good time."

"Thanks Mom, I needed that. Talk to you later."

"Don't call me until Hayden Grace has won that whole damn thing," she commented, hanging up.

"How's Grams?" Hayden Grace asked, coming up next me.

"Feisty," I replied, before adding, "She wishes you good luck."

"Cool."

The streets weren't too crowded when we arrived back at the city center of Aspen. Hayden Grace had asked to drive, but I explained that she needed to focus more on her riding than driving today. Secretly, I was terrified of her driving on the windy roads and small streets, and forget about her ability to parallel park – my nerves were better this way. We waited by the Silver Queen Gondola as Ron had instructed; within ten minutes the other riders from the Newbury competition started arriving. Hayden Grace started chatting with her friends, and I stepped to the side, trying to stay out of the way as I noticed I was the only parent escorting their child to practice.

"Hey Andy," Ron said, jogging up. He was the last to arrive, as usual, causing me to smile.

"Beautiful, isn't it?" he asked, waving at the surroundings. I nodded in agreement. He took roll call, and they headed toward the Silver Queen Gondola entrance.

"Mom?" I heard Hayden Grace call out, causing me to turn around. "What are you going to do all day?" she asked, with concern.

"Don't worry about me. Text me when you are done," I said, kissing her on top of the head and sending her on her way. I waited a couple moments before I set off into town. I was nearly a block away when my phone rang.

"Hello?"

"Andy, how are you?"

"Baby brother, how are you?" I said, shocked to hear Drew's voice.

"Mom told me that you had some big news. So spill the beans." He was just like our dad – always very direct. It made me smile.

"Well, you should start by asking me where I am," I said, trying to be difficult.

"I assume New Hampshire, but I don't know... you're at home?"

"I am standing on Hunter Street," I said, as if it were a good clue.

"So you're not at home."

"I'm in Aspen." I said, and I heard a low whistle on the other end.

"Hayden Grace," he guessed.

"Hayden Grace," I confirmed.

"That's amazing—when is the competition?" he asked.

"Qualifying rounds start tomorrow, and the finals are on Thursday for her event," I said.

"I'll be there."

"Drew, do not make any promises you can't keep," I said, worried my brother was just trying to be nice. He had a tendency to over promise and under deliver.

"Andy, I wouldn't miss it for the world. Where are you staying?" he asked, causing me to laugh.

"Nowhere you would want to stay," I continued to laugh. My brother liked the finer things in travel, hotel and women. He would never stay at the Comfort Inn, especially given its distance to the heart of Aspen.

"Okay, I'm booking a room at the Hyatt. I've stayed there before. You and Hayden Grace should stay with me. When are you headed home?" he asked, clearly suddenly distracted.

"Umm, I think Saturday morning," I said.

"Great. I don't know how long I can get away, but I will be there for the finals." We talked logistics a little longer; I was grinning ear to ear when we disconnected. Drew may have been my younger brother, but in the last couple years he definitely took on a big brother role, not only with me, but also with Hayden Grace. There was a reason he was one of Hayden Grace's favorite people—he was always there when it mattered. In the last six years, he never missed a holiday or a birthday. He always made himself accessible to Hayden Grace, no matter how busy he was. I remember two years ago when Hayden Grace and I had gotten into a particularly big fight, and she called Drew all upset. He drove up from New York the next day to see how we were both doing. He worked his magic and the fight soon ended, but his ability to make time for us in his life meant more to me than I could ever truly express.

Once off the phone I found a coffee shop, ordered a large coffee with peppermint and sat next to the big window, taking in the amazing view of the mountain. It was the best office view I could think of as I pulled out my laptop, needing to check work e-mails. Once everything loaded, I scanned through and saw that things were still progressing smoothly. After about an hour there was only one e-mail that sat unopened in my inbox; its subject line read: I DON'T GRANT EXTENSIONS and was from Malinda Mitchell. Finally building up the courage and taking a deep breath, I clicked on the e-mail. As I read through it my blood pressure dropped slightly. While her subject line was maddening, her e-mail was much less intense. She reiterated that she doesn't grant extensions, but would patiently wait upon my return and not a day longer. At the bottom of the e-mail, I almost missed the included notes on the project I had sent her. She had added in red one name in particular: Hayden Grace Parker with a question mark. Unable to resist, I hit reply to the e-mail and sent the following response.

139

Malinda,

Thank you for your patience in this matter. I saw the note at the bottom and I'm unsure what your additional notes mean? While I am flattered, Hayden Grace did not fit the criteria we had discussed.

Andy

Within seconds of hitting send, a new e-mail dinged in my inbox with the following response:

Not yet.

I sat and stared at the screen for a while, unable to process the implication of her meaning. Was she really after me as an employee or Hayden Grace as a client...maybe both? A knock on the window brought me out of my daze; looking up I found myself gazing directly into a set of familiar blue eyes.

CHAPTER 15

Paul Westcott was now sitting across from me, drinking coffee. There were side glances and whispers from the patrons sitting around us. I could tell some were trying to debate whether or not to approach the table.

"Welcome to Aspen," he finally said after a moment with a wicked grin.

"Thank you."

"Now do tell me. What are you doing here?" he questioned.

"I should ask you the same thing," I commented back dryly.

"I wasn't going to come, but at the last minute I was asked to fill in as a judge for the Regional 6 men's pipe competition, or so I hear that's the rumor," he said, dropping his voice to a whisper and winking.

"I've heard the same rumor."

"I'm usually penciled in for these types of things," he said after a moment with a wave of a hand.

"Penciled in?"

"I'm always penciled in," he said very matter of fact, as if it was normal to live life being a 'maybe'.

"Abbie…do you remember her?" I asked after a moment, and he nodded. "She got disqualified and so Hayden Grace got called up at the last minute," I explained.

"Practice?" he asked, tilting his head toward the mountain, and I nodded.

"What are you doing with all your free time?"

"Well, I was working until you happened upon me," I said, closing my laptop.

"Work is overrated," he commented.

"Clearly," I said sarcastically.

"Seriously, Andy, you only get to do this once."

"This?"

"Life…you need to live it on the edge, I always say."

"Do you always quote yourself?"

"Sometimes," he said, winking at me again.

"That's just not my life," I said after several moments, and he looked like he was about to protest. I raised my finger as a sign that I wasn't done. "Due to the improbable circumstances that we have run into each other half way across the country…I will give you the benefit of the doubt and agree that, in this case, work is overrated." Just then a little boy, about eight years old, approached the table. He very shyly asked 'PW' for a picture. It was a reminder of how different our lives were. I quietly packed up my laptop as the little boy and Paul posed for several pictures to the delight of his parents. They were almost done when another couple approached the table with the exact request. Smiling to myself, I got up from the table and walked out the front door of the café, shaking my head in disbelief.

"Andy!" I heard Paul call after me as I was halfway down the block. "Where are you going?" he asked, catching up to me. I paused and looked up at him in confusion.

"You were busy…I thought I would excuse myself," I said, as a way of explanation.

"But I just found you," he said, holding my gaze until I looked away. "What are you doing the rest of the day?" he asked before I could form a complete thought.

"I'm not sure. Hayden Grace was going to text me when she was done with practice and any other obligations that she has," I said, looking at my watch. It was now just past twelve. I suspected they would be busy until dinner time.

"Perfect. Spend the afternoon with me."

"Doing what?" I asked cautiously.

"It's my turn to show you the mountain," he said, flashing his wicked grin. I probably should have thought about it a little longer, but I nodded in excitement almost immediately.

"I would have to go back to the hotel," I said as I started to explain about getting my ski attire.

"Don't be ridiculous, come with me," he said, putting his hand on the small of my back and pointing down the block with his other hand. I would be lying to myself if I didn't acknowledge that feeling his touch gave me butterflies in the pit of my stomach.

"Do you frequent Aspen often?" I asked as we headed for the Silver Queen Gondola. It was the only landmark that I could recognize with any familiarity at this point.

"Often enough. I prefer Tahoe, but it's probably because that is where I learned to ride." He waved at an attendant as we entered the building, and we were escorted to the front of the line and given a private gondola for the ride to the top. During the 11,000 foot ascent in elevation I was quiet, speechless really, as I took in the view. The mountain peaks were covered in snow and clouds seemed to cling to their surface. The snow seemed whiter and crisper than it did back home. Everything about it was better: bigger heights, wider expanses of countryside and larger extremes. Simply put, it looked like heaven. When we reached the top I turned to find Paul staring at me.

"What?" I asked, suddenly self-conscious.

"I sometimes forget about the beauty of it all, but watching you take it all in…it's nice to see it through someone else's eyes," he said, stepping off the ride. A cold wind whipped by me as we reached the summit. I shivered, pulling my jacket tighter.

"Let's get you into something warmer," he said, leading the way toward a smaller building set off from the main building, which I assumed was the lodge at the top. Inside it was a beautiful log cabin with expanses of timber and leather. It was colorfully decorated in reds, oranges and yellows, giving the cabin a very intimate feeling. A large fire warmed the lobby as some skiers milled around. I figured out quickly that these were the private locker rooms for the professional or affluent skiers or snowboarders. Paul led me down a hallway and stopped at a closed door. He took out a card and scanned it, like at a hotel, and opened the door, allowing me to enter first.

The room wasn't big; it reminded me of an extremely large walk-in closet. Snowboards lined the wall in every color and design. Several more boards leaned by wooden benches, which were covered in ski jackets, pants, sweatshirts, hats and almost every accessory one could imagine. In the corner I could see more boxes piled up.

"Moving?" I motioned toward the boxes.

"No. I share this cubby space with some of the guys… you know, Scott, Davie and Trip. It's part of our membership here, and these are free samples and products from various sponsors or companies trying to sponsor one of us. Honestly, I don't really pay attention to it all—help yourself to anything," he said, watching me closely.

"Where are your friends?" I asked, wandering over to the boxes; I saw labels from Nike, Under Armour, Burton, NorthFace, Patagonia, Vans and even Guardian Apparel.

"Trip and Davie are back in California. Scott is somewhere in Europe. We all used to compete against each other regularly. We couldn't stand each other then, but now we all have our own interests and every couple of weeks those interests seem to intersect. It's much more manageable this way," he commented.

"So you are retired?" I asked, before thinking through the question.

"Mostly, I don't compete on the national teams or for the Olympic team anymore. Occasionally, I will still ride in the X Games or exhibition games, but that is happening less and less. Mostly I judge competitions, commentate for ESPN, do some odds and ends for sponsors…you know," he said with a wave of his hand.

"Not really," I mumbled to myself, pulling out several items that would work, and then I changed in the bathroom. When I emerged Paul was also dressed and putting on his boots. I scrunched my forehead in confusion. He may have extra clothes, but I didn't think he would have equipment to fit my size; I didn't see any skis lying around. While he finished getting ready, I looked away so as not to stare. Instead I found myself looking at the snowboards hanging on the wall when he suddenly came up behind me and pushed me, causing me to stumble forward.

"What the heck is wrong with you?" I shouted after regaining my balance.

"You're goofy footed," he said as a way of explanation.

"I know I'm goofy footed...you could have just asked," I said in exasperation. In snowboarding there were two stances: regular stance, which was the most popular, where the rider rides with the left foot forward on the board; and goofy footed, which was the opposite, where the rider's right foot goes forward. I had learned this from Stefan when we had gone snowboarding once, many years ago. He was a regular stance, but both Hayden Grace and I were goofy footed. Pushing someone from behind causes them to catch themselves with their dominant foot and is an easy way to determine how a snowboarder might ride. Clearly my exasperation had no effect on Paul, as he was already seated on the wooden bench tinkering with the bindings of a snowboard.

"I don't suppose you have a set of skis hidden anywhere in here?" I asked after a moment.

"What for?"

"For me?"

"I thought that you might snowboard with me?" he asked, looking at me almost innocently, standing up and leaning the board he had been working on towards me.

"I'm not a very good snowboarder." I hesitated before taking it from him.

"I find that hard to believe, but don't worry if that is, in fact, true. I am an excellent teacher," he said, glancing down in the cupboards under the bench. "I think these should fit," he said, pulling out a black pair of snowboard boots.

"Wow, you have everything you could ever need up here," I commented.

146

"Not everything," he replied, looking at me. Unable to keep his stare long, I sighed and looked at the board I was holding, resigned to the fact that I would not be on skis today.

"As a warning, the most patient of people have tried to teach me, only to regret that decision later." I thought of the two times Stefan had tried oh-so-very-hard to teach me how to snowboard. The first was right after we had met. He was cavalier in the way he rode, and I was unable to back down from a challenge. We were out on the mountain on a misty Sunday in February, and he asked me to board with him. I was just cocky enough at the time that I thought anyone could do it. It turns out that *not* anyone can do it. Stefan started out patiently with me, explaining the mechanics and the process. But the more I fell, the more frustrated he got. By the end, I was sore and bruised physically, and I think he was tired and bruised mentally. In the end Stefan agreed that I should just stick to my skis for the sake of our relationship. The second time was later, after Hayden Grace was born – when she took up snowboarding like her dad. They would always chide me and try to get me on a board. I was able to fend them off for a while, but eventually the heckling got to me, and I tried again. The second time was much like the first; it started out smoothly. Hayden Grace raced around me while I stood on the board, and even when I glided only a little, she cheered me on. Stefan urged me to take bigger risks, and things were going well until I hit a huge patch of ice and the board came out from under me. Unable to catch myself, I braced myself with my arms as I came crashing down. The pain was immediate and intense; I could feel the break just above my wrist. Hayden Grace started crying right away, and Stefan lost his cool between his hysterical daughter and injured wife. I even remember yelling at him that, and I quote, 'I never want to ride another stupid snowboard as long as I live.' 'Now I guess life has a way of surprising us,' I thought to myself as I stared at my boots.

"Snowboarding is more than just the technical lesson; it's about embracing the motion," he said as he paced the room, pausing to look at the boots sitting next to me which I continued to stare at. "Need help?"

"Sorry, I was just thinking back to the last time I tried this…it didn't end well," I practically whispered.

"Andy, you will be fine, you just need to relax," he said, standing in front of me.

"You really love what you do," I commented after a moment, sighing to myself in defeat and sliding into the boots.

"I wouldn't do it otherwise." It was a simple response, but it made me see him more clearly and understand his seemingly unwavering passion.

"Ready?" he said, holding out his hand.

"As I'm ever going to be," I said, reaching out and grasping his.

***

We made it out of the lodge and walked down to a smaller private flat area on the other side of the lodge. Paul helped me into my bindings and let me move around the area as I slowly tried to remember the pointers from Stefan's two lessons. I hit a small patch of ice almost immediately, and my instantaneous sensation was to pull my other leg around; however, with both legs being on the board, I quickly lost my balance and flopped onto my back with an unceremonious oomph. All those feelings of uncertainty, anxiety and fear crept back into my mind. Leaning up on my elbows, I could see Paul shaking with laughter as he tried to hold it in.

"Go ahead, laugh. I warned you," I said, flopping back down.

"No, it's okay. I just expected a little more grace after watching you ski," he commented, gliding over and putting out his hands to help me up.

"You would think, but no," I said, standing back up. He spent the next hour running through basic technique and function with me. It was all things I had seen snowboarders do a million times, but it was very slow going for me. To his credit he kept his patience, as promised. At one point he stood his board up in the snow and literally walked me through the motions.

"I think you're ready," he said at the end of the hour.

"Ready for what?" I asked in confusion.

"The mountain," he said, adjusting his equipment.

"But is the mountain ready for me?" I asked, trying to hide my extreme anxiety about the situation.

"You'll be fine. Just take your time, and if you need anything, I'll be right there," he said, flashing a small grin. He was so sincere, and I believed him. For the second time today, butterflies danced around in my stomach, but this time I knew it was nerves as we glided over to an intermediate trail.

"Couldn't we start at the bunny hill?" I asked meekly.

"It's a little late for that," he said, waiting for me to go first. I took a deep breath and started down the mountain. The first part of the trail was steep, and I was very cautious in my descent. True to his word, Paul never passed me or pushed me to go faster. He was able to catch me a couple times as I struggled with some of my transitions. I grew frustrated thinking about how quickly this would have gone with my skis and about half way down, with my calves and thighs screaming at me in pain and my stomach in knots, I swerved off to the side of the trail and bent over with my hands on my knees.

"Everything okay?" he asked, coming up next to me.

"Frustrated," I said, glancing at him and back down to the snow, trying to catch my breath.

"You're thinking too much, and it's causing you to work too hard. I've seen you scale the backcountry without even getting winded, and this is making you tired? I don't buy it. What's going on?" he asked, leaning over and getting close to me. His hand rested on my shoulder.

"I'm scared," I finally said.

"Of what?"

"Letting go." Once I said it, I knew it meant so much more.

"You don't have to let it go… just let it come to you. You know the basics…you know the snow…so trust yourself," he said, leaning back. I thought about what he said and knew he was right. Paul had been nothing but patient, and I wasn't being fair. What happened in the past shouldn't dictate my current situation. Snowboarding just felt so foreign to me, but I had truly never given it a chance.

"Okay," I said after a few minutes, getting up on my own this time.

"Alright," he said, waiting for me. I waved him on first and followed behind. I watched how fluid his movements were and how it had become second nature, like breathing or walking. I took another deep breath and closed my eyes, just for a second, sinking down a little deeper into my stance. I cleared my mind and let my body flow into the gentle back and forth movements as we glided down the mountain. Paul had slowed down a little so that we were now riding side by side as we neared the end of the trail. He was right—if I didn't think about it, it was a much more fluid movement. The more I relaxed, the less my calves and thighs screamed at me; the movement let me regulate my breathing and soon the movement was easy to recognize as I let it take over. Towards the very end I got bolder in my riding and took a turn much faster than I meant to, and I hit a patch of ice and tumbled forward.

"Andy!" Paul shouted. He was soon by my side looking worried. I took one look at him and started laughing. After a moment, he realized I was okay and started to laugh as well.

"That was really great towards the bottom," he said, finally helping me up. "Should we go again?" he asked, flashing me a wide grin.

"Why not?" I said, matching his grin with one of my own. We rode the gondola back up to the top and like last time, we were moved to the front of the line and given a private booth, only causing me to shake my head in disbelief. The ride up was much more satisfying after having ridden down, I realized. We rode another trail, and then another, and then one more. With each run my confidence grew, and I got a little bolder with my turns and my speed.

We had just reached the bottom after my fourth run when I felt my phone vibrate in my pocket. Pulling off my gloves, I reached my numb fingers into my jacket, grabbing the phone. I had one missed call and a text message from Hayden Grace. She was letting me know she was done with practice and wanted to meet up for dinner. I quickly texted her back, asking where she was; she responded immediately indicating the bottom of the Silver Queen Gondola where I had dropped her off. I scanned the crowd and saw her and the girls standing off to the side.

"Something wrong?" Paul asked, standing beside me.

"I have to go back to being a parent. It's time to feed the teenager," I said, pointing to Hayden Grace and her friends.

"Let me take you both to dinner," he said, quickly as if he wasn't ready for the day to end just yet. Secretly I knew I wasn't ready for the day to end either. Trying to hide my grin, I focused on the girls.

"I don't think Hayden Grace would mind, but let's ask her," I said, and he nodded. We glided down to where the girls were standing. I watched as confusion, and then surprise registered on their faces as we approached.

"Mom…? Mom!" Hayden Grace exclaimed, rushing toward me and knocking me over.

"So much for being graceful," I mumbled, and she laughed.

"You're on a snowboard…how in the world…?" she said, pausing and looking up, finally noticing my instructor.

"Paul?" she asked, and he nodded, pulling up his goggles. I could hear Lucie and Madison whispering to each other in excitement as they came to stand with us. "How did you get her on a snowboard? My dad and I tried for years," she said, clearly impressed – not by my new ability, but by his persuasion. He just shrugged casually. She finally stood up, allowing me to do the same.

"What are you ladies doing for dinner?" I asked Lucie, Madison and Hayden Grace.

"We have to meet up with our parents," Lucie and Madison lamented. "We were just waiting with Hayden Grace until you got here," Lucie added as an explanation. The girls begrudgingly waved goodbye to Paul and headed off down the block.

"I was hoping to take you both to dinner," Paul said once Lucie and Madison left. Hayden Grace's eyes got big, and she hesitated.

"Mom, I was hoping to go to that thing around eight," she mumbled in code. The party that wasn't a party at the Poppycock's, I remembered.

"We will be done in plenty of time," I said as Paul raised his eyebrows in a question.

"Okay great! I'm starving," she said as we walked back over to the gondola. Hayden Grace talked non-stop as we headed up to the summit to change and drop off the equipment. She talked about practice, the competition and of course, the pipe. Paul chimed in occasionally, but for the most part we just let her ramble on. Once in the lodge Hayden Grace was in awe of everything. She asked Paul questions about every single thing in the locker room while I changed. When Paul went to change, she ambushed me with another set of questions.

"So Mom… do tell," she whispered.

"Tell what?" I whispered back.

"Was this pre-arranged?"

"No, he saw me in the coffee shop window in town. It was completely by chance," I replied. She was skeptical, but kept quiet as Paul emerged.

"Shall we," he said, motioning for the door. We descended down the mountain in the gondola and headed to Brody's Tavern, a small restaurant several blocks away. As I was learning was customary when in the company of a certain well-known athlete, we were seated quickly and away from the main room. Dinner was good and the conversation flowed naturally between the three of us. Hayden Grace asked me in detail how the snowboarding was, Paul asked her how practice was going since he last saw her compete and I asked how her friends Madison and Lucie were doing. I had noticed that things seemed a little strained between the three of them since arriving in Aspen. Normally, in a situation like today, she would have asked to join them for dinner, but instead, insisted on separating herself. She told me things were 'fine', but that Madison and Lucie were acting different. I decided not to press what she meant by 'different' to avoid a fight at dinner. It was about 7:45 when I noticed she began to fidget in her seat.

"Hayden Grace, we are almost done and then I will walk you over to Poppycock's," I said, and she nodded. Again, I could tell Paul had questions, but kept them to himself as we finished up dinner. We were standing outside of the restaurant, and I was about to thank Paul for the snowboarding lessons and dinner, when Hayden Grace chimed in.

"Paul, would you walk me and my mom over to Poppycock's?" she asked in a hushed tone. Surprise crossed his face, but he recovered quickly.

"Not a problem," he said and pointed us in the right direction. The walk was mostly quiet except for the random questions Hayden Grace continued to ask about Aspen. It amazed me that she had any questions left at this point, but her curiosity seemed boundless.

"Mom, do you mind if I go in by myself?" she asked when we reached the door.

"No, that's fine. We should be heading back to the hotel around ten. You have a full day tomorrow," I commented, and she nodded in agreement.

"Thank you, Paul," she said, surprising both of us again as she embraced him in a quick hug and went inside.

"What was that about?" he finally asked.

"A boy," I said simply, and he nodded in some understanding. We stood idly outside Poppycock's as I watched through the window. Hayden Grace had already spotted Jonathan and walked right over and tapped him on the shoulder; he turned and smiled when he saw her. He started introducing her to the ten or twelve people that were already there, and they all started chatting away. I sighed in relief and turned to Paul.

"Thank you so much for a great day," I said, meeting his gaze. His eyes never ceased to leave me a little breathless.

"It's not over yet. I think from the schedule you gave Hayden Grace, I have you for at least two more hours." His enthusiasm caught me off guard, and I just smiled.

"What would you like to do?" I asked as we started to meander down the block.

"Nope, you're the guest," he commented. I thought about it for a moment before finally answering. "Do you ever get to play tourist in the towns you visit?"

"Rarely, it's mostly all about the mountain and boarding," he said in a serious tone.

"Okay, then let's do the touristy things you haven't done. I saw an ice rink earlier today," I said in a playful tone.

"Done," he said, suddenly turning me down another street, until we stood in front of the Silver Circle Ice Rink.

"Come on, it's equal ground for both of us," I said, pulling him forward, sensing he might be having a change of heart. We waited in line like normal people and rented two pairs of skates when it was our turn. It was only a matter of time, like at the coffee shop, before I could hear the murmurs from people around us as we waited for our skate time.

"Are you really oblivious to it all," I whispered to him.

"To what?" he asked, confused by my question.

"The whispers and stares?"

"Not oblivious, but I try hard to not let it affect me. The stares…the whispers…nothing lasts forever; it has died down some since I stopped competing so much. Plus, I still have my own life to live," he said as the women called our number. I have to admit we were a bit of a mess on the ice. At least I had skated

155

when I was kid, but Paul said he had never been skating. We were slipping and falling down, only to help each other up, just to fall down again. I had never laughed so hard in my life; at one point I was sure I had tears in my eyes. Little children were doing laps around us as we inched our way around the ice. While we attempted to skate, a novelty photographer skated around and asked us if we wanted our picture taken. At first I refused, but Paul insisted and in the end we got our photo snapped. At the end of our time, we made our way over to the gate and returned our skates. Paul bought a copy of the photo and handed it over to me, which I slipped into my pocket. He called it a 'memento' of our time together. Several kids finally worked up the courage to ask Paul for a photo before we left the rink. He looked at me as if to make sure I was okay with the distraction and that I wouldn't wander away like I did last time. I waved my hand at him indicating it was fine and stepped off to the side while he took photos with several different groups.

"It only really happens in ski towns," he explained after we left the rink, as we made our way down the street.

"What does?" I asked in confusion.

"The whispers and the stares you mentioned earlier. Put me in the middle of New York or LA and no one knows who I am—it's just these competitions and towns," he said, shrugging his shoulders. We still had about forty-five minutes before I had to get Hayden Grace. We stopped at a local shop, where we both got coffee and decided to split a large chocolate chip cookie, as we wandered the streets. I was finally beginning to feel more familiar with Aspen as I started to recognize shops and streets, much to my delight.

"What happened to Hayden Grace's father?" Paul asked after a lull in conversation. I glanced at him before replying. I had told the story a hundred times, but this time, telling Paul felt different.

"He died serving his country, six years ago," I said, glancing up to the sky.

"I'm so sorry," Paul said. I glanced at him, and I could see his genuine concern.

"Don't be. He died fighting for something he strongly believed in," I said almost automatically.

"Doesn't make it any easier," he commented, and I was slow to agree.

"How did you meet?" he asked after another minute.

"We met on a ski mountain, where else?" I said with a chuckle. "We shared a chair lift. I was practicing for a competition, similar to the Regional 6, and he and his buddies were there for the day. It was just one of those chance meetings, but after the meeting he just kinda stuck with me, you know?" I said, looking at Paul.

"More than you can imagine," he said, looking off in the distance. I glanced at my watch and saw it was almost ten.

"I need to get Hayden Grace," I said, and Paul nodded, directing us back to Poppycock's, saying little. I let him stew in his own head, knowing that he was working through something. I could see Hayden Grace standing by the front window, and I knocked on the glass, startling her. I chuckled to myself again, over my action. It was the same action Paul had done to me earlier in the day, and it seemed that only in Aspen did occurrences like these actually seem to present themselves. Hayden Grace came outside, and Jonathan followed closely behind her.

"Mom, I wanted you to meet Jonathan," she said, introducing me.

"Ma'am," he said politely, shaking my hand.

"Andy is fine," I replied with a small smile. I could tell by looking at

Hayden Grace, she was already completely smitten.

"Is this your dad?" Jonathan whispered to Hayden Grace as Paul stood next to me still lost in his own thoughts, causing Hayden Grace to giggle.

"No, this is Paul," she said, trying to clear her throat to capture his attention.

"OMG, it's PW," he said with delayed recognition and surprise. On cue over having his name mentioned Paul suddenly snapped to attention. Jonathan and Paul shook hands, while Jonathan stood wide-eyed. Hayden Grace gave Jonathan a quick hug and waved before we continued down the street towards the car.

"How was the infamous Poppycock's?" Paul asked after several moments.

"It was good. There are so many kids my age here, and Mom, did you know they have a snowboarding school?" she said with excitement. I was glad it was dark out so she couldn't see my eye roll, but somehow Paul didn't miss my gesture and let out a low chuckle.

"You don't need those schools Hayden Grace. You just need the mountain, your determination and passion. From what I've seen you have all three of those things already; that school won't teach you anything you don't already know," he commented. Deep down I was so grateful—I knew she wouldn't listen to me, but there was a good chance Paul's words would make it through to her. She looked at him with her head slightly tilted to the side as the advice sunk in. When we reached the car, Hayden Grace said goodnight to Paul and climbed into the car, quickly pulling out her phone and instantly starting to text; I didn't need three guesses to figure out who it was.

"Thank you for a completely unexpected day," I said, looking at Paul. In the glow of the streetlamp he looked like a sullen teenage, and I couldn't help but smile.

"What?" he asked defensively.

"You look like you're pouting."

"It has been a good day, hasn't it?" he asked and finally smiled, and we stood there for an awkward moment before Hayden Grace knocked on the glass inside the car.

"Mom, we have to go," she said, getting impatient.

"That's my cue," I said.

"Will I see you again?" he asked after a moment.

"I'm not sure...Hayden Grace has a lot going on," he nodded in understanding, but I knew it was a bit of a cowardly excuse. I could easily make the time if I wanted to, and part of me really wanted to see him again—those blue eyes had a pull I couldn't explain. But the sensible part of me was wary of Paul and how it would only lead to heartbreak. Like our last departure, Paul leaned over and kissed me on the cheek before retreating down the street. It took me another moment before I was able to get into the car as I savored the moment.

CHAPTER 16

Hayden Grace had to report early the next morning as she had drawn one of the first qualifying rounds. That morning there had been a flurry of activity as Hayden Grace raced around the room getting ready while also trying to eat breakfast and field texts on her phone. I finally took her phone away and helped her find Stefan's bandana which had somehow ended up under the bed, finally getting us out the door only a couple of minutes late. Now I sat in the grandstands as her wave of girls got ready. There were other competitions going on at the same times and occasionally I would hear cheers and excitement coming from different areas. I had a good view of the leader board so I could watch the scores coming in from the various competitions and already this early there seemed to be major upsets in different events, as I shamelessly eavesdropped on the people around me. Hayden Grace had told me that both Madison and Lucie had drawn a later qualifying round so they wouldn't be riding together today, but that fact didn't seem to upset her. I couldn't tell for sure, but I felt like I was witnessing the beginning of the end of those tight bonds between the girls. They had been so close for the last couple of years, but as they grew, their priorities started to change and each girl was going in a different direction. I wondered how Hayden Grace would handle the change, or if she would notice as they drifted apart.

My nerves increased as I watched Hayden Grace inch her way up in line, until it was finally her turn. I could see her perched at the top with a serious look on her face; Ron came up to her and said some last minute words of advice. She paused for a moment and patted the side of her jacket in what I knew to be a nervous tick, but it was also where the patches I had sewn in now were—then they announced her name. And just like that she headed into the pipe of her first national competition. I fought back tears, of pride and sadness, that Stefan wasn't there to witness it. She planned the same routine as she had done back at Mount Sunapee, but she felt she had more height and precision since then, as she explained in the car ride over. She dropped into the pipe, and her first trick was solid. I held my breath; the second trick she had a bit of a bobble, and I covered my eyes with hands as I peeked through the cracks, but she was able to recover. Her next two tricks were executed well, and I knew going into her last trick that as long as she landed it, she would have a pretty good chance. She went up and twisted two full rotations and came down in a clean landing. The stands erupted in cheers, and I exhaled. One run down.

As I waited for the second run, I could hear whispers around me, and I wondered what was going on. I even looked around to see if Paul was near, as the phenomenon only really happened when he was present. Not seeing him, I focused back on the competition. Everyone was now on their second run; the first two girls both wiped out and had not scored high enough to qualify for the finals. They were both in tears at the bottom of the pipe with their parents trying to console them as they quietly walked off into the crowds. I had been there before, and I did not pity what their parents had to go through at this moment. The next girl landed all her tricks, but her difficulty was low and her score reflected that. Another surge of excitement rippled through the crowd, but this time it was over something that was happening at the top of the pipe. Looking at the jumbo-tron, I saw Coach Davis, Hayden Grace and Paul. My heart sank, and my jaw dropped opened. 'What the heck was going on?' I wondered. His appearance electrified the audience and announcers. I could hear them over the loud speaker talk about his many accomplishments, and they speculated if he would participate in this year's X Games. Then they flashed a picture up on the screen, and my heart stopped. It was a picture of Paul and me at the ice skating rink from last night. Under the picture scrawled the words, "PW's New Snow Bunny?" I sank down lower in my seat, hoping that no one would recognize me. Again, they showed Paul and Coach Davis shaking hands, giving Hayden Grace a high-five and then Paul disappearing into the tent and from view of the camera. The murmur in the crowd continued after the announcer had moved on to the next competitor. Hayden Grace was three competitors away from her second run. The next girl came down and landed a really good run, which she needed because she had wiped out during her first run.

The whispers around me continued as people started to glance in my direction. Looking through my bag, I pulled out my knitted beanie hoping to discourage any onlookers. My anxiety started to climb as the next girl got ready to complete her second run. She hit the pipe hard and was going higher than any of the girls. She was a great rider but hit the coping or lip of the pipe on her last trick and slammed into the wall, a move I was all too familiar with having watched Hayden Grace do it in the past. The crowds went silent as we all watched in horror. Finally, after what seemed like forever, she slowly stirred and was sitting up by the time medical personnel made it over to her. They were taking their time evaluating her when I noticed a lady several rows down from me who kept turning around and staring at me. Hayden Grace was one competitor away from her second run.

"You're being paranoid, Andy," I muttered to myself, but took my sunglasses out of my bag and put them on for good measure. The next girl was one of the youngest competitors, according to the leader board, and she was good. Like the girl before her she had height on her tricks, but unlike the girl before her she finished her run, putting herself in first place. The crowd was going wild, and the camera panned over to a couple I assumed were her parents, who were crying with joy. The lady in the front row turned around again to look at me, and then snapped a quick photo of me with her phone. My heart skipped a beat, but continued to speed up at the same time. Thinking that the people around me could hear the loud thumping my heart was making, I took a deep breath trying to calm myself. Hayden Grace was next.

I could see Hayden Grace talking with Ron, and then they called her name and she got into position. She patted her jacket again and paused at the top. Between the whispers and Hayden Grace, I felt like the walls were closing in on me. I tried to breath, but it wasn't working. The pipe was 160 meters long, and her routine would take less than one minute…but it would feel like a lifetime. She looked up, and I imagined her talking to her dad but then in an instant she was heading full steam at the pipe. She dropped into the pipe a little higher than she normally does, and she was riding with an intensity that she often lacked. She hit her first trick and soared high. She landed cleanly and set herself up for the next trick. The lady in the front row turned around again and started to make her way up the bleachers towards me. I tried to focus on Hayden Grace. Her next trick was executed well, and she cruised into her third trick. She switched up her next trick, and instead of doing the Japan Air, she did the Backside 720 which was previously her last trick. Finally, setting up for her last trick, she went up….rotated around two and half times…it was the Frontside 900 she had been working on right before we left for Aspen…came down on the inside wall…and…she…landed…it. The stands erupted in applause; I saw her on the leader board throwing her arms in the air with excitement. I exhaled as I stood to clap and cheer, wiping the tears from my eyes.

The lady from the bleachers was now just moments away from approaching me. Frantically, I grabbed all my stuff and exited off the other side of the grandstand, as complete panic set in. I didn't know where to go; I needed to get to Hayden Grace, but when I got down from the bleachers, my instinct told me to head to the exit. As I headed for the exit I heard more whispers and someone ask:

"Isn't that the snow bunny?" I cringed and tried to move faster through the crowd.

"Excuse me! Entertainment TV; can I have a moment of your time?" It was the lady from the bleachers, and she was behind me now. I could feel the minor shift in the crowd as people began to point and realize what was going on. I could also hear the announcers announce the next competitor about to take the pipe. It was all happening so fast, yet slowly in the same moment. I was close to the exit, maybe another fifteen yards—'I could make it,' I thought to myself, picking up the pace. Suddenly, a strong arm wrapped itself around my waist, stopping my motion, causing me to inhale sharply.

"I got you," Paul whispered into my ear as he pulled me into his chest. Tears sprang from my eyes as my breathing became more erratic; my vision was getting blurry. I heard some more commotion around me, and soon he was leading me in a different direction. He had one arm around my shoulders and the other was up blocking any camera flashes – but more importantly, blocking people's faces as we went straight under a rope and into a draped tent. I was immediately instructed to sit and put my head down and take large, deep breaths. I did as I was told, and gradually my breathing slowed, causing my pulse to slow and the tears to stop.

"Andy, are you okay?" Paul crouched down in front of me with a look of concern.

"What just happened?" I asked when I was able to put coherent thoughts together.

"You just had a panic attack," another voice said. I squinted in his direction and saw a red jacket with a white cross and knew he was a medic. "Are they common?" he asked as a follow up, and I shook my head.

"First one," I whispered, wiping the last of the tears from my cheeks. As my mind raced to catch up on the events that just occurred, another wave of panic washed through me. "Hayden Grace," I said, trying to stand.

"Relax, she is fine. There are still three or four riders to go, and she is sitting pretty strong in second place," Paul explained, and I nodded. I discovered it was easier at the moment to nod than to try and carry a conversation. The medic watched me for a couple more minutes before he declared that I was fine and strode out of the tent.

"Andy, I'm so sorry," he said, grabbing my hands. "I didn't even think that picture from last night would make its way to the media. It's the life I deal with—it shouldn't be yours," he barely breathed. My thoughts weren't fully functioning, as I was putting the events back together.

"No, it's....it's just I never...how did you...?" I lied... my thoughts were not together.

"I saw the picture on the jumbo-tron from the top of the pipe, and I knew they would come after you. I didn't have your number, and I had no idea where you were sitting. I made my way down to the bottom just in case, and by the time I made it, I followed the excitement," he said, running his hands through his hair and sighing in exasperation.

"Hayden Grace," I mumbled again, and he nodded. He opened the tent flap, and I could see the leader board. There was one more girl to ride, but Hayden Grace was still in second place. "I could feel them moving in, but I couldn't move – not until I saw Hayden Grace ride...," I paused and looked at him in horror. "Are they going to go after her next?"

"They don't know your name, and they certainly don't know she is connected to you. You should be safe," he mumbled, clearly frustrated by the situation. I heard applause outside the tent, and I peeked out again to see the last girl had finished her run, but her score was only good enough for third place. Hayden Grace finished second. This automatically advanced her to the final on Thursday.

"I should go to her," I said, but just the thought of leaving was causing my blood pressure to rise.

"Let me leave first. Give it about five to ten minutes and you should be fine," he said, grabbing a jacket from the table I hadn't noticed.

"Where are you going?" I asked, horrified at the idea of him having to face a situation like that.

"I'll be fine," he said, clearly reading the expression on my face. "I have to go judge the men's first qualifying round." He started to leave and then realization washed over him.

"Andy, where is your phone?" he asked, coming back to stand by me. I reached into my coat jacket, pulled it out, and handed it to him. He punched something in and handed it back to me.

"My number," he said, answering my unspoken question. He rushed out of the tent before I could answer. I waited in the tent another ten minutes before I peeped out. As promised, most of the crowd had moved. Looking at the jumbo-tron, I saw Paul and several other individuals taking their place at the judges table. This was my chance; I took a deep breath and bolted out the door in search of Hayden Grace.

CHAPTER 17

It took me a moment to find Hayden Grace after leaving the tent. She was off to the side of the pipe, surrounded by a crowd of people I didn't recognize. As I pushed my way through the small group, I saw her face light up when she finally saw me.

"Mom! Did you see?" she asked as we embraced in a big hug.

"I wouldn't have missed it for the world. Congratulations!" I whispered in her ear.

"Guess what?"

"What?"

"Paul stopped by the top to see me," she rushed with excitement.

"Oh?" I asked, trying to be surprised.

"He was wishing me luck," she added.

"Is that all?" I casually asked, as I tried to move Hayden Grace from the crowd.

"No, he had a bit of advice for me. He told me I was entering the pipe too early and to go in higher. Coach Davis didn't think I should try that on a qualifying run, but I did it anyway," she beamed at me, finally taking a breath.

"You did amazing," I commented, remembering the scene at the top of the mountain.

"Mrs. Parker?" someone said from behind me, causing me to cringe slightly hoping that it wasn't a reporter.

"Yes," I said, slowly turning around, still holding onto Hayden Grace.

"My name is Gary Levinston, and I represent Monster energy drinks. What we saw today from Hayden Grace really impressed us. It's hard to believe she isn't sponsored yet. We would be really interested in sitting down and talking." He reached into his pocket and handed me a business card. I simply nodded. I could see Hayden Grace's eyes get real big next to me as he spoke. As he walked away, we were approached by three other sponsors from Vans, NorthFace and Burton—all handing over business cards with similar statements about Hayden Grace. The woman from Burton also invited us to a party later in the week, which caused Hayden Grace to squeal quietly next to me. Once we finally walked away, I could tell we were both overwhelmed with all the information.

"Mom, can you believe this?" Hayden Grace finally whispered.

"Of course, you have worked so hard for all of it," I said with a smile. "But you still have a long way to go…it's about the ending, not the beginning, as your dad would say," I said more softly, and she nodded solemnly. We still hadn't made it very far when my phone rang. Glancing down, I gave a slight frown.

"Hayden Grace, it's work, I need to take this."

"That's cool. Jonathan's round is about to start—do you mind if I go watch?" she asked, pointing further down to a crowded area.

"No, that's fine," I said, and she practically skipped over to the spectator area. I sighed answering the call. "Malinda, how surprising to hear from you," I commented dryly, wandering over to an unoccupied area.

"Hayden Grace is doing very well," she said without a proper greeting.

"Yes, she is," I said, unsure of what she wanted.

"Well, naturally the answer is yes, but I have another question for you," she said, confusing me. I felt like I had missed part of a conversation.

"Wait...yes to what?" I asked.

"Yes, Angel Apparel will be her major sponsor. Seriously Andrea, you need to catch up."

"Malinda, I don't..."

"But that's not why I called," she said, interrupting me.

"Really, I think Hayden Grace should..."

"I see you are cozy with Paul Westcott," she said, interrupting me again.

"What?" I asked again—this conversation was becoming harder and harder to follow. I rubbed my temples, trying to understand what was going on.

"The picture of the two of you—it's all over the internet. Really Andrea, you could have told me that you knew him," she said, clearly irritated with me.

"I don't...," her statement caused me to pause. Did I *know* Paul Westcott?

"I've been trying to land him as a client for Guardian Apparel since day one. He would be huge for the company, Andrea," she rambled on as if I hadn't been trying to talk. "Andrea, I need you to convince him to sign with Guardian. If you can do that, I will give you the vice president of marketing position." She paused, waiting for a response.

"Isn't that position filled?" was all I could muster.

"I will *unfill* it," she replied in a monotone.

"Malinda, I don't know Paul Westcott that well. I don't feel comfortable approaching him about this…"

"Andrea, let me make myself clear. You get Paul Westcott to sign with Guardian Apparel, or you can forget about working for the company," she said softly in a sinister way, and hung up the phone. I felt the phone vibrate in my hand. Glancing I could see that she had already sent me the proposed sponsorship contract for Paul Westcott. 'What the hell just happened?' I thought to myself, staring at my phone. I needed someone to pinch me. Two weeks ago I was living a life I was familiar with, a life I was comfortable with…and now – now I didn't know what to do. I stood there in the same spot for a while as I tried to process everything. My phone vibrating in my hand brought me back to the present. It was Drew texting me with his flight and estimated arrival; I texted him back as we arranged a meeting spot, and set off to find Hayden Grace.

To her credit, she was right where she said she would be. She was glued to her spot, watching the leader board and the standings. I actually startled her when I walked up to her.

"He's in third place, and he needs a good run to place," she whispered to me.

"Why are we whispering?" I whispered back, glancing at the leader board to see that Jonathan was racing in the slalom.

"This is nerve-wracking," she said, looking up at me.

"Now you know what it's like to watch you," I commented, giving her a tight squeeze. She looked at me intently and then back to the board.

"That bad?" she questioned.

"It's the worst," I said, looking at her. "But I wouldn't trade it for the world." She smiled at my comment, and we watched the rest of the competitors in silence. In the end, Jonathan finished third, but qualified for the finals on Friday. After texting Jonathan to congratulate him on his run, Hayden Grace decided she wanted to go back to the hotel and clean up. We would return to the mountain that evening to watch Lucie and Madison in the last qualifying run of the day.

***

When we returned to the mountain later, it was exponentially more crowded than it had been earlier. I quickly learned that Aspen had a larger night life than I could have ever imagined. People were everywhere just milling around—live bands placed under heated tents and everyone was in a good mood—the feeling was easily contagious. We found an open spot on the grandstand to watch Lucie and Madison. I wasn't at all surprised that Jonathan happened to run into us, and Hayden Grace happened to invite him to sit with us. I actually found Jonathan's company refreshing compared to that of Lucie and Madison. At least he didn't shriek and burst into giggles every ten minutes. For most of the competition Hayden Grace and Jonathan sat close, leaning in and talking to each other quietly. This left me to myself, and I took the opportunity to watch the crowds around me. Part of me was keeping an eye out for the crazy reporter from this morning, but in general I just liked to watch how people reacted to the riding—this was such a larger competition than I could have imagined. Occasionally, I did see people looking in my direction and whispering, but they quickly moved on and never bothered me. Hayden Grace stopped to cheer for Lucie and Madison during each of their runs, but otherwise was oblivious to everything around her. A sad smile crossed my face, knowing we would be leaving in a couple days and not knowing if she would ever see Jonathan again.

Overall, the final qualifying runs were pretty exciting for this group. Everyone was pretty equal as far as skill, but it came down to execution and completion. Lucie, for example, fell on both of her runs and did not qualify for the finals. Madison had one solid run and fell on her second run, but came in second place overall, thus qualifying for the finals. I felt bad for Lucie's dad afterwards, as he tried to console his daughter who was heartbroken. I saw Lisa embrace Madison, and they both giggled with excitement and jumped up and down. We waited for the crowds to thin, and Hayden Grace went over to talk to both girls while Jonathan headed out, explaining that he had dinner plans with his family. After ten or fifteen minutes Hayden Grace jogged back over—excitement danced in her eyes.

"Hey Mom," she tried to say casually.

"Hey Hayden Grace," I said, eyeing her suspiciously.

"Madison and Lucie invited me to stay with them in their suite tonight so we can hang out. Would that be okay?" She looked at me, full of anticipation.

"Sure, of course," I said, slightly hurt at being abandoned for the evening. "What about your stuff?" I asked, thinking of her schedule in the morning.

"I'll just text you the list of things I need?" she asked, slightly pleading with me.

"The finals are tomorrow Hayden Grace," I said, trying to stress the importance of tomorrow, without stressing it too much.

"I know. We are just going to watch movies. Lucie and her dad decided to leave early tomorrow morning, so it will be our last night together." Gosh, she looked so hopeful; I sighed in defeat.

"In bed by eleven," I said, and she nodded.

"Thanks Mom!" She hugged me quickly and ran back over to the girls and was greeted with those familiar squeals of excitement. I was about to turn and leave when she ran back over to me. "Mom, where are you going?" she asked in confusion.

"To the hotel," I replied, with equal confusion of my own.

"We are all going to do dinner together, and *then* I was going to spend the night," she said, pulling on my sleeve.

"Of course, why didn't I understand that in the first place," I replied in a mutter. Secretly, I was excited to be able to share in some of their excitement. Given the way the day had gone, I should have anticipated the evening would be anything less than eventful.

CHAPTER 18

Lisa decided everyone was too tired to venture into town for dinner and instead we should eat at the Trecento Quindici Decano at the St. Regis. Protesting slightly that Hayden Grace and I did not have attire to eat at such a fine establishment, Lisa dismissed my claim and shut down my argument immediately. Once we got to the hotel Madison led the way directly to the restaurant and asked to be seated. The waiter took her name and said that some of our party had already arrived. Confusion crossed the faces of nearly everyone with us; Lisa gave me a quick wink as we followed the waiter to a private room.

"Daddy...Laura," I heard Madison yell in surprise. I froze as my heart dropped into my stomach. I saw his figure from the back. He was wearing jeans and a bulky navy sweater, but I recognized his salt n' pepper hair immediately.

"Mom, are you okay?" Hayden Grace whispered to me, and I nodded. Lisa walked over to her husband and gave him a kiss on the cheek and half a hug. I nearly threw up watching the scene unfold. It was like a bad train wreck, and I couldn't make myself run in the other direction. Gregg shook Lucie's dad's hand, and Lucie gave a short little wave as she sat down next to Madison. She was still sullen over the results of the event.

"Gregg, have you ever met Hayden Grace's Mom?" Lisa said, putting her hand on Gregg's shoulder.

"No, I don't think so," he said, turning to face me. The recognition was immediate, as a look of surprise and horror washed across his face. His eyes grew wide and bore into mine, as his nostrils flared.

"Gregg, where are your manners?" Lisa said, giving Gregg a slight nudge in my direction.

'Yes Gregg, where are your manners?' I thought to myself snidely, but instead I extended my hand.

"Andy." I had to play pretend, I thought to myself. There were too many people in the room to make a spectacle, and I didn't need any of the girls to witness any of it.

"Gregg," he said briskly, barely touching my hand before he withdrew it and took a seat at the table. I sighed and settled in at the far side of the table, away from Gregg and Lisa. The waitress came by for drink orders. Lisa politely ordered a glass of wine, Gregg and Lucie's dad ordered a beer and the girls each ordered root beers.

"For you, miss?" she asked, getting to me.

"Jack. Straight."

***

Dinner continued on slowly. I was thankful that the girls carried most of the dinner conversation with chatter of the competition and their competitors. During a lull, Lisa cleared her throat and looked at me.

"Andy?" she asked.

"Yes?" I said on edge. Everything about this situation had me ready to run out the door screaming at any second.

"Is it true?"

"Is what true?" Lisa wasn't known for her directness.

"I heard a rumor that PW..."

"Mom, I already told you PW was here," Madison interrupted, trying to bring the conversation back to her.

"Madison dear, don't interrupt," she said, looking back at me. "Is it true that you and PW are an item?" she practically whispered the last sentence, not that she needed to. The room was completely quiet, and all eyes were on me; I could particularly feel Gregg's eyes as they focused in on me.

"Mom and Paul aren't dating. They are just friends," Hayden Grace interrupted, and for some reason I exhaled and nodded at Lisa.

"I heard a rumor..." she tried to continue.

"Lisa, we met at Mount Sunapee and happened to run into each other again here in Aspen. Just friends," I interrupted. Lisa didn't look convinced, but changed the subject. The rest of dinner was uneventful. Soon the girls announced they were bored and headed up to the room to start a movie. Taking that as a good cue, I excused myself to the bathroom. It looked like Gregg wanted to talk to me privately, but I avoided his eye contact as I headed out of the room. I decided to hide out in the bathroom until I was sure the coast would be clear.

About fifteen minutes later I peeped out of the bathroom and glanced around the restaurant. I sighed with relief when I didn't see anyone I recognized and headed towards the lobby. In the lobby there was a small bar area off to the side which caught my eye. Thinking about the day, I shook my head in disbelief, went in and sat down. I had an overwhelming urge to call Marla to tell her about my adventures, but refrained, unsure if I could actually verbalize everything. After a couple minutes, the bartender came over and asked what I was drinking.

"Jack," I ordered again. It still seemed appropriate, I thought to myself, and it would make Marla proud. He didn't ask any further questions and quickly poured my drink, setting it down in front of me. I slowly sipped on it while I tried to sort out the day:

Hayden Grace had qualified for the finals in Regional 6…and she was amazing;

She had legit sponsor interest…I would have to sort through that later;

Gregg and I had 'officially' met in person and it was awkward and he was still a slimeball;

Malinda wanted Paul Westcott as a client or I was fired…I wasn't sure how I felt about this;

Being around Paul Westcott drew unwanted attention, but his eyes…oh my!

I don't know how long I was in a daze, but it was long enough to finish my drink, when the bartender cleared his throat and placed another drink in front of me.

"I didn't order one," I said with confusion.

"It's from the gentleman at the end of the bar," he said, pointing down the bar. I glanced over and wasn't surprised to see those blue eyes looking back at me. It took him several moments to make his way down the bar to me. He approached me with the wariness one would use to approach a wild animal.

"Hi," he finally said.

"Hi," I replied, looking over at him.

"Are you still mad?" he asked.

"Mad at you?" I asked in confusion. I had a lot of emotion going on tonight but that was not one of them. "No," I said, glancing down at my drink. He visibly relaxed and sat down next to me.

"Long day?"

"The longest," I commented dryly.

"Andy, I'm so sorry…" he started to apologize.

"Paul, stop. There is no need to apologize. Of all the things that have happened today, that no longer ranks as the worst thing to happen to me." He raised his eyebrows in concern.

"Want to talk about it?" he asked. I looked over at him. 'Did I want to talk about it?' I thought to myself.

"Not really, to be honest," I said, taking a slow sip of Jack. "Are you participating in the X Games next week?" I asked, trying to change the subject.

"Probably not—I'm kinda working on something different," he said cryptically.

"Like what?" I asked with interest.

"Too soon to tell," he said, and I felt his glaze fall on me, sending shivers down my spine.

"How are you always finding me?"

"The coffee shop was a totally amazing fluke. I was leaving my condo on my way to run some errands when I saw you in the window. I thought about pinching myself to make sure I wasn't seeing things. I don't often get second chances," he admitted. "Tonight, I had a small function with a sponsor that I was required to attend. It just so happens that I was already in the restaurant when I saw you duck into the bathroom. Thought I might wait you out," he said, causally turning to look at me.

"Andy?" I heard another voice call my name. I closed my eyes and shook my head.

"This day just won't ever end, will it," I mumbled to myself, turning around to look at Gregg.

"Paul will you excuse me for a moment?" I asked, and he nodded with interest at the situation.

"Gregg, what are you doing down here?" I hissed.

"I had to see if you were still here," he said, as I nervously glanced around. "Lisa and the girls are all upstairs," he added.

"Gregg, you shouldn't be here," I said.

"Andy, you can't tell Lisa," he said sternly.

"You can't tell me what to do, and I have every right to tell her what a scoundrel you are," I said, feeling the anger rise up.

"Andy, think of Madison," he pleaded.

"Me?? Think of Madison?! What about you? She is the only thing that has prevented me from saying anything," I spat back.

"Andy, be rational, maybe we can still make this work," he said. A slew of expletives ran through my mind like ticker tape. Without thinking, I raised my hand and slapped him across the face.

"Gregg, you need to leave and never talk to me about this again," I said to his shocked expression.

"Dad?" We both heard from behind us. Looking past Gregg, I saw Madison with a confused look on her face. He tried to mumble something to me, but decided against it and turned to where she was standing. Gregg leaned over and whispered something to her, and she glanced in my direction, glaring at me with a cold expression before they both headed off. I heard a low whistle from behind me.

"Remind me never to make you mad," I heard Paul comment as I walked back to the bar. Only once I was seated, did I realize that I was shaking.

"No, I still don't want to talk about it," I said before he could ask, and I finished my drink in one gulp. He studied me for a couple more minutes before he spoke again.

"Wanna get out of here?"

"I thought you'd never ask."

***

We exited the lobby and I headed toward the town, when Paul caught my hand and pulled me in a different direction. Confused, I didn't say anything. When Paul didn't let my hand go, I realized I didn't mind. We walked near the Silver Queen Gondola and up a short path by some residential houses and condos, until he took a sharp left, where we ended up on a beautiful stone patio. He fiddled with a key pad and pulled the back French door open.

"You live here?" I asked, slightly surprised.

"No, one of my sponsors owns it, and they let me crash whenever I need to," he offered as an explanation. The interior was amazing—wide plank hardwood covered the floors, on the walls was a soft cream color and the living room had a huge fireplace with lots of stone work. Glancing up at the ceiling, I admired the exposed beam work. A large leather coach and two recliners flanked the fireplace. It felt like an intimate ski resort lobby.

"It's amazing," I finally breathed, and he smiled.

"I thought you might have had enough of Aspen today," he said, walking into the vast kitchen. "Want something to drink?" he asked. I stifled a giggle, looking at the great 'PW' standing in a giant kitchen. He looked so out of place in such a normal environment—'it wasn't somewhere he belonged' I thought to myself with a sad smile—just another instance of how different our lives were.

"I think I've had too much to drink...do you have coffee?" Relief washed across his face, as he started to pull open a cabinet and produced two mugs and a coffee pot. "Do you stay here often?" I asked, sitting on a bar stool at the counter, watching him intently.

"Whenever I'm in Aspen, which isn't too often," he said, concentrating on what he was doing.

"Do you need help?" I asked with a laugh.

"No, coffee I can do," he confirmed. After he had everything situated he turned to look at me, and those eyes locked with mine. After a moment he let out a sigh and dropped his gaze.

"Where are you off to next?" I asked.

"Depends. Right now I have plans to probably skip the X Games and meet up with the guys in Italy and do some riding out there, but plans can change," he said with a shrug.

"It must be so nice to live such a nomadic lifestyle," I mused.

"It has its perks – but it has a lot of drawbacks too," he replied, setting a cup down in front of me. "Can I show you something?" he asked, and I nodded after I wrapped my hands around the warm cup. He led the way up two short flights of stairs and into what looked to be the master bedroom.

"This is a little forward," I commented as we passed the threshold, and he snickered.

"No, through there," he pointed to another set of doors that led outside. We walked out onto a large balcony that was secluded from the lights and sounds of Aspen by the trees. Looking up, a clear view of the sky and stars was visible. A small gas fire pit sat in the middle of the deck that with a flip of a switch came roaring to life. I sat down in one of the comfy recliners and a slight shiver ran through me. Paul left the balcony and came back with a blanket, which he wrapped around my shoulders, and a small smile spread across my lips.

"It's amazing," I said, for the second time that night.

"It's the best part about this place," he said, referring to the condo. I leaned back and looked at the stars and sighed; the tension from the day seemed to melt away.

"Thank you," I finally said, meeting his eyes.

"Thought you could use it," he said, leaning back in his chair.

"Have you ever had a day that just knocks you off your feet?" I asked, and he nodded.

"Hayden Grace had a really good day and qualified for the finals. It's what her dad wanted for her for so long, and that should have been enough for today, but then all this other stuff happened. She got all these sponsor offers, which is fine, but overwhelming. Then, I had that panic attack after the picture of us flashed on the jumbo-tron." It was like the flood gates had opened, and I just continued to ramble on, only pausing to look at Paul – who looked like he flinched a little at my mention of the earlier incident. "Then my client calls with this preposterous demand, which will probably get me fired. To cap it all off, the guy I was dating ended up being the father of one of Hayden Grace's best friends…and while I figured it out last week, he just figured it out tonight, and then Madison watched me slap her Dad. I'm sure that will come back on Hayden Grace somehow. What a mess this whole day has been." 'If I was going to cry it should have been here,' I thought to myself, but no tears came; instead I sighed and my shoulders slumped forward. I could hear Paul get up and move toward me.

"Andy," he said, laying his hand on my knee as he sat on the edge of the coffee table. "From what I've seen you are stronger than most of the people I know—man or woman."

'I'm the strongest Parker,' I thought to myself as he spoke.

"Do you bring a lot of people here?" I finally asked, trying to change the subject.

"Here? No. Just you," he said.

"Why?" I couldn't hold it in.

"I can't quit you, Andy Parker," he said, taking my breath away. With that he leaned forward and took the coffee mug out of my hands, placing it on the table. Then he leaned in ever so slowly and kissed me. Surprise instantly registered throughout my body, followed by a tingling sensation that gave me goose bumps. Paul pulled away slightly and looked at me, bringing his hand up and caressing the side of my face, which softened to his touch.

"I've been wanting to do that since the day I first met you," he whispered, tucking a stray strand of blonde hair back behind my ear. I held his gaze only a moment longer and leaned back in for a kiss. This time there was an electric pulse behind the kiss as Paul moved his hands down from my face to my shoulders. I reached out my hand to touch his chest and moved it up to his face, eventually weaving my fingers through his hair. Silently he rose and took my hand, leading me back into the bedroom.

We stood in the bedroom for a moment as his eyes searched mine, connecting with something as he kissed me again with more passion and urgency. The energy between us felt so thick that it hung in the air around us as I poured myself into every kiss. Gracefully we moved to the giant poster bed, and he laid me down as he hovered over me.

"Andy…" he started to say something.

"Just shut up and kiss me," I said, reaching up and pulling him down towards me as he chuckled. He kissed my cheeks and then trailed kisses down my jaw-line towards my ear and down my neck. Each kiss sent shivers throughout my entire body. He carefully pulled off my sweater and continued trailing kisses to my chest. He paused, slowly unhooking my bra as his hands now cupped my breasts, causing me to inhale sharply. I pulled at his shirt, and it took him a moment to realize what I was doing. He shifted, letting me slip off his shirt, only to expose his finely-toned physique. As I ran my fingers down his abs, I could feel him shiver under my touch, causing me to grin. He continued to trail kisses down past my navel causing me to shiver this time; I could feel him smile as he continued to the waistline of my jeans. He slowly unbuttoned my jeans and knelt before me on the bed as he tugged my jeans and panties off in one movement. He held my foot and slowly kissed down my leg and up my thigh, making his way slowly back up to my lips. Every kiss felt sensual and sent a warm tingling sensation to the center of my core. When we kissed again, I grinned, and pushed him down on his back and returned the favor with a thousand small sensual kisses of my own.

I could feel the tension mounting in my own body as he rolled me over onto my back once more. 'He had to feel it too,' I thought to myself as his lips covered mine once more. We slowly made love until we both cried out in pleasure and he collapsed on top of me; his breathing matched my own erratic breaths. When I opened my eyes I was staring into his blue eyes.

"Your eyes are endless," I whispered, finally being able to say what I felt since our first meeting. He smiled, kissed my lips, and pulled up the blankets. We shifted so that I lay on his chest, and he wrapped his arms around me as I drifted off to sleep.

CHAPTER 19

I stretched in bed, only to realize that I was alone. Glancing at the clock, I could see that it was just after six in the morning. I sighed in relief, knowing that Hayden Grace didn't need to report for another couple of hours. The smell of coffee drifted into the bedroom and brought a smile to my face. I glanced around the room and settled on Paul's shirt as I padded down the hallway and the stairs. He stood in the kitchen with his back to me. He was wearing only his boxer briefs, so I took a moment to admire his sculpted back. I crept forward only for the floorboard to creek, giving away my presence in the room. Paul turned and gave me a wide smile, as I gave him a sheepish wave.

"You look so guilty," he said, striding toward me to wrap me up in an embrace and kiss me good morning.

"I hope you don't mind… I borrowed your shirt," I finally said.

"That fact was not lost on me, and no, I don't mind," he said, leaning down to kiss me once more before letting me go.

"Coffee?" he asked as he poured two cups, not really waiting for my response. "I have made this slight observation that you can't seem to live without it," he teased playfully.

"Thank you," I breathed into my hot steaming mug. I drank slowly, and the day's agenda started to form in my head.

"Stop it," Paul said, looking at me.

"Stop what?" I asked.

"You're thinking…I can tell because you get this spaced out look, and you tilt your head ever so slightly to the side," he observed.

"I was just going over the day's agenda: how I have to get to our hotel, get Hayden Grace's gear, check into the Hyatt, and meet my brother," I rambled.

"Whoa, one at a time," he said, leaning on the counter towards me.

"Your stuff is where?" he asked, and I told him about the motel and rental car. He paused to look at me, contemplating a response. "Jessica can get all that stuff for you," he finally said.

"Who is Jessica?" I asked in confusion.

"She is my assistant. My team hired her to more or less keep me in check; although, to be honest, I don't use her very much. She got here yesterday and is always asking me what she can do to help; this is right up her alley," he said nonchalantly.

"Of course, you have an assistant," I mumbled.

"Ok, next," he said.

"My brother, Drew, is flying in today and we are going to stay with him at the Hyatt," I said slowly.

"Okay, Jessica can bring all your stuff over to the hotel. Will I get to meet your brother?" he asked.

"Um…sure," I said surprised, and he nodded with approval.

"What time do you have to meet Hayden Grace?" he asked, moving on.

"Nine....the competition starts at twelve," I said.

"Makes sense...the men's final is at seven," he said.

"Are you judging that?" I asked, and he nodded.

"So what's next on your agenda?" he asked again.

"Umm, that's everything. I guess I need to shower and get ready," I said. I was unaccustomed to having any help—I had been doing it all by myself for so long, it was odd to have time to spare.

"Now there's something I can help with," he gave me a sly smile, and I laughed. "No, really, go upstairs and take a nice long shower. I will give Jessica a call," he said. I wrote down all the instructions, and he waved me on.

The hot water cascaded down my shoulders as I stood in the shower letting the tension run down my shoulders. I heard the door to the bathroom open and in slipped Paul. Turning to look at him, we stared at each other through the glass door for a moment before he slipped out of his boxer briefs and joined me.

"I told you I could help with this," he mumbled, kissing me once more.

***

We sat at the kitchen table drinking our second cup of coffee and eating muffins that the sponsor had left for Paul, talking about random things. I kept stealing side glances at him, and a smile I couldn't erase stayed on my lips.

"So in all this time we have spent together, you haven't shared your story," I said, looking to him.

"You want my story? It comes with a cost," he said, leaning over to me, causing me to automatically lean in for a kiss. "That's a good start," he said with a hint of mischievousness in his eyes. "My story isn't very interesting," he said.

"Try me," I said, hoping for more.

"I was born in San Francisco, but when I was four my parents moved to Lake Tahoe; they were both ski instructors, so I grew up on the mountain. I picked up a snowboard around the age of six, and they couldn't get me off of it. I was doing tricks by eight, and I entered my first competition at eleven. At fourteen I had won my first competition. Eventually competition wasn't enough—I liked to make up my own tricks and have tricks that no one else could do. I got to travel the world, snowboarding. It was amazing. Now I'm a little older, and my body doesn't really hold up the way it used to, so I've scaled back on the competitions, but I still love to ride and compete on occasion. Now my time is spent more on the business side of Paul Westcott," he paused.

"Now tell me something I can't read on Wikipedia," I said, interrupting him.

"Up until recently my favorite color was black, but now it's hazel," he said, looking up into my eyes which caused me to pause, and a shy smile to spread on my lips. "I meant it when I said I can't quit you…you are unlike anyone I've ever met."

"The feeling is mutual," I whispered, and he smiled, leaning over to kiss me again – once slowly and then again with such passion that it sent this electrifying pulse to my core.

"I need to get going soon," I finally said, pulling myself away. If I wasn't careful I could spend all day looking into his eyes and getting lost in his touch.

"Do you want me to go with you?" he asked. He was only dressed in his jeans, and his wet hair was slicked back as he stood up and padded around the table into the kitchen in his bare feet.

"No, I should be fine. Thanks for having Jessica do all that stuff this morning," I said, holding up the Hyatt hotel room key. She had apparently dropped it off at some point while we were upstairs. I had to admire a woman who works so quickly and efficiently.

"Happy to help," he said, coming up to me kiss me again. "Would you mind if I joined you and your brother to watch the finals?" he asked cautiously.

"No, it would mean a lot to Hayden Grace…and myself," I said immediately. I was kicking myself slightly at showing my over-eagerness.

"Andy, my being there might create unwanted attention," he said after a moment. I could tell he was struggling with something. I had answered so quickly that I hadn't thought about the extra attention that sitting with Paul would bring. I thought about what had happened in my life since he came into it and decided that some things are worth the risk.

"Live on the edge, someone once told me," I said, quoting him from the other day. He broke into a dazzling smile and laughed.

"Okay, I have some things to take care of, and I'll meet you over there," he said.

"Oh, do you need a pass?" I asked in confusion. Family members were given passes for special seating during the finals, but I had only requested two passes for Drew and me.

"Don't worry about me," he said, and I rolled my eyes. Of course he didn't need a pass.

***

I walked from Paul's condo to the Hyatt in less than five minutes because it was literally on the other side of the Silver Queen Gondola. My hotel key indicated that the room was on the top floor, and I rolled my eyes at the fact that

Drew had reserved a suite.

"Andy?" I heard as I entered the suite, causing me to jump.

"Drew?" I asked after getting over being startled.

"My flight got in early," he said, standing up from the recliner and stretching out his arms.

"Oh my God, I'm so excited you're here," I said, flinging myself into his embrace.

"Glad to see you too, sis," he chuckled after a moment. After I regained my composure, I scanned the room for our things.

"Looking for your stuff?" he asked casually, and I nodded. "Interesting thing about that, Andrea Parker," he said. His eyes danced in excitement as if he had a secret.

"What?" I asked dryly.

"Well, let's see...while I was sitting in the lobby, waiting to find out if it was possible for me to check-in early, or if I would have to leave my stuff with the bell hop, this lovely long-haired brunette strode into the hotel with a bellhop of her own, wheeling all this stuff in behind her. She speaks to the person behind the counter for maybe five minutes, and she has upgraded *MY* room to a suite, which was going to be ready momentarily for her," he paused to take a breath and to make his story more dramatic.

"Jessica, as I found out, sat down across from me as she waited for the room, and I couldn't help but ask if I had heard correctly that she had upgraded *MY* room to a suite. Then I asked why she would do that. Jessica seemed startled for a minute that I was sitting there, and she told me the most interesting story."

"Oh," I said, trying to fake disinterest and hoping that I wasn't turning

191

red in embarrassment.

"Oh, you want me to continue? Ok, here's where it gets interesting," he said, oozing with sarcasm. "Jessica said she worked for Paul Westcott. You know – the famous professional snowboarder – and that he was seeing a mysterious blonde-haired woman with hazel eyes, which I later confirmed to be you, much to my surprise, but more on that later. Anyway, Jessica had gone to get your things from that crappy motel you were in and was told to check us all into a suite for the duration of your time here. She also returned your rental car…in case you were wondering," he said smugly.

"Sounds like you and Jessica hit it off nicely," I commented, avoiding eye contact.

"Oh…we certainly did. I got her number," he said with a smirk.

"What about Stella?" I questioned back.

"That's casual. You know Stella can't be tamed. The best way to keep her interest is to be uninterested," he commented.

'It's like raising a teenager,' I thought to myself. "Sounds complicated," I said instead.

"With Stella things usually are. But that brings me back to you and Mr. Westcott. Would you like to tell me more about that?" he paused, and I could tell he was looking at me.

"Not really," I said, sliding a glance at his face.

"You know, I almost called mom, but thought I would give you a chance to explain yourself," he smirked.

"You wouldn't dare," I gaped, throwing a pillow in his direction.

"Kidding! I wouldn't wish that on my worst enemy," he said after ducking out of the way. When he straightened up, we both smiled and burst into laughter. I found my stuff, changed my clothes, and started pulling together Hayden Grace's things as I told Drew the whole story. Every detail from Tuesday two weeks ago: I told him about Gregg, Paul, Malinda and the competition; it felt good to get it off my chest.

"Now that sounds complicated," he finally said when I was done.

"Tell me about it," I said, flopping down on the sofa in exasperation.

"Nothing has ever been simple with you," he said, sitting down next to me.

"No, it doesn't appear to be."

"Have you heard from Jennifer?" he asked, referring to our youngest sister.

"Not recently. Last I heard, she was studying for her board exams and looking for residencies all over the place," I said, thinking back to the email I got from her about a month ago. She was supposed to be at Christmas, but backed out at the last minute, leaving everyone disappointed.

"That's more than I know. I hadn't talked to her since she called to cancel Christmas," he mumbled. Drew had always been the one in the family to hold grudges the longest.

"Just let it go. She is busy and will reach out when she needs too," I said, rolling my eyes at him. Just then my phone vibrated.

"It's Hayden Grace—she's waiting for me," I said, standing up to get her gear.

"She still doesn't know I'm here?" he asked.

"Nope."

"Well played," he said, helping me with her stuff as we left the suite and headed towards the elevator.

"What are you going to do about Gregg?" he asked.

"I think that situation is settled," I said tentatively.

"What about the famous PW," he said with a grin.

"Ugh, not you too. His name is Paul, and I don't know. You'll get to meet him, so you tell me," I said after a moment, and his eyebrows rose.

"I do, do I? This is really shaping up to be a very interesting trip." He laughed as we walked out to the Silver Queen Gondola. We were barely across the street when we heard Hayden Grace.

"Mom! UNCLE DREW!!" she yelled. I saw a flash of limbs and blonde hair whiz by me, and I heard the oomph as she collided with Drew. He had to balance to catch her as they embraced.

"Surprise," I said when she unlatched herself. She was wide-eyed and laughed.

"Best surprise ever," she smiled, and we walked the rest of the way to where she needed to be as she hung all over Drew.

"Okay, we will be in the family section," I told Hayden Grace as we were about to part. At bigger competitions, there were small sections that were designated for family members. The competition organizers would issue passes in limited quantity to the competitors that made it to the finals. I thought it was so the competition had easy access to parents and their emotions to plaster on the TV and jumbo-tron, though the organizers would tell you it was for the convenience of the family to be able to watch their competitor.

"Right," she paused for a minute.

"What…" I asked, thinking I forgot something.

"No, it's nothing," she said, clearly embarrassed

"Hayden Grace," I asked sternly.

"Do you think Paul will come and watch me?" she finally asked after leaning over and whispering in my ear. Oh! Clearly I was not the only one who had grown used to his company.

"He promised me he would be there," I said, and she gave me a huge smile.

"Good Luck," Drew said, giving her a hug.

"You got this Hayden Grace, so proud of you," I said, and reached into my pocket to hand her Stefan's bandana.

"Thanks Mom, love you," she said as she headed toward the competitors' entrance.

"Love you," I said quietly as Drew steered me toward the grandstands.

CHAPTER 20

We were led into the family section by a younger gentleman who appeared to be in his late teens. It was still early, but already the stands were packed with people, and there was an excitement in the air. I could see that the riders had not yet arrived at the pipe. An event coordinator walked by to explain the event to the parents; and that cameras would be panning over to the parents' section as the riders came down, especially if they were doing well.

'Great,' I thought to myself sarcastically. Drew, on the other hand, seemed to stand a little taller, excited by the prospect of being on TV. I nudged him and mouthed 'narcissist' to him, and he shrugged. Not ten minutes later Lisa and Gregg arrived. Lisa waved and started to walk over to where we were standing. Gregg grabbed her arm and mumbled something, and they moved to a different area. I just gave a small wave, but I was not saddened by the prospect of them standing somewhere else. I again nudged Drew and pointed out Lisa and Gregg to him; his eyes grew wide, and he nodded in understanding.

"This is like a soap opera," he whispered to me, and I couldn't help but giggle. All the years of growing up with sisters had rubbed off on Drew, although he would never admit it, he loved getting involved with drama and gossip; hence, his attraction to Stella. Everything finally settled down, and the announcers broadcast that the competition was about to begin. There were twelve female competitors for the final. Per qualifying scores, the one with the lowest overall score rode first, so the best score rode last. Hayden Grace was set to ride ninth, and Madison was tenth. I was nervous as we waited; I could feel a knot form in my stomach with anticipation.

"Relax. She is going to be great." Drew was always so laid back that it drove me crazy sometimes. But in this case, his calming attitude was helpful. The announcer called the first name; it was a girl from California, and she dropped into the pipe. And just like that the competition began. The girl from California was pretty good, but had several wobbles. 'She would have to clean that up if she wanted to contend for a top spot,' I thought to myself. The second rider was much like the first rider: good rider, but had some mistakes.

I started to hear the murmurs and whispers, and I knew Paul had arrived without even turning around. There was an energy and added excitement he brought wherever he seemed to go. It wasn't long before I felt his hand on the small of my back, and he leaned in and gave me a kiss on the check.

"I didn't miss too much, I hope," he said.

"No, we are only on the fourth competitor," I replied back, and I couldn't help but smile. Next to me, my brother cleared his throat.

"I brought more coffee," Paul said, presenting a tray of coffee.

"Perfect," I said, reaching for a cup.

"You must be Drew," Paul said, turning to my brother. "I figured if you were related to Andy and Hayden Grace, there was a good chance you were addicted too," he said, offering him a cup.

"You are correct," Drew said, looking grateful for the caffeine. They shook hands and exchanged pleasantries. Drew continued to stand on my left, and Paul now flanked my right. I felt oddly at home in that moment. Paul's arrival did bring an added attention our way as he had anticipated. The TV camera crew immediately swung over, and Drew and Paul waved; I just smiled, pulling my sunglasses down to shield my eyes. I could see people around us taking pictures and whispering as we continued to stand there. We were now on the sixth rider.

"She needed to bend her knees more going into those last tricks," Paul commented as the sixth girl from Colorado finished her ride. Drew leaned over and asked a question as if he was a snowboarding expert, eliciting a chuckle from me because I knew Drew knew very little about snowboarding—he was a skier through and through. Paul politely responded as they dissected the girls' performance. Listening to the conversation, I could tell that Paul would be an excellent coach or mentor to other snowboarders. He had an obvious understanding for the mechanics, but his observation to detail was amazing. He picked up on little nuances in every trick that I thought was impossible, given the speed at which everything was actually performed.

"PW?" I heard over my shoulder, causing the three of us to turn around at the same time. Lisa was smiling broadly and waving as she and Gregg approached. More accurately, it looked like Lisa was dragging Gregg across the family section against his will.

"Lisa, right?" he said when they got closer. She giggled and batted at him, mumbling something about him remembering her.

"PW…" she started to say.

"It's Paul," he corrected her, shaking her hand again, which only caused her to giggle more, and me to roll my eyes. Drew somehow saw it under my sunglasses and nudged me in the ribs.

"Paul, I wanted to introduce you to my husband, Gregg. He's a big fan," she gushed as Gregg looked embarrassed.

'Oh is he,' I thought to myself, and I was about to roll my eyes again when Drew nudged me again.

"Ow," I whispered at him, and he chuckled.

"Gregg, is it? Have we met before?" Paul said, shaking his hand.

"No," Gregg stammered.

"Are you sure? I could have sworn I saw you in the lobby bar last night," he said. My jaw dropped to the ground; Drew coughed next to me, trying to cover up his chuckle, and Gregg turned red.

"No," Gregg stammered again.

"No...my bad, then. Nice to meet you," he said as he leaned into Gregg and whispered something in his ear. Whatever he said caused an immediate reaction in Gregg, and he turned bright red, his eyes growing wide.

"Lisa, let's go," he said gruffly, pulling her away as she questioned him about what was going on. When they left Paul turned back to Drew and I innocently shrugging his shoulders.

"What did you say to him," I tried to whisper, but ended up laughing.

"I just thanked him for being a huge asshole," he said with a mischievous grin.

"You did not," I gaped, hitting him in the shoulder.

"Well played," Drew said from next to me and fist-bumped Paul. We were chatting and laughing and then without realizing it, they announced Hayden Grace's name. We were at rider nine. I held my breath, and my hands went up to my mouth to cover my anxiety. Both Paul and Drew laughed at my reaction, but stayed quiet as she began her run. She entered higher in the pipe just as she did last time, causing her to soar through her first trick. She was solid through the next two tricks, and she had just finished her second-to-last trick, when I heard Paul next to me.

"No. You know better Hayden Grace." Before I had a chance to ask, I saw it. She came in at a slightly awkward angle for her last trick and came down on the coping of the pipe with a soft thud. She tumbled to the bottom of the pipe and lay there lifelessly.

"Hayden Grace!" I yelled, trying to move forward as the crowd grew silent. Both Drew and Paul held me back.

"The medics have got her," Drew said. I knew logically that he was right, but I couldn't stand by and watch.

"She's a fighter," Paul said and squeezed my shoulder. Just then Hayden Grace stirred and sat up in her spot. It was a matter of seconds, but it felt like a lifetime. The medics arrived and quickly examined her. She finally stood and shook the snow off of herself. The crowds gave her a loud applause, and she waved back before gliding out of the pipe and over to the family section. I broke free of Drew and Paul and ran to the barrier to give her a big hug.

"Hayden Grace, are you okay?" I asked.

"Mom, I'm fine. I just got the wind knocked out of me," she said, slightly embarrassed. Drew patted her on the back, and she smiled. Paul leaned over and whispered something to Hayden Grace, and she nodded before the event coordinator called for her. I stood and watched her disappear behind the crowds of people before finally allowed myself to exhale.

"Andy, you have to breathe, you basket case," Drew commented next to me.

"I'm trying," I replied. The announcer let everyone know the course was clear and that the next rider, who was Madison, would be cleared to go. We watched as she took the pipe and ran through her run. It was a solid run, and it put her in third place. I clapped along with everyone, but at the moment I had ill feelings towards anyone in direct competition with Hayden Grace.

"She is trying too hard," Paul whispered to me when she was done.

"What?" I asked.

"Madison—she would be a better rider if she was looser and had more fun with it. She is trying too hard to be the best and won't let it happen naturally,"

"What did you say to Hayden Grace?" I asked after a moment.

"The same thing I told her on Mount Sunapee and earlier this week. I told her to stop overthinking it – to have fun."

"It's that easy?" I asked.

"It should be," he said, and I could see how he saw the sport and his love and passion for it. The rest of the riders finished, and after the first round in the finals, Hayden Grace was now in eighth place. Thankfully several other riders had also wiped out, and Madison was in third place. Hayden Grace would ride fifth, and Madison would ride tenth in the final round. That anticipation was killing me, and my anxiety rose even higher. By the time we got to the third rider, Drew and Paul both stopped talking to me, giving me my space. It was like the entire event had slowed down and everything was taking twice the time. It seemed like hours, but we finally got to Hayden Grace.

She sat at the top, waiting for the announcers to give her the final go ahead. I could see Ron talking to her as they waited. They flashed her picture on the jumbo-tron, and the announcers were talking about her history before she started…

…Hayden Grace, fifteen years old, from Newbury, New Hampshire showing remarkable talent here in Aspen. Her father passed away six years ago and she credits her love for snowboarding to him. It seems she has also made friends with the

great PW, as we saw her talking with him during her qualifying rounds and again today. But let's see if she can come back from that awful fall during her first run...

With that she took off full steam toward the pipe. She dropped in higher into the pipe, just as she had the previous two times. She soared through her first trick, landing solid and fluidly going into her second trick. She entered her third trick carrying more speed than she did on her last run. She added a bit of flare at the end of the trick, and I could hear Paul clapping next to me. Drew was whistling wildly as she entered her next trick, which was the backside 720. She landed it cleanly and set herself up for her last trick which was her newer one. I didn't know if I could watch, but my eyes were glued. The Hayden Grace that was riding this pipe was more confident and mature than the Hayden Grace that had left New Hampshire. She was on fire, but her last trick was hard and I still worried. She went up, bending her knees as she entered the last trick. She left the side of the pipe with lots of height, allowing her to twist and grab her board at the end... then she came down and landed high on the inside wall and...she...landed...it...cleanly. The crowds erupted in applause. I was swept up first by Paul, and then Drew in big hugs. She had done it! Regardless of the score, she had landed what was probably the best run of her life, when she needed it the most. She pumped her fists at the bottom; she knew she had done well. We all held our breath as we waited for the scores. Finally, after several minutes her score posted, putting her in first place. Again the crowds erupted, and Hayden Grace jumped up and down. She pointed at me in the stands, and I pointed back. The camera quickly swooped in and blocked my view of her. I tried to step to the side to see her, but she was already seated by the sponsor's banner. Now we waited.

When the camera left, Paul squeezed my hand and gave me a big smile. Drew gave me another hug and couldn't hide his excitement, but we had seven more riders. The wait was going to be long. We calmed down just as the next rider, number six, finished her run; her final score put her in fourth place for the moment. The seventh rider was the girl from California, and she finished her run again, but didn't score higher than fifth place. I glanced at Hayden Grace, and she fidgeted in her spot, watching the other girls come down the pipe. She had removed her helmet, but left her dad's bandana in place. The eighth rider came down and had some serious height on her tricks; when she was done she got a loud roar from the audience. Her score put her in third place, and she joined Hayden Grace by the sponsor's banner. The ninth rider fell after her second trick; her overall score was only good enough to keep her in fifth place. The next rider was Madison. I was nervous for her and for Hayden Grace. Madison entered the pipe aggressive, like she had before; she hit her first trick and landed it cleanly. She was flying through her tricks. Her final trick caused her to bobble slightly as she seemed to run out of steam, but it was a really good run for Madison. The crowd cheered, and she pumped her fist when she finished. Hayden Grace stood up, and the two girls embraced. Madison had scored third.

Two more riders were left. No matter what happened, Hayden Grace was going to get at least third. Tears welled up in my eyes—I thought about Stefan and how proud he would be, her first national competition. He had believed in this dream long before I did, and she had enough determination to make it happen. The next rider gave a solid performance, and the heights of her tricks were higher than Madison's; her score put her in second place knocking Madison to fourth. Out of the corner of my eye I could see her exit from the sponsor banner area, where Lisa and Gregg ran to embrace her. I could only imagine the tears and disappointment she felt after getting this far. The former first place rider took her mark and entered the pipe fast. Her tricks were bolder and harder, and she had such confidence to her riding. I exhaled when she landed her last trick. I looked at Paul, and he gave a slight shake of his head. He didn't think Hayden Grace had it either. I looked at Hayden Grace, and she held up two fingers to me. She knew it too. I made my way over to the barrier, and she came over to embrace me before the score had posted. She had, in fact, gotten second place – but it didn't matter.

"You did it," I whispered in her ear over the roar of the audience for the first place winner.

"You think…" she started to say.

"I know he's proud," I finished, and she smiled. It was a simple moment, but it was all we got before Drew and Paul came over to embrace Hayden Grace. Suddenly the TV camera crew came over for an interview, and she was quickly swept away for the awards ceremony, among other things. The TV crew tried to get an interview from Paul about the event, but he declined. My heart swelled with pride, as I beamed at the sight of Hayden Grace getting her medal. After the ceremony, I turned to find a crowd of sponsors descending upon me. There were several from the other day, and new ones who presented themselves—my smile quickly disappeared.

"Can I help?" Paul whispered, coming up behind me, and I nodded. I noticed that he knew almost all of the sponsors – he spoke with them and took some cards before sending them away.

"Thank you," I said, when he returned. He handed me the stack, and I instantly turned and handed them to Drew.

"You're the finance guy—do something about this for your niece," I said. He looked startled at first, then intrigued by the process.

"Certainly," he said, tucking the cards into his pocket.

"What next?" Drew asked, as the crowds started to disperse. A couple of people hung around the entrance to our area, eagerly waiting for Paul to leave.

"I should go," Paul said, looking at the crowd. "I have to get ready for the men's competition in a little bit," he added.

"Thank you for coming," I said, looking at him earnestly.

"You're welcome," he leaned in for a quick kiss on the lips, shook hands with Drew and disappeared into the crowd.

"I was hoping to have a reason to hate him, but I have to admit it…he's a cool dude," Drew said after several moments.

"I'm starting to think so myself," I said as we watched him walk away.

CHAPTER 21

After the ceremony Hayden Grace said she wanted a shower and to eat dinner. When we left the mountain she headed towards the area where I had been parking. At the last second, I caught her by the arm and steered her towards the Hyatt. Needless to say, she was beyond excited to learn that we were staying this close to the mountain *and* in a suite. She was in teenager heaven. I convinced her to call her grandparents before she showered, and they spent about thirty minutes on the phone with her before finally letting her go.

Drew and I decided to order room service while she was cleaning up. I was too tired to head out again tonight. She bounded out of the bathroom about an hour later, just as the food was arriving. She was already dressed in her PJs and had the same idea we did. I noticed she had put her medal back on after the shower, and I smiled. She had earned it; she could wear it as long as she wanted, I thought to myself.

Over dinner, Drew filled us in on his adventures and a little bit more about Stella. She had apparently invited him to be her guest at an upcoming wedding in North Carolina. We were dissecting what that could mean when Hayden Grace's phone buzzed. She looked at me expectedly, and I nodded that it was okay. She pounced on her phone and a smile instantly played on her lips.

"Jonathan," I whispered to Drew.

"A boy?" he whispered back, and I nodded.

"Look at both of the Parker women with men in their lives," he whispered back sarcastically, and I swatted at him. With Hayden Grace lost in her own world, Drew and I talked more about his career and our parents.

"Mom," Hayden Grace finally acknowledged me from the sofa, where she had been huddled texting on her phone.

"Yes?"

"Jonathan's finals are tomorrow…can we go?"

"Sure, what time?" I asked, mentally pleading that it wasn't an early competition.

"It starts at 10."

"That's fine. But Uncle Drew is here, so it would be nice to spend some time with him."

"Uncle Drew can come too," she said, not looking up from her phone.

"That's as close to inclusion as you are going to get," I whispered to him, and he nodded. There was a knock at the door, and we all looked around in confusion.

"Are you expecting anyone?" I asked Drew and Hayden Grace. They each shook their head 'No' as I got up and opened the door to find room service standing there.

"Andy Parker?" he asked, and I nodded. He rolled a small cart into the room and unloaded a bottle of champagne and two glasses with a small note. He looked around the room again.

"Hayden Grace Parker?"

"That's me," she said from the sofa. From under the cart he produced a small bunch of flowers that included several yellow roses, and handed them to her.

"Thank you," she squealed, getting up from the sofa.

"What, nothing for me?" Drew asked in mock surprise from the chair he was sitting in. The man looked confused and left.

"Mom these are from Paul," she said excitedly, reading the note out loud.

Hayden Grace,

Congratulations! A big finish at a national competition is a big deal. Hope you had fun.

Here is to many more finals!

Paul

"Suck up," Drew mumbled from his spot on the sofa.

"You're just jealous you didn't think of that," I retorted, and he looked a bit sheepish.

"What does your note say?" Drew asked, changing the subject with a devilish grin.

"Yeah, Mom, what does your note say?" Hayden Grace mimicked him.

I tore open the note, cautious of the many things it could say.

Behind every great athlete is an even stronger mother.

Congratulations!

Paul

After reading it to myself, I read it out loud, and Hayden Grace cheered with excitement.

"I couldn't agree more," Drew said, standing up to open the champagne. I smiled at them, happy they didn't pry further. I slid the note under the tray so they wouldn't see that the rest of the note held an invitation.

P.S. Backcountry tomorrow?

It was an intriguing proposition, but I didn't know if I could get away. We settled in and started watching a movie, each of us lost in our thoughts. Halfway through the movie, Hayden Grace rolled over to look at me sitting on the sofa.

"Mom?"

"Yes."

"Are you dating Paul?" she asked, seemingly out of the blue. If I had food in my mouth I would have spit it out all over the place. But instead, I just swallowed hard and tried to avoid the expression of humor on Drew's face.

"What makes you think that?" I asked.

"This picture Madison just sent me," she said, handing her phone over to me. It was a picture on some random gossip site, which showed Paul kissing me on the cheek this morning when he arrived at the competition.

"I guess so," I finally admitted out loud. I watched Hayden Grace's face to make sure it didn't upset her.

"Have you been on five dates?" she asked further.

"No." Not five official dates, I thought to myself.

"You broke your own rule," she commented, obviously pleased by this revelation and rolled back over to continue texting. I sat a little dumbfounded by her statement. She was right, and I didn't have a good response for that.

"Are you okay if I am dating Paul?" if that was, in fact, what was even happening – I asked cautiously, fully aware I might not want to hear the answer.

"Yea, he's super cool," she said after several minutes.

"Hell, Stefan would have dated Paul if he had ever had the chance," Drew said from the recliner, unable to stay out of the conversation. I think both Hayden Grace and I looked startled, before we burst out laughing.

"Uncle Drew, you are so silly," she said and turned back to her conversation.

"It's true," he huffed under his breath. It wasn't long after that, that Hayden Grace fell asleep and Drew carried her to bed. I made sure to take her medal off and put it on the nightstand, so she would see it first thing in the morning. We sat back down on the sofa and talked about her career and sponsors for a while, trying to figure out what to do next. I was so grateful Drew was here. I knew I would have been totally overwhelmed with all this information and would have been unable to process it.

"What are you going to do about Malinda, the evil witch," Drew said after a moment.

"I'm going to tell her that I don't want her job, I don't want her to sponsor Hayden Grace and I am not going to court Paul Westcott for a sponsorship deal, as she would like me to." It wasn't until I said it out loud, that I knew it to be true.

"You haven't even asked Paul – it might be worth an open conversation," Drew suggested. I knew it was a numbers game to him, and this job was a smart choice financially.

"No, because if I do that, it makes me no better than anyone else, who is always trying to get something from famous people," I said stubbornly.

"Has he said that?" Drew questioned.

"No, but he doesn't have to. I see it all the time, when hanging out with him. People are constantly asking him for something, expecting something from him. That must get tiring," I further defended my position.

"Okay, I get it. But what are you going to do about work and Hayden Grace?" Drew pressed. He always liked a well laid plan, especially when it came to Hayden Grace.

"I don't know yet." I said.

"Well, I will call these sponsors in the morning, since we have some time before we go and watch this boy ski," he said, with a bit of protectiveness in his voice.

"About that?" I asked and laid out my plan for the morning. He gave me just a little bit of flack, before finally agreeing.

"You are officially off the hook from mother duty tomorrow. Go have fun, you crazy kid," he mocked. I frowned, but gave him a big hug before heading to bed. Once in bed I texted Paul.

I'm in under one condition~ Andy

Moments later I got a response from Paul.

What condition?

I quickly responded with a smirk on my face.

I get to ski.

He responded again within seconds.

Naturally.

After that, we finalized plans and I went to bed excited about what the next day held.

***

Compared to the rest of the week, it was a nice lazy morning. Hayden Grace got up late and was now fussing over what to wear to the competition. I explained to her that it really didn't matter as she would be wearing her jacket, but she was unconvinced. I did encourage her to leave her medal at the hotel. It took several attempts before she finally agreed. Drew spent the morning on the phone with various people, furiously scribbling away, making notes on a legal pad. I had already briefed Hayden Grace on the change of plans, and she seemed un-phased, as long as she still got to see Jonathan compete. I had asked her if Madison was going to hang out with them, and she just shrugged her shoulders.

"She hasn't been responding to my texts since the other night. She has been acting weird towards me, ever since our movie night. I don't know what's going on," Hayden Grace mumbled. Uh-oh…I knew what was going on, but I couldn't tell Hayden Grace about it. I hoped it would blow over. When Drew was off the phone, he announced that the Parker clan would be attending the Burton sponsor party that evening and needed to dress accordingly. I rolled my eyes at him, but I was secretly glad that I had packed at least one presentable outfit.

At promptly nine-thirty, we emerged from the hotel and headed towards the Silver Queen Gondola. Waiting for us was Paul dressed all in black and ready for the mountain, with his board and a set of skis standing in the snow behind him.

212

"Good Morning, Parker ladies. Drew," he said, smiling.

"Morning," I said.

"I could use some coffee," mumbled Hayden Grace, looking at Drew after greeting Paul.

"Did I hear you ask for coffee? That's a problem I can fix," Paul said, reaching behind the board and pulling out a cardboard tray with three coffees.

"For you," he handed one to me, one to Drew and one to Hayden Grace, who beamed from ear-to-ear.

"Amazing," I breathed, inhaling the fresh aroma.

"Thank you, Paul," Hayden Grace said. Drew grunted from behind the group, but he was grateful. I nudged Hayden Grace with my elbow, and she looked at me confused for a moment, before realization washed over her. She ran over and gave Paul a huge hug, catching him by surprise.

"Thank you for my flowers," she said, releasing him. I could tell he was a bit embarrassed, but simply nodded.

"Alright kids, behave," I said, looking at Hayden Grace and Drew.

"Have fun on your date," Hayden Grace snickered, and Drew gave her a high-five. Paul looked a little alarmed, but took it all in stride. Hayden Grace and Drew turned and walked toward the competition. Hayden Grace wanted really good seats. Drew told her that he could deliver, so they were off in search of these 'great' seats.

"Are you ready?" Paul asked, with a mischievous twinkle in his eye after they walked away.

I simply nodded in excitement.

CHAPTER 22

I thought we were headed up to the Silver Queen Gondola, but Paul surprised me when he walked out to the street where a van was waiting for us. I started to ask Paul a question, and he told me I should just go with the flow.

"I feel like I have so much to thank you for," I said when we were settled into the van.

"What could you possibly have to thank me for?" he asked in earnest.

"Where do I start…the champagne, the flowers for Hayden Grace, the constant supply of coffee…" he put up his hands to stop me.

"Stop. I did it because I wanted to and I can." I nodded without knowing what else to say further. We sat for a couple minutes before I had to break the silence.

"Drew is making us all go to the Burton sponsor party tonight," I said finally.

"Those are fun; you'll have a blast," he commented with a wink, and I raised my eyebrow at him with speculation.

"Do you care to elaborate?"

"Not really, it would be too incriminating," he grinned back.

"Where are we going?" I finally asked after about twenty minutes.

"The airport."

"The airport?" A string of thoughts flashed through my mind. "I thought we were going backcountry skiing."

"We are. Just not here," he said with another grin. We arrived at the airport a short time later and were soon boarded on a charter flight to Telluride. "Have you ever been?" Paul asked me as I gazed out the window at the mountains and terrain below me.

"Never," I breathed against the window.

***

We arrived in Telluride, only to be whisked off to another facility where we had to sign several waivers for insurance purposes. The plan was to take a class about backcountry skiing, about safety precautions and how to react in an emergency. I was amused by the idea of taking a class on what I already knew about the backcountry from experience. I doubted a class could really teach you what you needed to know. However, the guide at the facility agreed that based on our extensive experience, we would be able to take an abridged thirty minute refresher course on safety precautions. Our tour guide's name was Ace Savage, and he was going to accompany us on our trip. Apparently he and Paul knew each other well based on the hugs they gave each other when we arrived. Ace packed our bags as we finished our course, and within an hour of touching down we were being loaded into a helicopter and headed toward the San Juan Mountains.

I always thought the view from the top of a mountain was amazingly breathtaking; I was wrong. The view from the helicopter was inspiring. All that I could see was mountains and crisp white snow. It was too loud to say much in the helicopter even with the headset, which was fine by me. I had no words left to speak. Paul, on the other hand, chatted with the pilot and Ace the entire ride, while I tried to take it all in. We landed about thirty minutes later and moved out of the way of the helicopter as it took back off.

"It just us now," Paul leaned over and whispered to me, giving me goose bumps; I nodded. Ace, Paul and I felt like the only people on earth at the moment, and we were surrounded by the most majestic view I had ever seen. I clicked my skis into place while Paul and Ace stepped into their bindings, making some final adjustments. The best thing about the mountain was there was no set path, and we could interpret the mountain as we wanted. Ace eyed me suspiciously as we started down the mountain. It made me chuckle; it was the same look I had given Paul, Scott, Trip and Davie when they came to ski the backcountry with me. I now realized how ridiculous that entire thing was. If they had skied this, then Mount Sunapee must have seemed like a hill. He started slow until he learned my riding style and my abilities. He soon figured out I was more than capable, and we set off at a faster speed.

We floated on the surface of the snow for about an hour before Ace slowed down to a stop to indicate that this was a good place for a break. We pulled off to an area with more trees and rocks, and I found a good place to sit.

"How's the riding going?" Paul asked.

"It's so cool," I said with a twinkle in my eye, and he laughed.

"Good choice?"

"The best." Paul grinned back and was about to say something when Ace came over to tell Paul there was an area up ahead that had some natural kickers and wouldn't need to be built up very much. I took kicker to mean jumps and quickly caught up with the conversation.

"Andy, are you in?" Paul asked with a grin. I shrugged, and Ace looked even more skeptical. I got up to put my stuff on, and Ace pulled Paul off to the side. I could tell the conversation was a little tense, but it was settled quickly.

"What was that about?" I asked Paul when I had a chance.

"Just old prejudices," he commented before asking me if I was ready to go. I gave him a thumbs up, and we set off toward the natural kickers Ace had described. Soon we came to a larger clearing, and I could see the natural jumps that Ace talked about. The boys both stopped and pulled out shovels from their backpacks and got to work rather quickly, building up one of the jumps. It really only took them a short amount of time before it was declared ready.

"Ladies first." Paul yelled when it was ready. Paul's motto echoed in my head, and I decided to go for it.

"Sure thing," I said and lined myself up. Thinking about what I wanted to do, I got myself ready and took off down the jump. I landed easily on the other side and climbed back up to where they were sitting.

"Nicely done, Parker," Paul said, giving me a wink before he set off down the jump and did a fancy trick with multiple revolutions.

"How do you know Paul?" I asked Ace, trying to make conversation.

"We used to be fierce competitors until I tore my MCL and ACL. Never could ride the same afterwards," he commented, getting into place for his turn. He went down the jump, but he didn't have the flourish that Paul had—I could see it in his riding style.

"Andy," I could hear Paul, climbing back up from the jump.

"Hey," I said with excitement and a smile.

"You really amaze me sometimes," he said quickly kissing me on the cheek. "Your turn," he said, motioning to the jump.

"Nah, I only have one or two jumps in me a day. I don't want to use them all up at once," I chided him, indicating he could go next. For the next thirty minutes I watched him and Ace take turns going off the jump. We finally decided everyone would take one last jump and then start heading towards the meeting point for the van. I went first, and I did a simpler jump, landed on my feet and swerved off to the side. Next up was Paul, who had flare and style in his trick as he practically sailed over me—I clearly did not move far enough away. I was chuckling about this when Ace came over the jump last. I could instantly see he wasn't going to land right. I couldn't tell, but Paul looked like he had the same horrified expression on his face as I did. All we could do was watch and wait for Ace to come down, but it was like time was suspended. When he finally landed, there was a cloud of snow as he tumbled several feet before coming to a stop.

"Ace," Paul yelled, getting to him before me.

"Don't move him," I managed to shout at Paul as I arrived. From our brief class before the helicopter ride, I had learned to my surprise, that Paul knew little about first aid. Ace was groaning, but not moving when I arrived; that, at least, was a good sign.

"My leg—I felt something pop when I was taking off on the jump," he said, and I felt a sudden instance of déjà vu. Paul unsnapped Ace's board, and I looked for any visible injuries; thankfully there were none.

"Ace, I'm going to splint your knee, and then we are going to get you help," I said calmly.

"How far are we from the bottom?" Paul asked, matching my calm tone.

"Far enough. Taking a straight shot would be about thirty minutes," Ace said, breathing through the pain.

"Andy, I can't do anything to help. I'll go down and get help," Paul said, fixing his eyes on me. I ran through several different scenarios in my head, but that seemed to make the most sense. I finally nodded, and Paul looked relieved.

"Okay, I'll be right back," he said, leaning over and giving me a kiss before taking off down the mountain. As he did, I took a deep breath to steady myself before evaluating Ace again. Taking the first aid kit from my backpack, I quietly set to work securing Ace's knee. I could tell he was in a lot of pain, so after several moments I started acting like Hayden Grace by asking him a million questions.

"How long have you been backcountry riding?"

"As a guide, four years," he mumbled.

"You said you and Paul were competitors...are you good friends?"

"I've known him my whole life, but not competing against each other makes things easier," he said, and as he grunted I tried to move my hand quickly under his knee to tie the restraint.

"How did you meet Paul?" he grunted.

"I was his backcountry guide back in New Hampshire," I commented, tying the last knot into place. "Ace, that's all I can do for now. We just need to sit and wait for help," I said, looking at him and his leg. I sat down next to him, and without thinking, I took his hand and squeezed it.

"I get it now," he said after a few moments.

"Get what?"

"Paul doesn't bring people backcountry skiing," he commented.

"People?" I asked.

"No one—not here at least. Here, he always rides alone. You're unique, and I didn't get it earlier. I actually accused him of bringing some random snow bunny up here, and that it was dangerous." I flinched slightly at the reference, but doubted that Ace saw it. "I get it now," he continued. "You ride aggressively, but with such grace and finesse; it's hard not to notice," he gritted again. I didn't know what to say further, so we sat in silence until I noticed he had stopped squeezing my hand.

"Ace? Ace!" I yelled, checking his vitals. His blood pressure was low, and he was still breathing, but barely. "Ace stay with me," I mumbled, squeezing his hand again, and I felt him lightly squeeze back. Paul better get her quickly or we were going to have a lot more than a knee problem. I heard Ace mumbling to himself, and I tried to get closer to hear what he was saying. I needed to elevate his head so I slid in behind him and rested his head in my lap. His breathing was labored, but better. Rather than sitting in silence, I started to tell Ace my life story. I didn't know if he was conscious or not, but I felt the need to keep talking. I started with my first memories of skiing on the mountain. I had just about made it to present day when I heard the sound of sleds coming up the mountain, and I breathed a sigh of relief.

"Ace, help is here. He did it," I said, giving his hand a squeeze. I didn't want to stand up for fear of jostling him, so I just waved my hands from where I sat. The medics arrived and quickly took over, loading Ace onto a sled and carefully heading down the mountain. Paul stood next to me for a moment before I leaned into him and wrapped my arms around him. I was shaking slightly as the adrenaline stopped pumping through my body.

"Andy, you were amazing. We make a great team," he said, rubbing my back. I just nodded into his jacket. He didn't say anything further, but let me stand there for as long as I needed. Finally, I had composed myself and let him go. I clicked back into my skis and motioned at him that I was ready. I followed him the rest of the way down the mountain as he retraced his steps from earlier. As we arrived at the bottom, they had just finished loading Ace into the EMS truck and then they took off toward the hospital. The guy driving the van asked if we wanted another go at the top, but we both declined. It was starting to get late, and I had to get back to Hayden Grace.

The van drove us back to the airport, and we took another charter plane to Aspen. The sun was just starting to dip behind the mountains, and the sky was filled with orange, purple and blue hues. I had run out of words to describe the scene. Paul moved closer to me and draped his arm around my shoulder, and we sat there watching the skyline.

"So, I wouldn't have classified this as a date. A date usually involves dinner, flowers, maybe even some dancing; wouldn't you think?" he playfully asked. I looked over to him and smiled.

"This has been one of the best dates – definitely in the top ten best dates I have been on in a long time," I commented, thinking back to all the lifeless dinners I had sat through since I started dating again.

"Is that so? I'll need to try and break into the top five," he commented, cuddling up until the pilot let us know we needed to prepare for landing. In Aspen, another van waited for us and brought us back into the city center. There we were, back at the beginning; it was only eight hours ago when we left and in that time, the adventure we had had was spellbinding, romantic, harrowing and testing all at once. I looked at Paul smiling, and shook my head – it was so him. I helped Paul carry the gear back to his place and finally checked my phone.

Surprisingly, there were no missed calls, but there were a couple texts updating me on Hayden Grace and Drew's day. It looks like Jonathan had placed third in his competition, and Hayden Grace was very excited about this from the picture she sent of herself and Drew holding his medal; the caption read 'I should have brought mine'. Drew had taken her shopping in the city center, and they were headed to dinner before getting ready for the sponsor party.

"Anyone miss you?" Paul asked, coming back into the living room.

"Nothing major," I commented, looking at him.

"Hungry?" he asked.

"Starved."

"Should we invite Hayden Grace and Drew?" I was touched that he would try and include them.

"Nah, they are having uncle-niece dinner, and I wasn't invited," I said, referring to the text.

"Well lucky for you, I'm free for dinner," he said, sauntering over and grabbing me by the waist as he kissed me, long and slow.

"You cooking?" I asked when he pulled away. His eyes got wide for a second, and I laughed. "Kidding!" I went into the kitchen and saw there was a decent selection to choose from. "Why don't I cook…my way of saying 'thank you' for today," I said, and he nodded. I decided on a pasta dish with a small salad. While I cooked we talked about the day and Ace's injury.

"Ace mentioned you usually ride alone, why is that?" I asked as I set out the dishes on the table.

"I like being alone, not worrying about another rider or having them slow me down," he shrugged. "I haven't needed any company, until I met you," he added, locking those blue eyes on mine. "Riding with you is more fun. Actually, everything with you is more fun," he added causally.

"Oh," it came out faintly, but it was all I had. We sat down for dinner, and Paul got two beers out of the fridge for us.

"Bon appetite," I said, once he was seated.

"It smells amazing," he said as he started eating. We talked for a while more about the mountain and the backcountry after we finished eating, until I had to finally leave to get ready for the sponsor party. I went to leave and then turned back as I remembered I needed to ask him something, and ran into him.

"Sorry," I said, taking a step back, but he caught me by the waist and closed the gap. He didn't give me another chance to say anything and instead leaned in for another kiss. My phone vibrated in my pocket, and he chuckled as I pulled away to check it.

"Hayden Grace," I explained. She had texted me that they were back at the hotel, also getting ready. "I have to go…are you going tonight?" I asked almost shyly.

"I don't really go to those parties anymore," he said dryly. I tried to hide the disappointment on my face and turned to leave.

"Andy?" he called after me.

"Yes?" I said, hoping he'd changed his mind.

"Will I see you again?" he asked.

"If you're lucky," I said, winking, and I headed back to the hotel with a smirk on my face.

CHAPTER 23

Back at the hotel, I was greeted with an assault of questions by Drew and Hayden Grace. Drew was already dressed in a brown pair of corduroy pants with a denim button up shirt and a blue tie with thin white diagonal stripes hung loosely around this neck. He had a navy blue blazer that hung off the back of the chair by the door that I knew he planned on wearing. Drew wasn't always the greatest dresser, but living in New York had improved his style, 'either that, or Stella had,' I thought to myself. Hayden Grace had already showered and was working on doing her hair. I was informed again, that Jonathan had placed third in his event and just 'how awesome' that was. I learned that Jonathan was going to be Hayden Grace's 'date' to the Burton party tonight as he had been invited as well. I raised my eyebrows in concern, but Drew looked at me and gave a look that everything would be fine. I also learned that the dress Hayden Grace was wearing tonight was one that her favorite uncle, Drew, bought her in town; I rolled my eyes as I headed into the bathroom. When I got out of the bathroom both Hayden Grace and Drew were ready. Hayden Grace looked so grown up—she wore her blonde hair down in loose waves. Her dress was maroon and came down to her mid-thigh; it had a scope collar and sheer bell sleeves. She wore a simple patent leather skinny belt at the waist. It draped her figure nicely, and I was shocked that Drew approved. She was missing something, and I fished through my bag until I found a long gold chain with several rings on it. I handed it to her to complete her look.

"Mom, are you sure?" she asked, recognizing the ring as my engagement ring and wedding ring. Both were pretty simple bands and did hold a lot of meaning to me, but I knew they meant a lot to her and she had a big weekend.

"You earned it," I said simply, before sending them on ahead to the party, primarily because Hayden Grace was pacing in the suite and driving Drew and I crazy.

"I'll be right behind you," I told them, as I pushed them out of the suite. In reality, it felt like heaven getting ready without having to worry about getting Hayden Grace ready or listening to Drew's sarcastic remarks.

I pulled the dress out of my suitcase. It was an older dress that Marla had talked me into buying a year earlier. It was a black, form fitted dress, with a low cut; the top and three-fourth length sleeves were covered in a lace. I paired it with black platform heels. Deciding that my hair was usually always up in a braid or ponytail, I opted to leave it down and wavy. I only added a few curls in hopes of taming some of the fly-away hairs. Keeping my make-up minimal, I grabbed my phone and coat and headed out the door to the Burton party.

I could tell where the party was about a block away from the venue. The music wasn't too loud, but there were people in and around the area, like they were headed to a rave. I pushed my way to the door and thought for a minute I might be turned away. However, my name was, in fact, on the list and I was let in without a problem. Inside the atmosphere was semi-dark, and a band played in the background at a reasonable level. There were a lot of people inside, but it wasn't wall-to-wall people. After I left my coat with the women at coat-check, I started to scan the party for my wandering family members. I spotted Drew first. He was at the bar chatting up a brunette.

"Drew," I said, as I approached. Instantly, the women looked uncomfortable.

"Jessica, this is my sister, Andrea Parker," he said quickly as an introduction, emphasizing the word 'sister'. The woman seemed to relax and then instant recognition flashed across her face.

"*The* Andy Parker?" she asked, shaking my hand.

"In the flesh," I said, more awkwardly than I meant. "Thank you for taking care of our hotel and moving everything," I said as sincerely as I could to Jessica.

"Not a problem. Paul doesn't ask me to do stuff for him too often so when he does I know it's important." I nodded in understanding.

"Have you seen Hayden Grace?" I asked Drew, wanting to leave him and Jessica alone; they looked like they had been in deep conversation before I interrupted. He pointed in the direction he last saw her, and I made my way through the crowd. I finally spotted her, and she looked more like a young woman than a teenager all dressed up. She was talking rather animatedly to a gentleman and, of course, Jonathan was by her side. I approached slowly, not wanting to invade her space, and waved. She saw me and waved back, flashing me a thumbs up. After accounting for everyone, I made my way to the bar and ordered a gin and tonic while I watched the scene unfold around me. There were business men and women working the crowds and mingling, shaking hands and getting to know the people. There was definitely a younger crowd as well, that was just about having fun and partying; the drinks were free—I didn't blame them. I sighed and leaned against the bar. I wasn't alone for long. A gentleman by the name of Roger approached me, and we talked about Hayden Grace and her opportunities as a rider and what Burton could do for her. I listened intently but knew I was out of my league, and the final decision would be Hayden Grace's. He was soon called away to talk to someone new, and I exhaled. I hadn't been at the party long, but I found it exhausting.

"Jessica was right," I heard behind me. I turned to find Paul standing there. He was dressed in black slacks with a black button up shirt and his sleeves rolled up to his elbows. I was surprised by his arrival. Normally, his appearance caused such a stir that you knew when he was coming before he got there.

"Right about what?" I asked, leaning back on the bar eyeing him closely.

"About you, being all dressed up and in need of decent company," he smirked, and I returned his smile.

"You clean up pretty well," I commented as he came closer, and ever so gently kissed me on the cheek.

"You look beautiful, Andy," he commented as he put his hand on the small of my back and ordered a drink from the bar.

"I thought you didn't come to these parties?" I asked after the bartender left.

"Clearly, an exception had to be made," he said, looking at me intently.

"Paul, you made it," I heard Jessica's almost melodic voice float over to us.

"Jessica, thank you for the advice. You were right, as always," he smiled, and pulled me in closer to where he was standing. I didn't know what it was about his touch, but it still sent shivers down my spine and in the pit of my core every time we connected.

"Where is Hayden Grace?" Paul asked after a moment.

"With Jonathan," I said, and pointed to the other side of the room where Hayden Grace was leaning over and whispering to Jonathan and laughing. I could tell he was working up the nerve to hold her hand. She glanced up almost as if she heard her name and saw Paul and smiled and waved back. I could tell she was in her element, and it was nice to see her so happy.

"Andy," Drew leaned over and whispered in my ear. "Go and get out of here. You don't get many nights like this. I'll make sure Hayden Grace gets home safely tonight, and I'll take her to breakfast in the morning. My flight leaves at noon and yours leaves at five, so you're off duty until ten-thirty tomorrow morning, officially." He winked at me and urged me again to go. I smiled, and he steered Jessica off to another corner of the party.

"Paul," I said, looking at him. He looked at me slightly perplexed.

"Yeah?"

"Let's go," I said coyly.

"Go where, I just got here," he said with confusion.

"Do you want to stay?"

"Hell no," he said with excitement as we made our way to the exit.

***

I felt like a high schooler ditching the prom. We got our coats at the door and headed back out into the city. I noticed snowflakes started to drift down as we walked the streets.

"I'm not sure why you came tonight, but thank you," I finally said.

"Andy, I came for you, always for you," he said simply, grabbing my hand as we walked. The snow was now picking up and was coming down in bigger flakes. Inevitably we ended up heading back to his condo.

"Why don't you like those events?" I asked.

"It's all about people trying to get a piece of you. Sponsor this, endorse that and say this. I mean, they do their job well, but it gets tiring. At first I was really into it, and those sponsors have helped my career, but now I just do what I need to do. It got to the point that people in my close circle were trying to get me to do things and I had had enough, so now I don't go—it makes me happier," he said, giving my hand a tight squeeze. I couldn't tell if he was always this honest or if this was hard for him. The streets were too dark for me to read his face.

"My feet are killing me," I commented, as we entered his condo. I quickly kicked off my heels and sank down on the sofa rubbing my feet.

"I don't know how you can even pretend to walk around in those things," Paul said, sitting down next to me handing me a beer.

"Years of practice," I commented dryly, rubbing my feet. He put his beer down and motioned for me to put my feet in his lap, to which I quickly obliged. He rubbed my feet slowly, and I took the scene in, slowly sipping on my beer. It had been so long since I had come to rely on another person; this current moment was something I wanted to try and remember for a long time.

"Andy, when do you leave Aspen?" Paul asked after a while.

"Tomorrow," I commented, thinking about our agenda. I heard Paul chuckle, and I looked at him.

"You're doing that thing with your head again," he said, still smirking.

"I can't help it—all the women in my family do it," I said with a half frown.

"You should stay," he said, looking at the fireplace after several moments.

"I don't have to be back with Hayden Grace until ten-thirty tomorrow morning," I said coyly, but when I looked at Paul, I could tell he wasn't paying any attention. "Wait, where do you want me to stay?" I asked with confusion as if I missed something.

"Out West…here," he paused and glanced at me.

"Paul, Hayden Grace and I have a life to get back to. This week has been amazing, but I have a job, a house and a dog that I have to return to," I said quietly, and he nodded.

"I know…it's just with you…I have all these emotions…. I haven't ever met anyone else like you," he said, turning to look at me and unleashing the full power of his blue eyes on me. I didn't know what to say. Instead I folded my legs underneath me so I was now kneeling next to him on the sofa. I leaned over and kissed him.

"Andy…" he started.

"Paul, I don't have any answers and I don't know what tomorrow will be like, but we do have tonight," I said again, and leaned over and kissed him. He kissed me back, moving his hand to the base of my neck and weaving it into my hair. Suddenly, he released my hair and stood up and leaned down to lift me off the sofa. He carried me up the short two flights of stairs, to the bedroom and laid me down on the bed. He kicked off his shoes, turned off the light and climbed into bed next to me…something about the mood had changed. I snuggled up next to him, and he stroked my hair; eventually I leaned up on my elbows to look at him. He was stoic as he laid there, a slight frown on his lips. I tried one more time, meeting his lips with my own. Surprise registered in his body, and he embraced me without hesitation. I sat up slightly and unzipped my dress and unceremoniously dropped it on the floor next to the bed. I slowly unbuttoned his shirt, halfway down he grabbed my hand, and I could see his blue eyes in the dark as he stared at me. In an instant, I was underneath him, and he was kissing me with the same passion he had earlier in the week. His fingers trailed down my neck to my breasts, causing me to groan. His fingers carefully traced my curves as they dipped down between my legs causing me to moan in pleasure. I then tugged at his pants, and he quickly removed them, rolling back on top of me. I gripped his back tighter as we made love with a sense of urgency and passion that was different from earlier in the week. But he couldn't keep up his pretenses, and I could tell that the flirty and fun atmosphere from prior was replaced with melancholy and a sense of sadness. It was like we were saying good-bye. I fell asleep with my head on his chest as he was stroking my hair.

Just like before when I had spent the night, the next morning I awoke to an empty bed, but the smell of coffee wafted up the stairs. Not wanting to put my dress back on, I looked through his clothes and found a pair of sweatpants and an old navy t-shirt that I slipped on. Making my way downstairs, I could hear the sound of pots and pans. Paul looked up when I entered the kitchen and smiled.

"Coffee?" he asked.

"Of course," I said, taking a seat at the counter. "What are you doing?" I asked after several minutes.

"Making breakfast," he said sheepishly.

"You don't cook," I pointed out.

"I thought I would attempt it," he said, clearly frustrated.

"Want some help?" I asked with a grin.

"I'm almost done…I think," he said as he concentrated on the eggs in the frying pan. After ten minutes, and only a few cuss words, breakfast was served. He had made scrambled eggs, toast and hash-browns. I had to admit that for his first time, the food wasn't awful. He watched me intently as I ate each bite and smiled when I finished.

"Well done, Mr. Westcott. I think there is hope for you yet," I commented dryly, and he gave me a small grin.

"What are your plans today?" he asked after a moment as I stood to clear the table.

"Hayden Grace and I need to work on her sponsor situation. She needs to make some decisions, and we need to make some calls. Afterwards, we need to pack up and get our stuff together. Our flight is at five-thirty so we will head to the airport around three or three-thirty," I said as I sat back down at the table.

"Need some help?" he asked.

"With?"

"The sponsors?"

"Really? You wouldn't mind?" I asked surprised.

"I offered," he said, and I got up again to get my phone out of my coat pocket.

"Here, there are several proposals and e-mails that I have already received not to mention the stack of business cards Drew has collected at the hotel," I said, giving him my phone as I went back into the kitchen to do the dishes.

"Some of these are not going to work out, and some sponsors tend to over promise and under deliver," he mumbled with authority as he worked his way through my e-mails. I let him read through the e-mails as I continued to wash the dishes and clean up the rest of the kitchen. While his breakfast turned out okay, he needed to work on not using every dish available to him for some scrambled eggs, toast and hash browns. Seeing as he was still intently reading the e-mails, I slipped upstairs to shower. After the shower, I decided to put the dress back on not having any other clothing options.

Almost an hour had passed since going upstairs to shower, when I padded back downstairs to find him still sitting at the kitchen table. A small vein throbbed in his forehead, and I could see tension in his jaw.

"Paul? Are you okay?" I asked, sitting down at the table. I put my hand on the table to reach for his, but he instantly removed his hands from the table.

"Is there something you need to ask me?" he asked his voice hoarse.

"No." I said with confusion.

"What is your relationship with Malinda Mitchell?" he asked, his voice still barely a whisper.

Oh shit—the e-mail.

"I'm currently the lead senior marketing executive working on an ad campaign for her women's Angel collection," I said quietly.

"Is that all?" he asked clearly furious.

"She offered me a job with her company. She wants Hayden Grace to represent her Angel collection and... she wants you to represent her Guardian collection," I said in a clipped tone.

"I know," he said without looking at me. He slid the phone across the table making sure that our hands never met.

"I was going to tell her no when I got home," I said defensively, as panic formed in my gut.

"You should have told me, earlier."

"There wasn't anything to tell."

"Nothing to tell?" he asked slightly raising his voice.

"I wasn't going to ask you," I said defensively.

"It takes a lot for me to trust people. People always want something from me, and I just thought you were different."

"I am different."

"If it wasn't this time, she would have asked you again and again until you couldn't refuse her anymore—that's how she works. It's how she has worked for years...I bet she didn't tell you that she was once my first sponsor."

"No," I said surprised.

"Shocking. She is very one-track minded, and with her it's the bottom line. She kept demanding more and more, and it started to affect my family and my riding. I broke off the contract, and she started to spread lies about me, hoping I would come back. She made it hard for me to get more sponsorships until I started winning consistently."

"I had no idea."

"As long as there is the possibility that she is in your life then you can't be in mine. I think you should leave," he finally said.

"But what about this week? What about all the things you said?" I asked, looking down at the table playing with my phone.

"Sometimes things fall apart just as quickly as they come together," he said, rising from the table.

"Seriously? That's it?" I asked, looking up at him.

"That's it...can you see yourself out?" he asked, and I nodded as he head upstairs. I could feel the tears start to well in my eyes as I rose. I didn't know what to do; I cared for Paul Westcott more than I thought until that very moment. I wanted to go upstairs and try to explaining the whole thing, but I wasn't sure what good it would do. Instead, I grabbed my coat and shoes and quietly left the condo, locking the door behind me.

I tried to get myself together as I walked back to the Hyatt. 'How quickly things can go so wro5rng,' I thought to myself as I entered the lobby. I put the best smile on my face I could, as I entered the suite.

"Hello? Hayden Grace? Drew?" I asked, walking around the suite. I spotted a note on the table that read that they had gone to breakfast. Sighing with relief at having a few moments to myself, I changed my clothes. I kept replaying the conversation in my head and anger kept building up inside me. I was angry with myself for not deleting the e-mail...for even considering Malinda's offer. I was angry with Paul for not getting the whole explanation and for giving up too quickly. I didn't know how to fix the rift between Paul and I, but I knew I needed to make at least one phone call before Hayden Grace and Drew returned.

CHAPTER 24

The phone rang several times before her voicemail picked up. Not leaving a message, I set down the phone and waited. It wouldn't be long before she called me back. Just then, the door opened, and in walked Hayden Grace and Drew.

"Hey Mom, how was your evening?" she asked, coming over and giving me a hug.

"It was good," I said, not wanting to ruin her very chipper mood. I could see Drew give me a look that he was clearly not convinced.

"How was the rest of your night?" I asked, changing the subject.

"It was amazing! Jonathan is so great...he held my hand at the end of the night...he's so great" and then she squealed, and I had to try to not laugh as Drew rolled his eyes behind her.

"How was breakfast?" I asked, after I clearly wasn't going to learn any more information about her evening.

"It was good; Uncle Drew walked me through the sponsor stuff. He said I needed to take a vested interest in my career and future," she mumbled, already distracted by her phone.

"Vested interest?" I said, raising an eyebrow at Drew, and he just smiled.

"Drew, how was your evening and breakfast?" I asked.

"It was good," he said vaguely. Then looking around to see if Hayden Grace was paying attention, he leaned over and whispered, "I don't know how you do it." I smiled and patted him on the knee; sometimes I wasn't sure either. We chatted for a bit more and then Drew announced he had to leave to make it to the airport on time.

"Bye, Uncle Drew, thank you so much for coming!" Hayden Grace said, hugging him tightly.

"You're so welcome. So proud of you this week Hayden Grace," he said, hugging her back. Watching the interaction warmed my heart.

"Bye sis…I know something is up, I can see it in your eyes…hang in there," he said, whispering to me before giving me a hug. "These last two days have been so interesting. We will have to do it again," he commented coyly.

"Thank you for coming—it meant a lot to Hayden Grace and I," I said, hugging him back. Then he was gone, and Hayden Grace and I were left to our own devices.

***

My phone rang, and I excused myself to the bathroom, as it seemed the only private room in the suite.

"Malinda," I said, when I answered.

"Andrea, I hope you have some good news for me. I'm not a patient woman and the suspense has been killing me" she replied, with no inflection in her voice.

"Sorry, it's not good news. Paul Westcott won't be signing with Guardian," I hesitated for a moment.

"What do you mean? I have seen how cozy you two have gotten, and it's been all over the news. How could you not make this deal?" she was calm, but her tone had an edge to it.

"It's not my deal to make. I was appointed to run your ad campaign, not track down sponsors who I may, or may not, know." I could hear my voice rising slightly.

"Andrea, I told you that if you couldn't make this happen," her voice was becoming frost.

"You said you would fire me. Go ahead, I don't even work for you, and frankly, I don't want to work for you, and I don't want Hayden Grace affiliated with your company. I don't like the way you do business," I said, trying to steady my voice.

"I underestimated you, Andrea, and I am clearly disappointed with all this information. You're missing out on something big, Andrea. I hope that Gary can overlook you losing his biggest client and that you still have a job to go home to," she practically hissed with ill-intent and hung up the phone.

'Me too,' I thought to myself as I exited the bathroom.

"Mom?" Hayden Grace confronted me as soon as I came out of the bathroom.

"Hayden Grace?" I asked, trying to create some room and space.

"What's going on?" she asked with concern.

"Remember that job I told you about?" She nodded.

"It's no longer an option. Malinda and I have had some creative differences," I said with a slight smile.

"What do you mean—*it's not on the table?*" Hayden Grace cried. "I don't want to go back to New Hampshire. I love it here," she said.

"This isn't home," I said, trying to calm myself.

"But with everything that has happened, I don't fit into that life anymore," she said, raising her voice.

"Hayden Grace, I'm sorry. There will be other opportunities; I'm sure we can make things work," I said gently.

"No, you have ruined everything," she yelled.

'There is all that teenage angst I had missed since we arrived here,' I thought to myself.

"Hayden Grace things are not ruined…"

"Have you talked to Paul? Maybe he can help," she said desperately.

"Paul is gone sweetie—I don't think that's going to work out anymore," I said, fighting my own tears at the moment.

"What did you do Mom? Did you have to ruin *everything?* I hate you!" she yelled at me and grabbed her phone, running to the door.

"Where do you think you're going?" I asked, standing up and moving to the door.

"Out," she said, very emboldened by the conversation.

"You can't just walk out on this conversation," I said, trying to catch the door.

"Watch me," she said, and bolted out the door and down the stairwell. I thought about chasing after her but flopped down on the bed instead. Aspen was a pretty safe town, and she clearly needed some time to cool off. Plus, I suspected she was going to go find Jonathan so that she could be 'consoled'.

"Where did today go wrong?" I mumbled to myself.

***

Not knowing what else to do I took out my laptop and checked e-mails. Gary had already heard from Malinda and was livid about losing the account, but also over the fact that she had tried to steal me away for her company. He said that he expected to see me at the Boston office first thing Monday morning so we could straighten this whole thing out.

'At least I have a job for one more day,' I thought to myself.

Drew sent me an e-mail of sponsors that he and Hayden Grace had talked about and that had serious offers on the table. I needed to look over the list and confirm, and then contact them all per his instructions.

"Easier said than done," I mumbled, rolling my eyes at his e-mail. Since I didn't have anything else to do, I started in on the list. The first three companies listed I called and declined their interest offers; from the notes that Drew left, they really didn't seem like a good fit for Hayden Grace. My next call was to Burton with whom Hayden Grace was most excited about. It wasn't a big sponsorship but it was a start, and as she progressed there was potential for growth within the company. Coincidentally, it was Roger from the party that I spoke to on the phone. He was excited over this new partnership but made mention that Hayden Grace needed to keep competing and getting her name out there to stay on everyone's mind. I reminded him that by coming in second at Regional 6, Hayden Grace had automatically qualified for the Big Bear Exhibition in Vail in two weeks. Depending on the outcome, he said there would be other competitions in and around the West Coast for Hayden Grace. He hinted that living on the West Coast would make things easier, and probably be cheaper for us.

"I couldn't agree more," I replied before ending the call with him.

I called the four other sponsors on the list that Drew had indicated were promising, but a more detailed conversation would be needed. Vans, Monster and NorthFace were all excited over the start of this sponsorship and had offered Hayden Grace a small entry-level deal. It was more than what we left New Hampshire with. The fourth company I called was Vail Resorts Company which owned about eight different resorts in the California and Colorado area. I spoke with a woman named Gina, and she was very up front and honest with me that they only had a small sponsorship deal for Hayden Grace, but that my name had been given to them by Joel from Mount Sunapee. They were very interested in my talents and should I ever consider moving out West, she would love to sit down and meet with me about what I could possibly offer them as a company.

'What an intriguing opportunity,' I wondered to myself.

After I had that all sorted out, I tried to call Paul, but he didn't answer, and I didn't leave a message. I tried to call Hayden Grace, and she didn't answer, but I did leave her a very specific message. It was now just a little past noon, and I had no real plans and a couple of hours before we had to leave. I decided that I would do the only thing that had ever made any real sense or provided any clarity in my life – I grabbed my ski gear and headed to the Silver Queen Gondola. I had time for a quick run down the mountain. At the top of the mountain I caught myself walking toward the private lodge in the back before I remembered that that wasn't my life; he had made that abundantly clear.

I got in line with everyone else and soon found myself at the top of a trail ready to go. I explored the trails and mountains for as long as I could, until I couldn't ignore the rumbling in my stomach any further. I still wasn't sure about anything, but I knew that the mountain in Aspen was different than anything back home, and like Hayden Grace I wasn't ready to part with it either.

When I got off the gondola I decided to swing by Paul's condo to see if he was home; I wanted the chance to explain myself. When I walked up, I saw all the lights were off. Peering in the window, I saw that all his things were gone. My heart sank a little at the finality of it all. Sulking, I ventured into town for something quick to eat. The town was thinning out as the competition was coming to an end. Making my way back to the hotel, I saw Hayden Grace and Jonathan in the lobby, and it looked like she might be crying. Deciding it was best to leave it alone, I kept going until I got to the suite. Having too much idle energy I started to pack our things and had everything packed and waiting by the door when Hayden Grace returned.

"Hayden Grace," I acknowledged, when she entered the suite. She glared at me and grunted a response and then headed into the bathroom. I sighed and went and knocked on the door.

"Hayden Grace, come out," I said. I could hear her fumbling in the bathroom but no response.

"Hayden Grace, let's talk about this," I said again, after several minutes.

"There's nothing to talk about. You ruined my life," she said through the door, and I could hear the tears through her voice.

"Fine, I agree. I ruined your life," 'and probably mine,' I thought to myself as I stared at the back of the door. "It's time to go."

***

Hayden Grace continued with the silent treatment. She didn't speak to me again until we landed in Boston.

"Mom?"

"Yes?"

"Do you miss him?"

"Who?"

"Paul."

"Yes," I said, after a moment's hesitation.

"I miss Jonathan," and then she put her headphones back in and continued her silent treatment. Given that it was almost two in the morning when we landed in Boston, we had little traffic; we were able to make it to the house in record time. We had only been gone a week, but everything felt so different. I felt like a different person.

Molly was the first one to meet us at the door, and she was clearly excited. My parents woke up when they heard all the commotion and were so eager to see Hayden Grace. I was impressed by how well she faked her excitement. She answered all their questions and showed them her medal, which they 'oohed' and 'awed' over, of course. After about thirty minutes she put her headphones back on and disappeared to her room. My mom and dad gave me questionable looks, and I shrugged my shoulders. I didn't have the energy to relive the entire story; I was starting to think it was a dream.

CHAPTER 25

On Monday, Hayden Grace and I fell back into our normal routine. We got up early that morning, and I dropped her off at school. She mumbled something about staying late to make up some homework and then practice. I nodded in acknowledgement, sipping on my second cup of coffee. She still hadn't really spoken to me since Saturday; we were communicating in mostly grunts and nods.

The traffic into Boston was horrendous, and I was an hour late getting to the office. I don't know what I expected. I thought things would have changed while I was gone, but everything looked just like I had left it; it felt like I was walking into a stranger's life. Marla got to me first when I entered the office.

"So…?" she asked with excitement.

"So?" I mumbled, dropping my things at my desk and turning on the computer.

"I heard that Aspen was exciting."

"Not in the way you think it was," I commented. She was about to say something further when Gary barked my name from his office.

"Good luck with that," she whispered, slinking away to her desk. Moments later I was sitting in Gary's office. He was agitated and looked like he had aged immensely since I last saw him.

"Andrea, things have taken an unfortunate turn since you left for Aspen. This was why I was even hesitant to let you go. As you know, Malinda called in a panic on Saturday threatening the withdrawal of her entire campaign. I don't have to tell you what a big blow that would be for this company," he mumbled, looking past me at something in the distance. "But since then, Malinda and I have spoken, and I have smoothed things over. She has agreed, rather reluctantly, to keep the Angel account with us, but she no longer feels comfortable with you on the account." I stared incredulously at him, as he continued to speak.

"I am going to put Marla as the lead on this account, and I'm going to have to let you go. I simply cannot keep you as part of the company; you really messed up big on this one."

"She wanted me to leave the company and work for her, then I refused her offer, and *I* messed up big on this account?" I asked with disbelief in my voice.

"Andrea, its business—don't take it personally."

"Don't take it personally?! Are you kidding me? That's bullshit because this is completely personal. She wanted me to sign my daughter and my…date to a contract deal with her company. That wasn't my job; my job was marketing. Now she is getting me fired?" I shouted back, as I felt the anger rise within me.

"Please clean out your desk," he said after a moment, and dismissed me. I sighed in exasperation as I left his office, slamming the door. I heard him buzz the secretary for Marla next. We passed in the hallway, and the look on my face must have given away my true feelings as she instantly looked skeptical about what was going on.

"Good luck," I mumbled to her as I went to my desk and packed my things up. All I wanted to do was get out of there. I could hear a slight commotion coming from Gary's office, and a small smile played on my lips.

'Give 'em hell, Marla,' I thought to myself and walked out of the office.

Instead of going home I went straight to the mountain. It was well after lunchtime by the time I arrived, and I stopped to eat something in the café before heading out. Several people asked how the competition had gone and how I enjoyed Aspen.

"It was like a dream," I responded to Rachel who pestered me with a thousand questions, mostly centered on 'PW'. I had practically made it to the chairlift when I heard my name.

"Andy?" I turned to see Joel lumbering toward me.

"Joel."

"Where are you going?" he asked with suspicion.

"Where do you think?"

"I need a favor," he started.

"This all started with a favor."

"It's not what you think," he said, holding up his hands in surrender.

"What can I help you with?" I said, realizing I was being difficult.

"I need you to call Gina back at Vail Resorts. She has called me several times since your conversation on Saturday."

"Why didn't she just call me? What is your relationship with Gina?" I asked.

"I don't know what it is about, but I think it would be worth your time. Gina is my sister," he said and turned away. Oh!

"Joel...thank you," I called after him, and he just raised his arm and waved in my direction. I had no idea Joel had a sister and that she also worked in the ski industry—'must be a family thing,' I thought to myself with a small smile. I made my way up to the mountain and backcountry without running into anyone else. I had skied in the backcountry so many times, but today, it had a different feel. I felt bigger than the mountain; everything seemed smaller, more finite. I no longer felt lost in the landscape. As I made my way down the mountain I paused at the table top jumps, but as the memories flooded me I continued on—it was better to forget and move on.

I finished just as Hayden Grace started pipe practice. I stood off to the side and watched. She rode differently today than she had on Thursday. She rode with such aggression and recklessness, but it kept getting the better of her causing her to wipe out. I could tell Coach Davis was getting frustrated with her as he kept yelling from the top. I don't know if she could hear him or if she chose to block him out. After practice I observed her trying to talk to several of the other kids, but they seemed to move away from her; even Lucie and Madison barely spoke to her at the end of practice.

I waited outside the locker room, and I could see surprise registered on her face when she left the locker room and saw me standing there. I had already seen Lisa and told her I would take Hayden Grace home. Lisa seemed cordial, but something seemed off; by now I would have guessed that Madison had told her mother that she saw her best friend's mother slapping her father. Knowing Lisa, she was going to handle her family business privately, keeping a happy façade. Hayden Grace and I walked to the car in silence. On the drive home she put her earphones in and continued to ignore me, which was probably for the best as I didn't have anything to say. When we got home she went straight to her room and closed the door. Moments later, music could be heard through the door.

Setting my stuff down I half-heartedly made dinner and knocked on her door to let her know. She emerged ten minutes later and quickly ate before heading back to her room. I looked at my phone, and I had missed calls from Drew and Marla. I ignored both; instead, I curled up on the sofa with Molly and fell asleep to the TV.

***

Tuesday felt like it was going to be a better day than Monday. At least today I couldn't be fired, I reminded myself. I got up and took Hayden Grace to school. She continued not to speak to me. When I got back home, I didn't know what to do with myself, so I sat on the sofa and clicked on the TV. It wasn't ten minutes later when my phone rang. It was the coordinator from the Big Bear Exhibition. The young woman confirmed that Hayden Grace had qualified for their competition and asked if she would be competing. We already knew she had qualified, and without hesitation, I responded that she would be there. Really, that decision made the rest seem easy. I felt different since Aspen, and I knew Hayden Grace felt different; this no longer felt like home, and it was time to move on.

After getting off the phone with the competition organizer, I called Gina from Vail Resorts. We had a long discussion, and she asked if I could fly to Denver for a meeting as soon as possible. Knowing that I no longer had any obligations at work, I agreed. I called my parents, and learned they were still in Boston visiting friends. I asked if they could come back and stay with Hayden Grace for a couple of days, and they agreed. I made flight arrangements and started packing. I was so focused on the plans for the rest of the week that I didn't realize what time it was until I heard Hayden Grace open the front door. Molly let out a bark and ran to greet her. My plan only held water if Hayden Grace was on board. Although I didn't think it was going to be tough sell.

Hayden Grace paused at my suitcase in the hallway but continued to her room and closed the door. I made dinner and knocked on her door; several moments later she emerged and came to sit at the table. I was about to speak when she started to speak.

"Mom, I don't think I fit in here anymore," she said quietly, not looking at me.

"I don't think we do either," I said after a moment. She instantly looked up at me, as a puzzled look crossed her face. "I think it's time for a change," I added.

"What do you mean?"

"I was fired from work on Monday," I sheepishly admitted.

"But why…the campaign—they loved it," she said, coming to my defense.

"Remember Angel Apparel?" She nodded in understanding. "Malinda, the CEO, changed her mind and would only give me the contract if I signed Paul and you to sponsorship deals. I refused, and I got fired." It was the simplest explanation.

"That's not fair," she commented, looking big-eyed.

"Life's not fair," I said with a sigh. "Anyway, Hayden Grace, I have been doing a lot of thinking since then, and your snowboarding career is taking off and you need to be out there. Everyone has told me so, and I couldn't agree more. I think we need to move," I said, but before I finished Hayden Grace had launched herself from her chair and hurled herself at me and buried her face in my shoulder as she asked a thousand questions.

"Is that a yes?" I laughed, and she nodded and continued to repeat her questions.

"Whoa. I don't have any answers. I'm flying out tomorrow for a job interview, and then we will take it from there." She pressed me for more details, but I refused to tell her in case it didn't work out.

"What am I going to do?" she asked when I told her my travel plans.

"You are going to get ready for the Big Bear Exhibition in Vail," I said, and she erupted in excitement.

"So I did qualify?"

"Yes, the event organizer called today to confirm," I said with a smile.

"Mom?" she asked after several moments.

"Yes?"

"I'm sorry," she barely whispered.

"For what?" I asked, eyeing her closely.

"For everything I said in Aspen. I didn't really mean it; you didn't ruin my life, and I don't hate you."

"Apology accepted," I said and walked over to kiss her on the cheek. We sat at the table for the rest of the night talking about the competition and possible plans. She filled me in on what Jonathan was up to and how Lucie and Madison were acting weird and no longer wanted to hang out with her. I felt like we had reached normal again, and I smiled.

"Oh, Mom?" Hayden Grace said on her way to bed.

"Yes?"

"I thought you would want to know that Paul took a pretty bad spill while riding in Italy, but that the report says he's going to be okay." She just shrugged and disappeared down the hallway. I sat quietly for a moment as my heart skipped a beat.

"Okay," I whispered to myself, when I was finally able to think again.

CHAPTER 26

I was exhausted when I pulled back in the driveway of my house on Saturday night. It had been such a long week. My body was reeling from the long back to back trips to Colorado, knowing I had another one coming up in less than a week. I had just pulled my suitcase out of the trunk when the front door swung open and Molly and Hayden Grace bounded out towards me. Molly jumped up and barked while Hayden Grace latched on in a huge hug. In reality, the time apart was probably the longest time we had been apart since Stefan died.

"I missed you, kid," I said to Hayden Grace, setting her down.

"You shouldn't go away again like that," she commented.

"Why? Is everything okay?" I asked with concern.

"Ummm…it was okay…," she whispered, causing me to look at her more closely. It was only then that I noticed the black eye.

"What the hell happened to you?" I exclaimed.

"I got into a fight," she replied sheepishly.

"You got into a what?" I asked again in disbelief as we made our way inside. Once inside, I set my stuff down before everyone started asking me a thousand questions.

"No. I ask the questions first," I said, standing in the kitchen with my hands on my hips, staring at Hayden Grace and my parents. "What happened while I was gone?" I repeated.

"I got into a fight with Madison," Hayden Grace finally said.

"Why? Where? When?"

"It was yesterday at club practice. She made some remark about you and her dad, and then she wouldn't let it go. She shoved me and said you were using Paul the same way you probably used her dad. I don't know what came over me but I punched her, and then she hit me back and we were rolling around in the snow until Coach Davis separated us," she admitted quietly.

"Coach Davis called us at home and let us know they were both suspended from the team for the rest of the week," my mother added.

"And you didn't call?"

"We wanted you to focus on your interview. Nothing was going to change," my dad added. I mulled over the information for a minute.

"Hayden Grace, how are you feeling?" I asked, a bit more calm.

"Well, my hand hurt really badly afterwards but now its fine...but overall I feel frustrated, mad, sorry..." she said all in one breath.

"No matter how mad people make us, that is no reason to punch them," I commented, and she nodded.

"Gramps has already told me, and then he showed me the correct way to throw a punch," she said, and he nodded as I raised my eyebrows.

"Mom, why would Madison say all those things?" she questioned. I took a big sigh.

"Remember that guy I was seeing before we left for Aspen? Well, it turns out that it was Madison's dad—I just didn't know it was Madison's dad because I had never met him. I confronted him in Aspen after that awfully awkward dinner we had, and Madison saw me slap him," I confessed much to the astonishment of the group.

"What a mess," my mother commented.

"He probably deserved worse," my dad said, clearly frustrated.

"What an ass," Hayden Grace said.

"Hayden Grace...language," I said, internally agreeing with her.

"What? It's true," she said defensively.

"Still," I said, and she slumped in her seat a little bit.

"Have you and Madison spoken since?" I asked.

"No. Her mom came and got her, and she was so angry. Rumor has it Madison is not coming back to the club team." That didn't surprise me. Knowing Lisa, they would probably move or start over somewhere else; she didn't seem like one that dealt with conflict well.

I hadn't been in touch too much since I left with such focused purpose and now I realized what a mistake that was. I was a mom first and most importantly, and I was proud of that, but I had to admit that the time apart had been refreshing. It gave me a lot of time to be still for a moment and think as I planned our future, but I realized I should have checked in more often. Hayden Grace handed me a cup of coffee, and my dad pulled out a chair at the kitchen table for me. I sat down, taking a sip of coffee as they all sat around me looking very intently.

"So?" my mom finally said, breaking the silence and changing the subject.

"So…" I said, keeping my family in suspense. Unable to keep the story to myself much longer, I grinned.

"I'll start at the beginning," I said vaguely. "My flights over were good, no turbulence or delays."

"Oh spit it out already…did you get the job?" my dad interrupted.

"I got the job," I finally said with a broad smile. The room erupted in cheers and applause. Hayden Grace jumped up and did a little dance before hugging me. Molly even started barking in all the excitement, causing us all to laugh.

"What is the job?" my dad asked after a couple of minutes, when everyone settled back down.

"Well, through April I will be a ski instructor/backcountry guide at their NorthStar property at Tahoe. After April I will move into their marketing department as Director of Marketing Services," I said with a grin. "But I haven't accepted anything. We don't have to make any decisions until after Big Bear next week," I added, much to the dismay of everyone in the room. In truth, it had been a great visit. Gina was warm and inviting from the second I got there. She personally picked me up at the airport on Wednesday, and we had dinner. Thursday she toured me around the headquarters in Colorado and mostly we sat and talked about what my experience was, what my desired future outcomes were, and how they fit in with Vail Resorts. We then talked about Hayden Grace and how she fit into the picture. My overall impression with Vail Resorts was that it was very family oriented and might just be the perfect fit for Hayden Grace and I. On Friday we skied at Breckenridge most of the day, and then at dinner that evening she offered me the two positions. She finally admitted the reason she had called Joel was that she didn't want to seem over eager with me, considering that the current Director of Marketing had just given his notice and this would be a perfect opportunity. It was a huge decision, however, and I wasn't sure I wanted to make it without talking to my family first, which she understood.

"I think that's enough for tonight," I said standing. "I will see everyone in the morning," I added, before heading to bed. Everyone nodded in understanding and headed towards their respective areas. Sighing with relief that the conversation had gone well, I crawled into bed thinking about Hayden Grace and her altercation with Madison. I had just turned the bedside light off when I heard a knock on the door.

"Yes?"

"Mom, can I come in?"

"Of course," I said, sitting up. She came in with Molly in tow, and they both crawled into bed with me. "What's going on?" I asked, slightly surprised.

"I missed you. I don't need a reason," she mumbled.

"Hayden Grace?" I asked, poking her with my finger.

"Mom, I want to move so badly," she whispered, wiggling slightly under my poking.

"Why, what's going on?"

"Well, there was the fight with Madison, but she really hasn't been talking to me since Aspen. At first I thought she was just mad that I placed at Regional 6 and she didn't. Then I heard rumors on the club team that she was saying I was better than everyone else because I placed and 'PW' was dating my mom," she paused, and I cringed inwardly.

"What about Lucie?" I asked.

"Lucie is leaving the team after this season. She said she no longer enjoys the riding and would rather be doing other things. So she hasn't really been into hanging out so much," she mumbled again.

"Hayden Grace, I just want to make sure that you aren't running away from something rather than facing it head on," I said, leaning over to face her.

"I don't think I'm running away from anything, there just isn't anything keeping me here anymore."

"Well said," I said, rolling back over and closing my eyes.

"Love you Mom."

"Love you Hayden Grace."

***

The next morning my parents were waiting for me at the kitchen table when I rolled out of bed. I felt like I was sixteen again, and I was in trouble. They both sat there and motioned for me to join them. Someone had the forethought to prepare a cup of coffee which was on the table as I sat down.

"Andy, we are worried about you and Hayden Grace," my mom began.

"You both have been so different since you returned from Aspen," my dad commented.

"Aspen was a pretty life changing experience," I commented back, taking a long sip of coffee.

"We want to be supportive, but we just don't know how," my mom carefully added. There was a long pause as I waited for them to get to the point.

"What your mom and I are trying to say is we can't move with you to the West Coast, but we want to make things easier for you. We have been talking for a while about selling the house on Long Island, and we wanted to move further north in order to be closer to you and Hayden Grace and some of our friends," my dad said.

"But we won't be here." I said in confusion.

"We understand that, but we would like to put our house up for sale and live in yours," my mom finished my dad's thought.

"Really?" I asked skeptically. It seemed too easy.

"I see you thinking, but there are no strings attached," my dad said.

"Okay," I commented, not knowing what to say. The fact was that it would be less stressful having my parents move in to the Newbury house. The house held sentimental value for me and Hayden Grace as it was the house that Stefan and I bought together; it was the house she had lived in her whole life. But at the same time that it was the house that Stefan and I bought together, it was also the house she had lived in her whole life; maybe it was time to let it go.

"So that's a yes?" my mom pressed.

"It's an okay. I need time to think it all through," I said, getting up and leaving the kitchen table.

"Where are you going?" my dad asked in confusion.

"It's Sunday, so I'm going to work on the mountain," I said, and headed for the bedroom.

***

Being at the mountain finally felt somewhat normal, and everyone gave me the space I wanted; no one had any questions for me, and no one had any favors. It was my normal routine. My parents dropped Hayden Grace off at the mountain around eleven so she could practice while I finished up lessons. I got done early and went to watch her practice. Her riding was good, and it looked to be consistent with her week in Aspen; she seemed more relaxed. Hayden Grace saw me standing at the bottom and asked me to watch one more run which I did, happily. When she was done she glided down to me, and she was beaming.

"Was that a new trick at the end?" I questioned.

"You did notice! I had a bet with Coach Davis that you would notice, and he said you wouldn't," she grinned.

"I hope you bet big," I laughed as she headed into the locker room. As she did I slid a glance to my left and saw a gentleman standing there. He looked familiar, and my heart started to race; I quickly approached him.

"Paul?" I questioned. The man turned around, and I stared into his pale green eyes.

"Excuse me?" he said.

"Umm, so sorry, I mistook you for someone else," I mumbled, walking away. The same thing had happened to me when I was in Colorado at the airport. I mistook the Starbucks barista for Paul Westcott. It was humorous now, thinking about it, but then it was mortifying. My mind was playing tricks with my heart, and I felt like I was going crazy.

***

Monday and Tuesday went by quickly and before I realized it Hayden Grace and I had a flight in the morning for Vail. My parents were set on staying with Molly and even offered to start packing things for our move. I had told them we weren't set with anything, but they insisted that it made the best sense. I finally agreed to have them pack up specific things that I knew would have to go to Goodwill regardless of if we were moving or not.

Hayden Grace wasn't as excited about going to Vail as she had been about going to Aspen. Things were different; her friends weren't going, let alone talking to her. Her coach wasn't going; her uncle wouldn't be there and neither would Paul. Jonathan, on the one hand, was going to try and meet Hayden Grace for a day or two before he had to travel to his own competition at Breckenridge. Those plans were still up in the air, but she clung to the hope that they would happen. Hayden Grace had gone to Aspen as an unknown but at Big Bear she was going to face spectators and competitors she had already beaten, and I could tell the added pressure was weighing on her shoulders.

"Don't worry…we will tackle this as we always do—together," I told her the night before we left, and she nodded.

CHAPTER 27

This time, unlike in Aspen, we were staying in sponsored housing for the competition that Gina had insisted on setting it up for us. We were in the Vail Village which was really close to the mountain and the ski lift. Actually, it was probably less than a hundred yards from our front door to the ski lift. The room was a good size and had a kitchen and living room so we could eat in instead of eating out the whole time; it was an added bonus for sure. When we got into our room, a welcome basket was waiting on us from the entire Vail Resort family. Hayden Grace was very impressed with the accommodations and gift basket, but I could tell she was nervous.

Once situated in the room, we went to walk around and check-in for the Exhibition. Check-in went smoothly and from the schedule we saw that Hayden Grace had time to practice on Thursday; qualifying was on Friday, and the finals would be on Saturday. There would be no time to spare on this trip because our flight home was first thing on Sunday morning. We had just left the check-in tent when Hayden Grace got a text that caused her to gasp.

"Mom, we have to go back to the village right away," she said, grabbing my arm and pulling me along.

"Why?" I responded, trying to catch my balance.

"Because of this," she turned her phone to show me she had just gotten a text from Jonathan, and it was a picture of the lobby of our villa. He had made it.

"Okay," I said, finally understanding. We made it back to the lobby of the Villa in no time. Once she saw him she let go of my arm and ran to Jonathan, giving him a big hug. I smiled—it was such a sweet moment; I couldn't help but feel happy for her. Jonathan wasn't alone, and his parents came over to introduce themselves; their names were Cindy and Matt. We chatted together for a while as the two of them had their own moment. From his parents I learned they were just staying the one night and hoping to watch Hayden Grace's practice rounds before leaving for Breckenridge. Jonathan's tournament was a day off from Hayden Grace's, and he would practice on Friday, qualify on Saturday and then have the finals on Sunday.

"Mom, can we go to dinner?" Hayden Grace asked, after about fifteen minutes.

"Can who go to dinner?" I clarified, knowing that I wasn't going to let her go by herself with Jonathan no matter how much I liked him. I may have been into breaking Stefan's rules lately, but even I agreed she was still a little young to be dating.

"All of us," she said, reading my expression.

"That would be fine with me if Jonathan's parents also agree," I said, looking at them, and they nodded. It was then decided we would eat at Tavern on the Square before calling it a night. Overall, dinner was great. Jonathan and Hayden Grace carried on much of the conversation. Occasionally, Cindy or Matt would ask a question, but eventually Hayden Grace or Jonathan would take over.

"Hayden Grace, have you heard from PW?" Jonathan asked at one point.

"It's Paul," she said automatically.

"Sorry, Paul," he replied, a little sheepish. I don't think that was his first reminder.

"No, not since Aspen,"

"Sorry, you must be disappointed," Jonathan replied.

"Don't be sorry; he's just a normal person," she replied, glancing at me, and I smiled but Jonathan looked unconvinced.

"Did you hear about his accident," Jonathan asked across the table. I couldn't help but lean in a little to eavesdrop on this conversation. I know it was probably all over the internet, but I wasn't going to seek out information about Paul; however, if it happened in my company, I wasn't going to reject it either.

"Yeah, it was bad," Hayden Grace whispered, looking up at me. She had known it was worse than she had led on when she mentioned it last week. Look at her trying to protect her mom.

"They said he will make a full recovery," Jonathan continued on.

"I hope so…he is a great rider," Hayden Grace said before changing the subject. My mind reeled over the little bit of information shared. I had done a good job of trying to forget Paul Westcott, but just as I thought I had the lid on that tightly sealed, someone would say something and it all came gushing out. Sigh.

***

Hayden Grace had an early morning practice time, so I met Jonathan and his parents at the bottom of the pipe as we watched her take her runs. She was focused and determined with each run. The longer she practiced, the more people stopped to watch. Jonathan clapped and cheered with each run. His parents seemed impressed with her abilities, as they got caught up in the excitement and started clapping and cheering along. She finished her practice runs a little after one, and we all had lunch together before they left. Jonathan leaving was bittersweet for Hayden Grace, but she handled the departure well as she wished him luck on his competition. I shook hands with Cindy and Matt, and then they were off to Breckenridge. We had just settled back into the hotel when my phone rang.

"Drew," I said, looking at Hayden Grace who perked up.

"Andy, you should have told me," he said, skipping the pleasantries.

"Told you what?"

"About Paul, about your job, about Hayden Grace," he said with frustration.

"Well Hayden Grace is right here, if you want to talk to her," I said, trying to alert him to the fact I wasn't alone, and I wasn't going to openly talk about everything in front of her.

"Well let me talk to the professional snowboarder," he teased, changing his tone. I handed the phone off to Hayden Grace, and they chatted. She told him all about Vail and how her practice runs had gone. She even filled him in about Jonathan and his visit. When they were done, she handed the phone back to me and said she was going to watch a movie on her laptop. I waited for her to put her headphones in before I started to talk to Drew again.

"What did you want me to tell you?" I finally said.

"Everything…instead I have to learn from Mom and Jessica about everything."

"Jessica?"

"You remember…"

"I remember who she is; I didn't realize you had kept in touch," I said, irritated.

"We have kept in touch…some," he said, suddenly vaguely.

"Is she there with you now?" I hissed, as realization hit me.

"Not at this moment," he said sheepishly, causing me to laugh. "But you can imagine my surprise over dinner last night…"

"In the city?" I interrupted.

"Yes, she was in New York," he said, laying it out for me, "…my surprise over dinner last night when she mentioned Paul and his accident. I knew you wouldn't have been with him in Italy, not my sensible, responsible sister Andrea Parker. But I figured you would have been there when he returned to nurse him back to health and all, and so I told her as much. Then Jessica drops a bomb on me and informs me that she didn't think that the two of you had spoken since Aspen," he paused, and I was about to interject before he continued. "Then I talked to Mom, and she said you were fired from work and things started to click into place. He found out about the evil witch's plan didn't he?" Drew accused.

"Yes," I replied meekly.

"How? You were going to reject that plan, or did you change your mind?"

"He saw it on my phone, and he didn't give me a chance to explain. Malinda was furious and convinced Gary that it was my fault, and he fired me to keep her contract," I mumbled.

"Andy, why didn't you tell me?"

"It wouldn't make a difference—it is what it is," I said.

"Well, if it makes you feel better, he's a wreck," Drew added.

"Who?"

"Paul."

"Oh," it was the only phrase to escape my lips. Drew grilled me a little while longer before he asked about my job prospect. I relaxed and told him about Vail Resorts and the offer. He asked further questions until he was satisfied with all the answers. We disconnected about thirty minutes later, the conversation leaving me drained. I curled up with Hayden Grace and finished watching the movie she had started.

***

Hayden Grace was up and dressed and ready to go before I even opened my eyes the next day. I told her she could go on without me, but she said she would wait. Although she said she would wait, she paced nervously while I got ready.

"Are you going to be okay?" I finally asked, as we were about to leave.

"Yeah, I just need to get into the pipe," she said…I was unconvinced, but I let it slide.

Just as in Aspen, we parted at the competition entrance. She went off to get ready for her qualifying rounds, and I went to find a spot in the grandstand. It was still early, so I was able to find a good spot and within no time the announcers were announcing that we were ready to start the qualifying round. There were a total of ten girls in the first qualifying round. I recognized two of the names from Aspen; neither girl had done exceptionally well, and I sighed in relief. The qualifying round was uneventful, and Hayden Grace repeated her final run from Aspen and came in first in her qualifying heat. She made it look effortless. The event organizers quickly announced the next qualifying round would begin in fifteen minutes and that the current riders needed to clear the area. The events at Big Bear were on a tight schedule. I found Hayden Grace off to the side, taking off her gear, and she smiled when she saw me.

"That felt good," she said, whispering in my shoulder as we embraced.

"It looked good, too. You looked more relaxed and in control," I commented, and she nodded.

"I had a lot of time to think about everything since Aspen. I want to be riding more than anything, and I love being on the mountain every day. I love the height of the tricks and the rush you get when first entering the pipe. I was meant to do this, and now that I know I can do this; I feel more relaxed," she said, looking at me.

"Who are you and what have you done with my fifteen-year-old little girl," I said in awe of her observation.

"I'm still her, mom," she said, rolling her eyes at me, causing me to laugh.

"You're more like your dad than you know," I commented, causing her to grin as we headed back to the room.

The trip to Vail was much less exciting than the trip to Aspen had been. There were no backcountry adventures, sponsor parties or romantic encounters. Both Hayden Grace and I instead decided to stay in for the rest of day. She didn't want to know what the scores of the other girls were, and she had no interest in window shopping or wandering around Vail. She mostly texted on her phone and watched movies, and I, for the most part, sat with her and watched movies until I grew restless. I finally announced I was going out to get dinner, and she nodded but made no move to join me. I got dressed and headed out into the Village to find something to bring back.

I had finally decided on pizza and was waiting in line when someone tapped me on the shoulder, causing me to spin around.

"Andy Parker," Scott said, grinning back at me.

"Scott…I don't know your last name," I chided back.

"Savage," he said as I puzzled over the last name.

"Wait, are you…"

"Related to Ace Savage? Yeah, he's my brother," he completed my thought.

"I met him; he's a great guide," I said unsure if he knew about his brother's injury.

"Don't play coy with me Parker. You saved my brother's life in Telluride. He told me all about it," he said, dropping all the playfulness in his voice.

"It was nothing, really. How is he doing?"

"Ace? He's doing fine. He had a concussion and tore his MCL again, but all things considered he's fine. Nothing he can't handle."

"That's really great to hear," I commented back, as the cashier called me forward to place my order.

"You can't get away from me that easily," Scott quipped, stepping up with me and placing his own order, telling the cashier he was paying for everything.

"Thank you," I finally said in disbelief.

"Thank *you*. First Trip and then Ace—too bad you weren't around when Paul got injured," he said, shaking his head. Just the mention of Paul's name felt like a punch to the gut leaving me breathless.

"Was it that bad?" I asked, afraid of the answer.

"Man, it was the worst. We weren't even in the backcountry; we were just riding the slopes on the mountain, ya know?" he asked, not really expecting a response.

"It's like he just lost his concentration for a second and that's all it took."

"None of us knew what to do while we waited for ski patrol; he was in a lot of pain. I went with him to the hospital," he paused, looking at me before he continued.

"He asked for you."

"He asked for me?" I asked confused.

"Before the doctors were able to give him the pain meds and while he was lying there. He was barely conscious, and he asked for you."

"I had no idea."

"I figured the guy is so stubborn he would never admit it, but I thought you should know." Then before I could form a reply Scott changed topics.

"But enough about that...what brings you to Vail?" he asked cheerful again.

"Hayden Grace."

"Oh, how is the younger Parker?"

"She is riding in the final tomorrow."

"No shit," he said with such enthusiasm causing me to laugh. Just then the woman called our number at the pick-up window.

"Thank you for the pizza," I said, suddenly feeling very awkward.

"I'll stop by the finals run; I'd like to see the younger Parker ride. I feel like it's the least I can do since you have done so much for my family," he gushed.

"It was nothing," I said again.

"Oh, the modesty, I love it," he said, waving good-bye. I was able to return to the room with the pizza without running into anyone else I knew, but my mind was spinning. It seemed that everyone had so much to share about Paul but Paul himself. He continued to keep radio silence, only adding to my frustration.

CHAPTER 28

Every competition day was different. Hayden Grace didn't have a set routine or ritual she had to go through, and for that I was grateful. She rolled out of bed around eight, and we had breakfast before she got ready. On this particular morning she kept her headphones in and listened to music as she got ready. She continued to listen to her music as we made our way back to the pipe. I kissed her quickly and wished her good luck, and she just nodded heading to check-in. I went and got my pass for the family section and found myself a good spot to watch everything. I did love the energy that came with competition days. You could hear the excitement buzz in the crowd—it was almost something tangible you could reach out and touch. The announcers were going through their analysis of the riders when I felt someone tap me on the shoulder.

"Gina?" I asked, completely surprised by her presence. "What are you doing here?"

"I wanted to check on you and Hayden Grace. How were the accommodations?" I was skeptical that that was the only thing she was checking in on.

"They are great; much better than the motel we stayed at in Aspen," I added, and she smiled.

"How is Hayden Grace feeling?" she asked, causing me to grow weary.

"She is good—she mostly kept to herself this morning," I said cautiously.

"That's great," she said earnestly, and made no attempt to leave.

"Gina?" I heard behind her, and we both turned. Coming toward us with a goofy grin was Scott.

"Scott, what are you doing here?" she said with alarm, as they embraced.

"Checking on the Parker ladies," he said, leaning over and giving me a hug. "What are you doing?" he asked.

"Checking on the Parker ladies," she said, mimicking his statement playfully.

"The Parker ladies are doing great," I interjected, causing everyone to laugh.

"How did you both get in here?" I asked, thinking about my pass.

"I work for the company—automatic pass," she said, flashing her ID.

"I'm me…it gets me into a lot of places," Scott said, flashing a grin and eliciting a chuckle from Gina.

"Does anyone abide by the passes?" I asked, in slight exasperation.

"No," they said in unison. Gina and Scott knew each other well I learned. They both rode together growing up, and then Scott went professional and Gina when to college. They had kept in touch some, but mostly their paths crossed at competitions or other big events. It turns out, as they explained, that the snowboarding community was actually pretty close, and everyone had a good camaraderie with each other. We chatted away as the first couple of riders took the pipe. Hayden Grace's top qualifying score held, and she was going to be riding last during the first run of the finals.

My anxiety was pretty low when Hayden Grace took the pipe for her first run. Having been through this once before, I had a better understanding of what to expect of such a large competition and of her. I was still nervous for her, but I was able to breathe and enjoy her performance. She sat perched at the top by herself as they called her name. She patted her jacket and took off toward the pipe. She dropped in high and soared to her first trick. I thought the height was going to be a little too much for her, but she maintained control and transitioned to her next trick. She was in control the entire way through the run; I waited at the end to see if she would do her new trick, but she didn't, instead opting for the same run she had done in Aspen. Although it was the same run, this one was stronger, and she was more confident. Her score reflected it, keeping her in first place. She pumped her fists in excitement and waved to me. I could see some surprise cross her face when Scott waved back, but she took it all in stride. I rolled my eyes, knowing I would have a thousand questions to answer when this was all over.

"That was killer," Scott said next to me, and I smiled in pride.

"She has really gotten to be a better rider in a short amount of time," Gina commented. I gave her a questionable look, and she looked guilty. "Joel sent me some video of her riding. I needed to know about her before we could offer her a sponsorship." I nodded in understanding, but I was slightly irked by the comment. I started to understand what Paul had meant about everyone always wanting something from you, regardless if they were close to you or not. Gina wasn't trying to pry, but it was her job to know everything about Hayden Grace and with that would be certain obligations and expectations. It would always be a business relationship no matter how friendly or nice she seemed, I thought to myself, understanding the business side a little more.

"Her style reminds me of Paul a little bit," Scott said nonchalantly, causing my head to spin around quickly.

"Do explain," I said when I was able to put the words together.

"She rides with a certain abandon, but it's fun to her—you can tell she enjoys it. He always said that you need to have fun riding, and it doesn't always translate with some riders. But with her it does." He shrugged his shoulders again, and we stood in silence as we watched the riders start their second runs. The biggest competition for Hayden Grace in the second round was the girl that had beaten her in Aspen; she was currently in third place. When she was done with her first run, she was clearly frustrated with something, and she shouted something in anger when her scores were announced. I wasn't close enough to hear her, but the faces of those around her let me know it wasn't good. You could tell she was not used to losing, and she would come out strong in the next round. I was not wrong.

Nothing changed in the standing as we neared the final three riders. But this time my anxiety was spiking as we got closer to Hayden Grace. The third place rider, as expected, came in aggressive into the pipe, throwing new tricks into her run. She was trying hard; you could see it in her riding, but it wasn't a clean run. There was a slight bobble on her final landing, yet overall it was a better run than her first one. The scores reflected it, putting her into first place.

I could hear Gina and Scott whispering something to each other about the rider, but I ignored them as I focused on Hayden Grace at the top. She sat at the top listening to her music not paying too much attention to the other riders. The previous second place rider started her run and got halfway through it before she nicked the coping, causing her to lose her balance and wipe out. Her score from the first run was still high enough to give her third place—'not bad' I thought to myself as Hayden Grace got ready. I had my hand covering my mouth as I shifted nervously. They announced her name; she patted her jacket and slid into the pipe. She had the same height as before on her tricks, but she had changed the order of her tricks. With each landing I exhaled just a bit, but my nerves were still on high alert until she was done. She setting herself up for her last trick, and I could tell it was going to be the new trick she had showed me earlier. She rode with such relaxation, as if she had done this a million times. She twisted and grabbed her board making a clean landing at the bottom, and the stands erupted in applause. She pumped her fist in the air and looked for me as I waved back, finally exhaling.

"That was sooo sick," Scott shouted next to me as he started high-fiving everyone around us. It didn't take long for the scores to come out...she was in first place. She jumped up and down and ran over to where we were standing.

"You did it," I said into hair, as she gave me a big hug.

"I did everything dad and Paul told me to do," she said proudly, still jumping up and down. Scott gave her a high-five, and so did Gina. I knew Gina and Hayden Grace hadn't been formally introduced, but there would be time for that later. She was quickly ushered away for an interview and the medal ceremony. I was grinning from ear to ear as I pulled my phone out to take some pictures. I could see that Drew and my parents had already texted me; they had been watching online. Scott and Gina congratulated me again, and then left the area. It took about another hour for everything to be concluded. I took enough pictures that would satisfy my parents throughout the whole process. When it was done Hayden Grace came over and showed me her medal. She was smiling broadly, and she had every right to do so. We both knew that based on her score in this event, she could qualify for one of two events next. It would either be the Revolution Tour in Seven Springs, Pennsylvania or the Sprint US Grand Prix at Mammoth Mountain in California. The Grand Prix was the larger event, but Hayden Grace was still young and newer to this circuit so they might take someone with more experience. We would have to wait for the call on Monday or Tuesday.

We went back to our room, and Hayden Grace called her grandparents and her Uncle Drew. She told them all about the competition and sent out pictures of the medal; everyone was so excited. I asked if she wanted to go out and explore the area. I thought given the excitement she would want to be out and about, but instead she said she would rather stay in and watch some more movies.

I sighed, secretly hoping she would want to go out since I was getting more than a little restless. But I complied with her request. She continued texting, and I suspected this time it was Jonathan while I pulled my laptop out and checked e-mails. There was a knock on the door, and I glanced at her and she shrugged. I got up and opened the door, and there was a gentleman there with flowers.

"Hayden Grace Parker?" he asked, and I pointed to Hayden Grace sitting on the sofa. He came in and set the flowers down on the table. It wasn't a huge bouquet, but it was a nice arrangement. I thanked the man and walked over to where Hayden Grace was now standing with the note in her hand.

"Who sent the flowers?"

"From Jonathan and his family," she gushed, turning the most impressive smile on me, causing me to laugh.

"That's so sweet," I said secretly disappointed. Deep down I had hoped they had been from Paul. While he was clearly still mad with me, Hayden Grace had done nothing, and I hoped he had been watching.

CHAPTER 29

We were back in Newbury by dinner time on Sunday. When we arrived home Hayden Grace had several packages waiting for her. Some of her sponsors had sent her promotional items. Burton had sent two boards and a new set of bindings. Vans and NorthFace had sent clothes, and Monster had sent some energy drinks and other promotional materials. Hayden Grace was excited as she sifted through the items, eventually dragging them to her room.

My mom and dad had decided that we should all go out to eat as a family to celebrate. I did not object knowing my refrigerator had seriously been neglected the last couple of weeks. Hayden Grace picked the restaurant, and we all got dressed up. Hayden Grace wore the dress her uncle had bought her in Aspen. I wore the dress I had bought at Nordstrom for dinner with Malinda. It was there at dinner that both Hayden Grace and I decided that we should move to Tahoe and I should take the job with Vail Resorts at NorthStar. We talked logistics as a family; the timing would depend on which competition Hayden Grace qualified for next. We could swing through Seven Springs on our drive out West as that competition was the following week. The Grand Prix was two weeks out and would give us time to drive across the country. At first, I was convinced that I should drive by myself, and Hayden Grace should fly so as to keep her in school longer, but both my parents and Hayden Grace disagreed. I would have to make some calls on Monday about her transferring schools. My parents smugly let me know they had already put their house up on the market, as they knew I was going to take the job. They didn't know if they would stay in our house permanently, but it was a good solution for now while they figured everything out. By the end of dinner things seemed to be falling into place; I felt good about this plan, and Hayden Grace was happy so that was all that mattered.

***

On Monday when I dropped Hayden Grace off at school I went into the main office and completed the paperwork for her school transfer. The principal said they would be very sad to see her go but wished her luck. When I got home I called Gina next and told her I would be accepting the position. She was thrilled with the news and would start making arrangements for our temporary housing on the mountain until we could get situated with something more permanent. I called Joel next and gave my notice effectively immediately. He said he understood and told me that I had a place there whenever and if ever I came back, which I appreciated.

My parents and I spent the rest of the morning packing and organizing things into piles. Things that we didn't need were getting packed up and moved into the attic. Things that were going to Goodwill were getting piled in the garage—which meant moving things out of the attic and into the garage…it was a juggling act. I thought I had done a good job of moving things when Stefan died, but I was wrong: I had done a good job at hiding things when Stefan died. Things that would move with Hayden Grace and me started to pile up in the living room.

It was after lunch when my phone rang. It was the competition organizer for the Grand Prix. Hayden Grace had qualified, and they wanted to extend the offer. I accepted on her behalf and squared things away with the organizer. I was beyond excited, and in a spontaneous move I called the main office at Hayden Grace's school and asked that she be paged to the office. It was about ten minutes later, that I heard a breathless Hayden Grace answer the phone.

"Mom? Is everything okay?" she questioned with alarm.

"Everything is fine," I said pausing.

"So…"

"The Grand Prix just called…" I didn't get much more out because of the shouting on the other end.

"Are you freaking kidding me," she cried into the phone, joyous.

"No joke," I said, knowing that this was not a joking matter.

"This is so rad," she said, at a much more appropriate level after someone said something to her.

"I know…I'm proud of you Hayden Grace."

"Thanks Mom!"

"Okay, have a good rest of your day, and I will pick you up from practice," I said, thinking I would go to practice and tell Ron in person we were leaving.

"Not likely after this news, but thanks Mom…Love you," she said, hanging up the phone. I was grinning ear to ear about her accomplishments. I was so proud it was hard to put into words. I felt a tinge of sadness thinking about these moments that Stefan was missing out on. I took a deep breath as a small realization came over me that he was there with us and he was basking in Hayden Grace's accomplishments just like I was.

Knowing that Hayden Grace was competing in the Grand Prix made it easier to plan our move; we had a specific amount of time to get to Tahoe before heading to Mammoth. Apparently news had traveled fast because after I hung up with Hayden Grace, I got several calls from other sponsors congratulating Hayden Grace on the accomplishment and tweaking her sponsorship contracts. I made sure to take good notes so that I could call Drew that evening to discuss the amendments.

At about seven I left for the mountain to get Hayden Grace. By the time I got there she was already in the locker room changing. I found Ron in the main lodge, talking with some parents. I waited patiently until he was done.

"Ron," I started.

"I know," he said with a smile on his face.

"How?"

"News travels fast. Not many Newbury boarders get a shot at the professional level, and the kids have been gossiping about each other since Regional 6," he admitted.

"I just wanted to thank you for everything," I said, leaning in to give him a hug.

"You have an amazing young lady and an even more talented rider there," he whispered, and I nodded.

"She is going to need a new coach," I mumbled.

"Oh, she will make do…I think you will find that prospect easier the better she does," he said, winking at me before excusing himself to talk with another parent. Hayden Grace came out of the locker room with extra bags, and I went over to help her.

"Where did you get so much stuff?" I questioned, lugging it to the car.

"I don't know, but there is more of it," she said slightly horrified.

"We haven't even gotten to your room yet," I said laughing, thinking it was going to exponentially worse.

We had set to leave on Wednesday in hopes of arriving in Tahoe by Sunday, giving us about ten hours on the road each day. This would also give Hayden Grace several days to practice before heading to the next competition. It was a very fast turnaround, but I was confident I could make it work. Hayden Grace was going to go in for a half day on Tuesday and then attend her last practice that evening. I hoped to have the U-Haul mostly loaded by then with the help of my parents.

***

Wednesday morning arrived quickly as we loaded the last of our belonging into the U-Haul. Molly, Hayden Grace and I would be riding in the cab, and we would tow the car behind. It was going to be tight, but we would make it work. My parents were teary-eyed as they set us off on the road. They promised to travel out to Tahoe as soon as we had settled down and found a permanent living situation. I had talked to Drew the night before about contracts, and he bid us a good trip. I even called Marla back and told her we were moving. She apologized profusely about putting Malinda on my scent. I told her not to worry about it as things work out for a reason. She also promised to come out and visit when she was able too. Hayden Grace had much less of a tearful goodbye. She had said good-bye to Coach Ron and several kids on her team. Lucie did wish her a safe journey and told her to stay in touch. Madison had not yet returned to club practice and didn't respond to any of Hayden Grace's texts, leaving the situation as it was with no closure. The biggest surprise was my sister calling to wish us a good trip. She was great but so caught up finishing medical school that she often missed major milestones or important dates. I had a secret suspicion that Drew or my mother had called her as a reminder. Hayden Grace was happy to talk with her for a while before she finally had to head to bed.

Now we were on the road headed to a new life with new adventures, and I couldn't be more excited. It was probably something we should have done several years ago. A clean slate is good for everyone, and we were no exception.

Hayden Grace patted Molly who was in the seat between us as she plugged in her music.

"No way," I said, leaning down putting my hand on hers.

"We have five days on the road; if you're going to listen to music then you have to share," I said, knowing that driving in silence for five days would make me very cranky.

"Okay," she said with a mischievous grin and leaned over, plugging her music into the AUX outlet in the cab. Soon Fall Out Boy could be heard in the cab. It was better than silence I thought, but we were only an hour into a fifty-plus hour drive, I thought, rolling my eyes.

CHAPTER 30

It had been nearly two weeks since we arrived in Tahoe. The road trip had been pretty uneventful. Hayden Grace even helped with some of the driving—it was a great way to get her road experience we otherwise hadn't had time to do. Molly loved every moment of being in the car but like the rest of us, was super excited when we arrived at our final destination. We got unpacked, and Hayden Grace was able to practice at Tahoe before we headed to Mammoth.

The Grand Prix was a huge competition that made Aspen look like a hometown event. Hayden Grace rode well and finished in fourth place ahead of many competitors who had been riding for several years. She was excited with her performance and ready for the next competition. We only had two more left this year before the end of the season. She was already talking about next year and dropping hints about qualifying for the next Olympics which was only two years away. She had started school and was adjusting well. She hadn't been at school too much given everything going on, but she had made one friend who was not a snowboarder, and they were texting daily. She continued talking with Jonathan, and they had planned to hang out once both of their seasons were over. With our move we were now only about an hour away from where he lived, and I saw many road trips to visit him in my future because much to her protest she wasn't allowed to officially date until she was 18.

***

It was the Monday after the Grand Prix, and I had just finished my second cup of coffee. I was sitting at the front desk of the ski instruction area of the mountain. My group lesson didn't start for another hour. The set up at Tahoe was larger and a little bit more structured than it had been at Sunapee, but I didn't mind a little more structure. Most mornings I worked with a young women named Bethany. She was a local in the area and reminded me of Rachel. Bethany came rushing into the building late on this particular morning.

"Case of the Mondays?" I questioned as she bustled around, trying to get herself all set up.

"No…kinda…I don't know," she said in exasperation. "There is a circus going on out there. The mountain is all abuzz with rumors that PW is here," she said in excitement.

"Paul Westcott?" I stuttered.

"Yea…you know him?" she questioned suddenly eyeing me closely.

"I used to but not anymore."

"Too bad. Apparently they are doing some promotional work or something…but I'm not sure…it's all just speculation," she shrugged, finishing getting ready for her lesson. I closed my eyes and sighed to myself. He was so close, but it had been seven weeks since I last saw him. I wouldn't even know what to say at this point, but it didn't matter because while I knew he was here, he didn't know I was here. Sighing over the depressing realization, I finished my coffee and went to help Bethany get ready for our lessons.

Again at lunchtime, I heard the same murmur of Paul being on the mountain. The rumor was always different—he had made a miraculous recovery and was doing tricks in the half pipe, or he was just shooting a commercial for a sponsor. The craziest rumor I heard was that he was there giving private lessons to some celebrity clients. Whenever I inquired where he was, the location always changed and circumstances started to vary. I began to wonder if any of it was real. When I was leaving at the end of the day I had to drop off some paperwork in the main lodge, and I could feel the energy when I entered. It was that electric buzz that carried through a crowd whenever Paul was around. I had no doubt that he was there; I could feel his presence. A sad smiled crossed my face. I wasn't going to go looking for him; I was trying my best to move on.

That evening after dinner I was unpacking a box in my bedroom and came across the photo of Paul and I at the ice skating rink in Aspen. I couldn't help but smile as I looked at it intently. We both had huge grins on our faces, and we looked so happy. Carefully I put it back in the box between two books so as not to crush it. I thought about everything that had gone on since then and the ups and downs that had followed. It wasn't ideal, and Hayden Grace and I were in a better place, but we had gotten there without Paul Westcott.

***

Tuesday was much the same as Monday. There continued to be rumors and excitement around the resort, but I tried my best to ignore it and focus on my lessons. I had just finished giving ski lessons to a group of 6-8 year olds, and I was waiting on my next client who was late, giving me the opportunity to grab a snack from the back office. It was a private ski lesson; the client had called last minute and requested me specifically.

"Andy, someone is here to see you," called Bethany from the front office.

"Be right there," I called from the back room, shoving the rest of the granola bar in my mouth. I rounded the corner quickly from the back office to the lobby and unexpectedly collided with someone causing me to be off balance. When I straightened up I gazed into a set of electric blue eyes.

"Paul," I whispered.

"Parker," he whispered back, never taking his gaze off me. I don't know how long we stood there, but I heard Bethany clear her throat.

"I'm so sorry, but I have a client," I mumbled, not knowing what else to say.

"Private ski lesson?"

"Yes," I said suspiciously.

"It's me," he said, standing back and giving me a slight smile.

"Why?" I asked in confusion. It was only then that I noticed he was leaning on a cane, and he was limping slightly. I could also tell that he had dropped some weight; he looked different than when I last saw him.

"What happened?" I asked, motioning to his leg.

"Can we talk privately?"

"Yeah, as my client you have me for the next sixty minutes," I said, glancing at my watch. "Want to grab some coffee?" I asked unsure of what to say next.

"Oh, thank God," he said with a sigh of relief. I gave him a questionable look, and he continued.

"I was slightly concerned you might have given up caffeine since we last saw each other, but I took a gamble." He walked over to the counter where Bethany was sitting and held up a cup of coffee.

"No need to worry…I'm still addicted," I said with a smile.

"It's a peace offering," he said as an explanation, and I approached him, accepting the cup of coffee. I couldn't help but smile at the gesture; when I looked I saw his signature grin, causing me to sigh in relaxation. We left the instruction center and made our way over to the lodge. Paul insisted that we go up to the second floor via the stairs, and he do so under his own ability. I didn't protest; we took our time and eventually found a small corner that was set off from the crowds. As we made our way through the lodge his appearance, though different, still elicited the same energy and buzz it had previously. When we finally sat down,

I could tell he was tired, but I didn't say anything. Paul adjusted his leg slightly before looking at me.

"Andy, I have so much I need to say…," he said, running his hands through his hair like he did when he was frustrated.

"Start with, what are you doing here?" I asked, interrupting him.

"You are a hard woman to find," he said, looking at me. "I went to Mount Sunapee looking for you a couple weeks ago."

"You went to Mount Sunapee?" I asked skeptically.

"I was looking for you," he said.

"You could have called," I said dryly.

"No. What I need to say should be done in person… Anyway, after realizing you weren't there, I called Jessica, who, by the way, has apparently stayed in contact with your brother. So imagine my surprise to find out that you were here in my own backyard." He gave a small smile. "I didn't know if you would even talk to me so I booked a private lesson, and here I am," he said, finishing his explanation.

"How long have you been here?" I asked, narrowing my eyes in suspicion.

"I was here yesterday doing some consulting work for one of my sponsors, but I didn't know how best to approach you. I didn't even know if you would talk to me," he replied sheepishly. "I didn't know what to say…"

I had thought about this moment a lot right after Aspen, but as time went by, it had started to become a distant memory, but now Paul was here, standing in front of me.

"Andy, I'm so sorry," he said, reaching across the space between us and grabbing my hand. His touch was electric as I felt the knot in my stomach turn.

"What are you sorry for?" I asked. I didn't pull away from his touch, but I didn't make any attempt to lean into it either.

"When I saw that e-mail from Malinda, I overreacted. It's just that it can be hard to trust the right people, and she had been so cunning and sneaky trying to land my sponsorship. For a while she was always showing up at sponsor parties or places where I was eating dinner. After a while, she stopped coming and instead would send messages through people I knew or other sponsors. I just felt like you were handpicked to try and seal a deal," he rushed.

"Paul, I'm so sorry about that. I should have told you earlier. She demanded that I get the sponsorship, but I refused and it cost me…"

"Your job," he interrupted, and I looked surprised.

"Jessica was a wealth of information," he said with a look of guilt.

"My job, among other things…," I looked into his blue eyes, and they still took my breath away, "…it cost me you…" I finally admitted, closing my eyes. "But you just left. I called you," I said as the anger and frustration rose.

"I know."

"You didn't just hurt me…you hurt Hayden Grace too!"

"I know."

"How do I know what you're saying is for real?" I said in frustration, closing my eyes for a minute. It was easier to concentrate when I didn't have to stare into his eyes.

"Andy…" he breathed my name, and it sent goose bumps to my core. I slowly opened my eyes, and there he was right in front of me. I could feel the energy between us, but I resisted. I couldn't be pulled into his world again. "Andy...I'm so sorry I pushed you away... It is the biggest regret of my life," he said, looking at me. He leaned towards me and tucked a stray strand of blonde hair back behind my ear, letting his fingers linger on my check and neck. I couldn't fight the urge any longer; I leaned in and met his lips. Our touch was electrifying as the kiss deepened. I finally pulled away—the emotion was too strong, and it took me a moment to catch my breath.

"What happened?" I asked, motioning towards his right leg, changing the subject.

"Snowboarding accident in Italy," he mumbled, putting his hand on his knee.

"I heard that, but what happened?" I knew the news story, but I wanted to know the real story.

"It was a fluke..."

"Paul, you don't have to tell me, but please don't lie to me either," I said, as he started his non-answer. I had gotten enough of those from Hayden Grace that I knew how to spot them a mile away.

"Fair enough," he said, but he didn't elaborate further. Our time was running out as I glanced at my watch; I was still unsure of why he had come.

"Can I take you to dinner tonight?" he asked, watching me closely. His expression was so open; he looked like a nervous fifteen-year-old boy.

"I can't tonight, I have to work..." I saw his expression fall as I contemplated having dinner with him.

"What about tomorrow?" I added after a couple of moments, and he nodded, looking relieved.

"Speaking of work, I need to head back," I said standing. I wasn't going to ask if he needed help; I didn't want him to think that I pitied him. Walking away was harder than I imagined…every part of my body told me to stay, told me to hold on and never let go. My hands were shaking slightly when I got back to the instruction center as I got ready for my next group lesson. My head was spinning, and I wasn't sure what to do next. Taking a deep breath, I focused on the task at hand and tried to push everything else out of my mind until I could deal with it later.

***

Hayden Grace got home early from the mountain, and we sat at the table eating spaghetti, salad and garlic rolls.

"How was school?"

"All right."

"How was practice?" Hayden Grace rolled her eyes at me. She didn't currently belong to a club nor did she have a coach, so what she was doing wasn't really the structured practice she had become so accustomed to. Instead, she was going to the mountain every day on her own and trying new tricks and practicing her runs. She was slightly worried that she might be missing something and told me so, daily. Everything happened so fast that we didn't have time to work out those details, but for the remainder of the competition season, I felt like she was going to be fine as long as she continued to go to the mountain.

"It was good. I did see these two guys on the pipe; they were practicing this really cool trick, so I tried to copy it," she commented.

"How did it go?"

"I nailed it after four or five times," she said triumphantly.

"How banged up did you get?" I asked with concern.

"Not too bad…just a couple of bruises. I have had worse." I nodded in agreement.

"Hey Mom, I heard a rumor," she asked quietly.

"Oh?"

"I heard that Paul was on the mountain the last two days," she asked, looking at me intently. Rumors travel so fast; it blew my mind that anyone could keep secrets in this day and age.

"I can confirm that rumor to be true," I said after a moment.

"Did he come see you?"

"Yes, we talked for a little bit," I said vaguely.

"How does he look?" she asked, with curiosity.

"Good…weaker…but good," I said after a moment—it was what I had been thinking since the moment I saw him.

"His injury…bad?"

"It looks like he's getting better, but injuries take time. Healing takes time," I commented, more for myself than Hayden Grace.

"Are you going to see him again?" she pressed.

"Yes, we are going to dinner tomorrow night," I replied cautiously. "Are you okay with that?" I asked her. I had every intention of eventually bringing up the subject tonight, but since she brought it up, I thought I should ask.

"I think so. I don't really like how he just left our lives after Aspen. I expected more from him," she paused.

"Why? Because he is a well-known athlete?"

"No, because I thought he cared for us, and normal people don't do that when they care for someone, do they?" she asked.

"No, they don't." I replied.

"Everyone deserves a second chance," I commented, not trying to defend Paul, but more to teach Hayden Grace that sometimes life isn't that cut and dry.

"I suppose so. We will see," she said, looking at me.

"Where are you going?" she asked, moving on to the actual date part.

"I don't know. I texted him our address, and he told me to be ready at seven. He asked if you would be around" I added, thinking back to the text.

"Do you want me to be?" she asked, tilting her head to the side.

"That's up to you if you want to be around. You know Paul and have a right to see him if you want too," I commented.

"Okay, I should be done with practice by then. You might need some help getting ready anyway," she commented, smirking at me. After that she brought up Jonathan, and we spent the rest of dinner dissecting their latest conversation.

CHAPTER 31

I was excited-nervous the following day thinking about dinner with Paul. My lessons seemed to drag on, and time seemed to crawl by until I got home. Once I got home time flew as I struggled to get myself ready. I made Hayden Grace something for dinner and then put it in the oven to keep warm. I sat and stared at the closet a while longer than I intended until I finally settled on a short red dress with long sleeves and an open back. I had a pair of nude pumps in a box in the back of the closet I hadn't yet unpacked that I had to fish out. I let my long blonde hair hang loose, adding a slight wave and a bit of hairspray.

"Mom?" Hayden Grace called, coming in the front door ,causing Molly to bark.

"In here," I said, calling from my bedroom. The temporary apartment Gina had arranged for us was very nice, but it was a bit tight compared to the large home we were in previously. It wouldn't be hard for Hayden Grace to find me.

"Mom, you look amazing," Hayden Grace said, plopping down on the bed.

"You think so?"

"You should make Paul work for it."

"Excuse me? Where did you learn that and work for what?" I questioned in alarm.

"Uncle Drew said that when a person messes up, we should make them work for it...it will show you how much they truly mean it," she commented.

"I'm sure Uncle Drew said that, but it's not an entirely accurate observation," I said, mentally cataloging a note to have a long conversation with my baby brother. Just then the doorbell rang, and Molly jumped up and ran to the door barking.

"I'll get it," Hayden Grace said, getting up and walking to the door. This gave me just a couple more minutes to myself as I finished my make-up. I looked in the mirror one last time and sprayed a bit of perfume on before walking out of the bedroom to the living room. In the living room, Hayden Grace was standing and talking to Paul. He looked up when I entered, and our eyes meet instantly; my hazel eyes connecting with those electric blue eyes.

"Andy, you look beautiful," he said, coming into the room further. He was still limping slightly, but I saw that he didn't have his cane with him today. He was dressed in dark gray dress slacks and a black belt. He had a lighter gray button down shirt which was open at the top, and he wore a matching dark gray blazer.

"You look pretty dapper, yourself," I commented, still not having moved from my spot.

"Mom, Paul brought us flowers," she said, bringing over a bouquet of flowers to me. It was a full dozen white roses wrapped with a red ribbon. They were beautiful; I could smell them before Hayden Grace even handed them to me.

"I got some too!" she gushed, taking her smaller bouquet into the kitchen for some water.

"What I was telling Hayden Grace was that I wanted to apologize for my quick exit in Aspen—it was uncalled for," he said, not taking his eyes off me.

"I forgave him already," she called from the other room.

"She was a quick sell," I commented swiftly, and he chuckled. I finally willed myself to move, settling the roses on the counter and picking up my coat from the back of the sofa.

"Hayden Grace…" I started to say.

"I know…dinner is in the oven, and I will put your flowers in water too. Go have fun you crazy kids," she said with a laugh as she headed back into the kitchen. I chuckled again and shook my head.

"Shall we?" Paul asked, and I nodded. He was close enough now that I could smell his cologne, and it was intoxicating. He placed his hand on the small of my back and started to usher me out. Glancing at Hayden Grace in the kitchen who wasn't paying attention, he leaned over and gave me a quick kiss on the check.

"Amazing," he whispered as we exited the apartment.

I didn't know what to expect when we left, but a black town car waited for us by the curb.

"I can't drive anywhere that's more than ten minutes away… yet," Paul said, motioning to his leg, and I nodded in understanding.

"Where are we going?" I asked curious about our final destination.

"Dinner," he replied vaguely, and I didn't press further. Once in the car he reached for my hand and brushed the back of it with his thumb.

"Andy, I know I said it inside, but you take my breath away," he said after a couple of moments. I was glad that the car was dark, and he couldn't see me blush in response.

"Where is your cane tonight?" I asked, changing the subject.

"It's in the trunk in case I need it, but I was hoping to make it through the night without it," he replied with only a hint of worry in his voice.

"How is rehab going?" I asked, trying not to pry.

"It's going as well as it can go for a torn ACL and MCL. I do have a brace I have to wear," he said, patting his leg. I couldn't really see the outline of the brace in the dark car, but I had been around enough ACL and MCL tears on the mountain to know what he was talking about.

"It's the same injury Ace had …and it ended his career," he added as an explanation after a couple of silent moments.

"Are you worried about that for your career?" I asked.

"I'm not worried…I'm terrified," he said, and I instantly understood. It was his livelihood, his passion, and he was worried about losing it all.

"You are stronger than Ace; you can come back from this if you want to," I said fiercely.

"You can't know that," he commented back. I took my other hand and put it on top of his, causing him to look at me.

"Yes, I can. I know you, and you can do anything."

"I used to think that."

"You still should," I said, as the car came to a stop.

"Hungry?"

"Absolutely," I said, and he smiled. He led me into the restaurant; the name on the sign read Village Café. His pace was a little slower, but I was in no hurry. We were seated quickly, not because of who he was but because he actually had a reservation. The waiter took our order and left us alone. There was a moment's pause before Paul spoke.

"I got injured because of you," he said as an explanation and not an accusation.

"You're going to need to elaborate," I said, slightly choking on my water.

"I had been distracted and moody since I left Aspen. The guys thought that going out for a ride would help improve my mood. I had reluctantly agreed, and everything was going fine, and I was enjoying myself. We had decided to camp out a little around these jumps, and we were just goofing off. When it was my turn I went off the jump, and at the last minute I could have sworn I saw you. I twisted to get a better look which caused me to tweak my knee; I lost my balance, and I had no chance of landing the jump regardless of the air I had. I came down hard on my knees, and then I don't really remember anything else. But I could have sworn it was you; it didn't make sense, but I wanted to believe it so badly," he whispered, looking relieved before dropping his head. The information startled me and validated me at the same time. I felt better knowing I wasn't the only one seeing things during our time apart.

"I saw you everywhere I went too," I said shyly, and he looked up at me. "One time I thought you were the Starbucks barista," I commented, trying to lighten the mood which caused him to chuckle.

"Paul, if you felt this way…why did you wait almost seven weeks?" I questioned.

"After the crash it took a couple days before I was conscious and aware of what was going on. Once I was alert they transferred me to a rehab facility back here in California. I thought about reaching out to you a thousand times since then, but I didn't want your pity. I didn't want you to come back to me because you felt sorry for me. I was actually going to wait until I was walking better," he glanced to the side at something that wasn't there. "But I couldn't stay away any longer. It wasn't a lie when I told you in Aspen that I couldn't quit you. I tried that first night after you left in Aspen and then while I lay in the hospital bed, but I couldn't stop thinking about you."

"That is quite a story," I finally said after a moment. I reached my hand across the table and held his hand. We sat there in silence holding hands and staring at each other until the food arrived. It broke a trance we had woven, and we were able to move on to other topics. We talked about his rehabilitation and a couple of setbacks that he had. Full recovery was still going to be almost seven months away. He talked about having a new appreciation for competing and that if he was able to, he was going to recommit himself to competing and all the things he had taken for granted. He actually made the same statement Hayden Grace made that the Olympics' were only two years away, and he needed to start focusing on that as soon as possible. I listened intently when he spoke. He asked me about Hayden Grace and her competitions; he knew a little bit having followed along with final score postings online. I told him about being fired and how the opportunity with Gina presented itself.

"It sounds like it's been a long seven weeks for both of us," he commented when we were done with dinner. "Would you like desert?" he asked, and I declined. He paid for the check, and we made our way to the door where the car was waiting. I was a little worried the date felt like it was coming to an end, and I wasn't ready for the night to end…I didn't feel like things were settled yet between us.

"How about some after dinner drinks?" Paul asked, once we were seated in the car.

"That sounds great," I replied, relieved.

"I know the perfect place," he commented, tapping the driver on the shoulder and whispering something to him. When he leaned back he had a small grin on his face as he held my hand again.

"Have you enjoyed the Tahoe skiing yet?" he asked, trying to make small talk.

"No, not yet. With the move and all the travel with Hayden Grace, I haven't seen anything but the small area where I teach lessons," I commented.

"If you get the chance you should, it's an experience," he added.

"How about I just wait for you to show me?" I said, lifting my eyes to his.

"Andy, we don't know if…"

"Just promise me that when the mountain opens for skiing this fall, you'll show me the sights," I said with an edge in my voice.

"I promise," he said, nodding solemnly.

***

The driver came to a stop, and again Paul opened the door for me. We stood in front of a house that looked like a log cabin with its exposed beams and stone façade. Inside the lights were on, illuminating the large windows.

"Is this owned by one of your sponsors?" I asked as he opened the door.

"No, I own this one," he said, setting down the keys and glancing at my surprised expression.

"I'm going to send the town car away but know that I have a truck and I can bring you home at any time. I know you have to get back to Hayden Grace. Make yourself at home," he said, and I nodded in understanding. He turned and headed back out the door to speak with the driver, and I took off my coat and wandered through the first floor. There was an expansive living room with a large deep chocolate brown sofa overlooking a fireplace and view. In the corner I could see boxes piled up with what looked like more sponsor logos. The back wall was entirely made up of windows and faced the mountain. The living room flowed into the dining room where a large wooden table was pushed up against the wall and several brown leather chairs were stacked up. In their place a makeshift rehab center was set up with stretching mats, bands and other assorted equipment. The kitchen was expansive but hardly looked used, causing me to smile. I could see the corner of a pool table in the loft above the kitchen and something that possibly led to a bedroom.

"What are you thinking about?" Paul asked, coming up behind me.

"How do you know I was thinking about anything?"

"You have a 'tell'," he whispered. He leaned over and hit a small button on the wall, and music filled the air as he wrapped his arm around my back pulling me close.

"Do you stay here often?"

"It's my primary residence," he commented, and we began to sway to the melodic sounds of John Legend.

"Nice choice of music," I commented.

"I have a new appreciation for it, since I met you," he said, twirling me slowly.

"Should you be dancing?" I asked, looking at his knee.

"Who knows, but some time ago, I promised you a real date with dinner, flowers…"

"…and dancing," I finished, leaning in for a kiss.

"…and dancing," he repeated when I pulled away. The song changed, and we slowed to a sway.

"Andy, there is something I need to tell you," he said slowly.

"Anything," I said, looking into his eyes as they pulled me in.

"The last seven weeks have been the hardest in my life and not because of my injury. I find myself falling in love with you more every time I see you—when I first saw you on Mount Sunapee, finding you sitting in that café in Aspen, teaching you to snowboard, watching you watch the stars, backcountry skiing, the Burton sponsor party, seeing you here in Tahoe—each and every time you have left me breathless and unsteady...being away from you is becoming a problem...you ground me the way no one else has," he breathed, leaning in for a kiss. We had stopped dancing, and I put my hands on his chest as the kiss deepened.

"That's the best thing you have said all night," I mumbled between kisses with a smile, and his eyes twinkled back.

"This is normally the part where I would lean down and whisk you away upstairs," he chuckled.

"Who needs to go upstairs?" I whispered, pulling him down onto the sofa.

***

Paul dropped me off at home around one in the morning; apparently our apartment was only three miles from his home. I leaned over and gave him another kiss before I exited the truck and walked to the apartment. He waited for me to go inside before his headlights receded into the dark. I had invited him to dinner with Hayden Grace and myself that evening and he accepted. He mentioned that he had rehab for his leg in the morning but that it shouldn't be a problem. He wasn't getting as tired afterwards anymore. We were only going to be in town a couple more days before we needed to leave to head to Park City, Utah for another competition.

CHAPTER 32

Paul arrived at our apartment promptly at six that evening; he was using his cane again tonight so I figured he was fatigued after rehab this morning. Molly was barking and circling his feet until he reached down and scratched her behind the ear. Hayden Grace had come home from the mountain in time for dinner, but she was obviously agitated as she stomped to her room. I had prepared lasagna, salad and butter rolls before setting the table. Once Paul was seated, I went down and knocked on her door; she muttered something about being there in a couple of minutes.

Back at the table I just gave him a quick smile as I started serving. Paul gave me a questioning look, and I just shrugged. With Hayden Grace it could be something or nothing causing her grumpy demeanor. About five minutes later Hayden Grace emerged; she was wearing jeans and a hoodie and her hair was twisted up in a bun. She made the effort to be polite and apologized for being late to dinner.

"What's going on Hayden Grace?" I finally asked after ten more minutes of her brooding.

"It's those stupid guys on the mountain…the ones that were doing the cool trick the other day. They said that because I was a girl, I would never be able to do their stupid tricks. Well, I told them I could do it better than they could, and I did—I nailed the trick. You know what they did? They just mumbled some things under their breath and left…they just left! I did figure out they are on the snowboarding club on the mountain. If the club is full of people like them, then no-thank-you," she fumed, pausing to breathe. I tried to hide my smile, and Paul bit his lip, trying to cover up his laughter.

"Anything else bothering you?" I asked. It wasn't like Hayden Grace to get so worked up over something so trivial.

"I guess I'm a little homesick. I miss having club practice and Coach Davis. I even miss Madison…but only a little bit," she finally mumbled, looking down at her food.

"Hayden Grace, I get it. It's a lot of change in a short amount of time. You are allowed to miss the things we left behind," I said, and she lifted her eyes slightly.

"It will be okay…" she mumbled and dug into her lasagna.

"How is the riding on the pipe? It's been a while since I have ridden it," Paul asked, distracting her after a moment.

"The conditions are perfect," Hayden Grace said, getting animated. Then she went off on a tangent about how the pipes out West were bigger and faster than the ones back on the East Coast. I wouldn't say her mood was fixed, but it was much improved by the time dinner was over. Paul kept her busy with questions about her riding and the competitions he had missed. I couldn't help but smile; the entire interaction felt so normal and natural…I felt happy in that moment.

After dinner Hayden Grace and Paul cleared the table much to my surprise. We settled in the living room, but instead of putting the TV on Hayden Grace suggested a board game. I was a little surprised but delighted by the idea. She ran and found Monopoly in her room, explaining that it was in a box she unpacked recently which is what made her think of it. We played until around eleven when Hayden Grace and Paul both started to yawn. I chuckled to myself by how similar they could be at times. I kissed Hayden Grace and sent her to bed. She mumbled goodnight and something about a Monopoly rematch, as Paul had beaten us both hands down. I stood with Paul at the door, and he leaned in and kissed me before he left for the night.

***

The next morning Hayden Grace was quiet as we sat at the table drinking coffee. It wasn't that unusual with her as she was not a morning person, but something seemed off about her behavior. I finished making her lunch, setting it down on the table in front of her, startling her.

"Mom?"

"Yes?"

"Can we invite Paul over again for dinner? It was really nice having the company, especially someone who talks snowboard…no offense," she said, looking at me.

"No offense taken. I will call and ask," I said unable to hide my own grin. She perked up a little after that as she finished getting ready for school. The bus route ran right by the apartment so I didn't have to drive her to school, but I did have to make sure she was on time, which was challenging at times. Today she caught the bus without a problem. I got ready for work; glancing at the clock, I had a little bit of time before I had leave so I called Paul.

"Good Morning," he answered.

"Morning," I said, smiling.

"To what do I owe this unexpected phone call?" he asked.

"Hayden Grace requested your presence at dinner tonight," I chided him.

"She did now. How do you feel about that?" he asked.

"I feel pretty good about that," I said with another smile.

"I would love to," he finally responded.

"Okay same time, same place?"

"Great, see you then," he said and disconnected.

***

After ski lessons I came home and again cooked dinner. Tonight's menu was chicken, green beans and potatoes au gratin. I even had time to make chocolate chip cookies for desert, much to my surprise. Hayden Grace came home and quickly bounded to her room, not allowing me to see her.

"Hayden Grace? What's going on?" I asked, knocking on her door.

"It's not a big deal," she said, opening the door. I could see the bruising under her eye immediately when she finally opened the door. Another black eye.

"What happened?"

"I fell learning a new trick," she sighed as I examined her eye.

"Any other injuries?"

"Just some new bruises," she commented. I told her to go sit at the kitchen table as the doorbell rang. Molly started barking and pacing by the door; it was like she knew who it was and was just as excited as the rest of us.

"Make yourself at home," I said quickly, opening the door for Paul and then heading back into the kitchen. Puzzled, Paul followed slowly behind me into the kitchen. I put a bag of ice together and handed that to Hayden Grace with a dish towel. Paul sat down across from Hayden Grace and looked at her intently.

"You meet the wall?" he asked after she put the ice on her eye, and I fussed for a couple of more minutes.

"Yeah, I was trying a new trick, and I didn't get the rotation down," she said with exasperation. Paul asked her more questions about the trick, and by the time I had set the table and plated everyone's dinner he had figured out her mistake. He even drew a little picture on the napkin in order to better explain it to her.

"That makes so much sense, doesn't it, Mom" she said, looking at me, and I just nodded.

"I would have known that if I had a coach," she commented, looking directly at me. Paul raised his eyebrows in my direction, and I ignored her remark and his look.

"When do you leave for Park City?" he asked several moments later.

"Our flight is at six tomorrow. We have a town car coming to get us around three-thirty," I said, thinking about the schedule.

"Park City has a good pipe," he commented in approval. That comment caused Hayden Grace to launch into a battery of questions about Park City and the pipe there. After about thirty minutes, all of the snowboarding talk was done, and we had moved onto different topics of conversation. We talked about Paul's rehab some more, and the progress he was making. We even talked about my ski lessons some. After dinner Hayden Grace and Paul again cleared the table. When they were done, as a surprise, I brought out the cookies and three tall glasses of milk. Hayden Grace put a movie on and the three of us settled in on the sofa.

Halfway through the movie I looked over and Hayden Grace had fallen asleep, and she was now leaning on Paul's shoulder.

"Sorry," I whispered to Paul, getting up and getting a blanket to cover her up.

"No, it's fine...it's just..." he paused, searching for the right words. "I never thought I would get this," he said, pointing to us both on the sofa. "The love of a beautiful, talented and strong woman and then the relationship with Hayden Grace... it's more than I could have dreamed off," he paused, looking at my face.

"I love you, Paul Westcott. I am so grateful for the day you glided into my life," I said, leaning over and kissing him, and he nodded. I leaned over and rested my head on his shoulder as the movie continued to play. Falling in love with Stefan was all at once—it was all or nothing and fast like driving a car at 100 mph down a highway. Falling in love with Paul was different; it was slow and relaxed, almost like floating on the surface of the water.

I woke up a little after two in the morning. Hayden Grace was still sleeping on Paul's other side. Paul was now asleep in the middle with Molly at his feet. I leaned over and kissed him on the cheek, causing him to stir. He looked at me with his sleepy eyes, and there was a deep emotion that danced around in them. It was more than love...it was the feeling of comfort...of home.

"You should stay here for the night," I whispered, kissing him again. I then leaned over and shook Hayden Grace slightly. She mumbled something and curled up even tighter next to Paul. I smiled and again shook her slightly; this time she opened her eyes and looked at me.

"Time for bed," I said, and she nodded as she got up and headed toward the bedroom.

"Goodnight Mom...Goodnight Paul," she mumbled when she was half way down the hall with Molly sauntering behind her.

Paul was now standing and stretching.

"I should go," he said, obviously not wanting to impose. "I have rehab in the morning," he quickly added, sensing my disappointment, but I nodded in understanding.

"When will I see you next?" he asked as we stood by the door.

"We get back from Park City on Monday," I said, rubbing my temples.

"You look stressed...anything I can do to help?"

"Not unless you can find Hayden Grace a coach. If I keep letting her coach herself, she is bound to break something or punch someone," I said, and he chuckled.

"I know a couple of people that might be good for the job. Let me make some calls and get back to you," he said.

"See you Monday?" I said hopeful.

"Wouldn't miss it," he commented, kissing me before heading off towards his truck. Monday now seemed like eons away, I thought to myself as I climbed into bed.

***

It was just past three-thirty when my phone rang, causing me to jump slightly before I answered it. It was the town car company; they were there outside waiting for us. I motioned to Hayden Grace, and we grabbed our things and headed out the door, but not before giving Molly a treat and explaining to her that Gina would be by to look after her while we were gone. I locked the door and turned to find Paul standing in front of our town car. He was dressed casually in jeans and a long sleeve thermal shirt; he was leaning on his cane. Our eyes connected, taking my breath away; I hoped that it would never stop doing so. Hayden Grace paused in front of me in confusion. He had a bag set down on the ground next to him with a smirk that I had come to know and love.

"I thought I might tag along, I heard someone needed a coach."

On the Edge

Acknowledgements

There are so many people I want to thank who have supported me along the way. Writing may appear to be a solo career but it's a very false façade and I couldn't do what I do without the constant support and advice from those around me. First to my husband – thank you for letting me bounce my crazy ideas off of you. Thank you for being my proofreader, my manager, my financial advisor and most importantly my biggest fan. To Caitlin at Royal Social Media, you have the innate ability to know what I want or need before I do sometimes. Your support, advice and collaboration enabled this process to continue. To my friends who allow me to send them unedited or unfinished drafts, thank you. Your ability to see the final product and provide support and feedback have been invaluable. Every writing project is different and the research behind each varies. For this project, I could not have done it without Hana Beaman who answered my questions without tiring. Her perspective and knowledge gave this story more depth and life.

Finally, thank you to the book bloggers, reviewers, interviewers and booksellers; for your time, your work and your patience. Thank you for bridging the gap between writer and reader.

About the Author

T.S. Krupa was born in New Haven, Connecticut. Raised in a Polish household with a blended American culture, she is fluent in Polish. She graduated with her bachelor's degree from Franklin Pierce University, where she also played field hockey. She earned her Master's from Texas Tech University and graduated with her Doctor of Education from North Carolina State University. She lives in North Carolina with her husband and dog. *On the Edge* is her second novel. Learn more about her other novel *Safe & Sound* and future writing projects at www.tskrupa.com.

Reading Guide

1. Andy comments, "My daughter was a product of me regardless of my flaws, just as I was a product of my mother and she of hers. There was no greater compliment." Do you agree or disagree with her statement? Why or Why not?

2. Hayden Grace draws her confidence from real physical items. What are some of those items and what significance do they hold for her?

3. Andy is a single mom raising a rising snowboarding professional. How would her life be different if Hayden Grace was not into snowboarding?

4. Hayden Grace's character is modeled after the many people who dedicate themselves to get to the next level. What are the sacrifices one makes to get to the next level? What sacrifices did Hayden Grace make? Do you agree with the demand and pressure placed on these people at such a young age?

5. Andy says, "Falling in love with Stefan was all at once—it was all or nothing and fast like driving a car at 100 mph down a highway. Falling in love with Paul was different; it was slow and relaxed, almost like floating on the surface of the water." Do you think that each love is different? How have you experienced this?

6. Hayden Grace struggles with her friend relationships. How does she value those relationships at the beginning and how does that change throughout the novel?

7. Family is a strong theme throughout the novel. What are some examples of this? What other themes did you observe?

8. Andy realized she was dating a married man. Do you agree with her choice in how to handle the situation? What would you have done differently? Does the fact that children were involved change your perspective?

9. Hayden Grace attends a party where she finds herself in trouble. Do you agree with her choices? Do you agree with Andy's choices?

10. Andy struggles to honor her husband's wishes when it comes to parenting Hayden Grace. Do you agree with her decisions? How would you have handled the situations that arose?

Made in the USA
Middletown, DE
27 September 2021